THE YEAR WE BECAME MORE

A Novel By

Amber Irene

To the little girl who asked, "Why me?"

This is why.

Content Warning

This story contains references to:

- Suicide and suicidal ideation
- Substance use and addiction
- Self-harm (accidental/non-intentional)
- Mental health struggles (depression, anxiety, trauma)
- Mild sexual content
- Strong language

If you or someone you know is struggling, please know that you are not alone and help is available:

- **988 Suicide & Crisis Lifeline (U.S.)** – Call or text **988**, or chat via 988lifeline.org
- **Crisis Text Line** – Text **HOME** to **741741** (U.S. & Canada)
- **SAMHSA National Helpline** – 1-800-662-HELP (4357) for substance use or mental health support
- For international readers, visit **findahelpline.com**, which lists global mental health hotlines and crisis services.

Reader discretion is advised.

Book Soundtrack

B.o.B - Airplanes (ft. Haley Williams)
Alessia Cara - Scars to Your Beautiful
Addison Rae - Fame is a Gun
The Weeknd - Cry For Me
Bruno Mars - Talking to the Moon
KSI, Tom Grennan - Not Over Yet
Ashes of Eden - God, Save Me From Myself
Billie Eilish - BLUE
Michael Gerow - Rewrite the Stars
Selena Gomez - Souvenir

Addie's Soundtrack

"CAROLINA" – KAROL G
"ALAMBRE PúA" – Bad Bunny
"LA CANCIÓN" – J Balvin & Bad Bunny
"New Woman" – LISA, ROSALÍA
"Te Boté - Remix" – Nio Garcia, Casper Magico, Bad Bunny, Darell, Ozuna, Nicky Jam

Jax's Soundtrack

"The Hills" – The Weeknd
"Swimming Pools (Drank)" – Kendrick Lamar
"Unforgettable" – French Montana, Swae Lee
"Work Out" – J. Cole
"Mask Off" – Future
"Mirror" – Lil Wayne, Bruno Mars

Zahra's Soundtrack

"Neva Play" – Megan Thee Stallion, RM
"Essence" – Wizkid, Tems
"Jiggle" – Soun Bwoii
"ExtraL" – JENNIE, Doechii
"Under The Influence" – Chris Brown

Matthew's Soundtrack

"SICKO MODE" – Travis Scott
"Hotline Bling" – Drake
"Taste" – Tyga, Offset
"Saturn" – SZA
"Alright" – Kendrick Lamar

Yoona's Soundtrack

"KAZINO" – BIBI
"Physical" – Dua Lipa, HWASA
"CAKE" – KARD
"Blood Sweat & Tears" – BTS
"MONA LISA" – j-hope

Liam's Soundtrack

"Stressed Out" – Twenty One Pilots
"Take What You Want" – Post Malone, Ozzy Osbourne,
Travis Scott
"Better" – Khalid
"Self Care" – Mac Miller
"Sweater Weather" – The Neighbourhood

TABLE OF CONTENTS

Chapter One 13
Chapter Two 19
Chapter Three 23
Chapter Four 31
Chapter Five 39
Chapter Six 49
Chapter Seven 55
Chapter Eight 67
Chapter Nine 75
Chapter Ten 81
Chapter Eleven 89
Chapter Twelve 99
Chapter Thirteen 107
Chapter Fourteen 115
Chapter Fifteen 129
Chapter Sixteen 143
Chapter Seventeen 153
Chapter Eighteen 161
Chapter Nineteen 179
Chapter Twenty 195
Chapter Twenty-One 207
Chapter Twenty-Two 223
Chapter Twenty-Three 233
Chapter Twenty-Four 239
Chapter Twenty-Five 249
Chapter Twenty-Six 261
Chapter Twenty-Seven 271
Chapter Twenty-Eight 277
Chapter Twenty-Nine 289
Chapter Thirty 299
Chapter Thirty-One 305
Chapter Thirty-Two 317
Chapter Thirty-Three 329
Chapter Thirty-Four 337

CHAPTER ONE
Adelina

It's the first day of senior year, and my stomach twists like it can't decide between nerves and excitement. The mirror stares back, catching the places I avoid looking too long, the parts of me I still don't know how to carry into the world. My reflection holds my gaze, sharp where I wish it were soft. I focus on my hair, on the fit of my jeans, skipping the parts of my face that never sit right with me. If I pretend long enough, maybe that's what people will see first.

Mami says I have my father's wavy chestnut hair and fair skin, but I get my brown eyes and short height from her. I wish my father were here to see me off on my first day like he had for many years. I still hear his voice in my head, "Chin up, Addie, it's your time." But instead of crumbling, I tuck the memory into my pocket, like armor. I know he's watching over me and that always gives me a sense of comfort.

A loud honk goes off outside, waking up butterflies within me. That would be Zahra waiting for me. I take one last look in the mirror, avoiding the faint lines that scar my upper lip. They're always there, waiting for me to notice, even on days I wish they weren't. Mami is in the kitchen, grabbing her car keys.

"*¿Ya te vas?*" Mami asks, dangling the keys.

"*Sí,*" I nod. "Zahra is already outside."

"I thought I heard a honk." Her Spanish accent is subtle when she speaks.

As we head out, Zahra rolls her window down to wave at Mami, who waves back with that big proud-mom smile. At the curb, Mami kisses my forehead and wishes me good luck on my first day. I mumble a thanks, trying not to sound too nervous, and jump into Zahra's car. I toss my backpack in the backseat and give her a quick hug before she starts the engine. As we pull away, I catch Mami getting into her own car in the rearview mirror.

"Well, you look nice, Addie. Trying to impress anyone?" Zahra asks. She's focused on the road, but I see her peer at me, waiting for my response.

"No! Who do I have to impress? By the way, you're the one who's dressed to impress," I scoff.

Zahra's rocking her usual main-character energy: black ripped jeans, leather boots, and a hot pink tank top under her jacket. The color pops against her deep brown skin, making her glow even brighter in the morning light. Her curls are perfectly defined, bouncing just above her collarbone, and her gold hoops catch the sun every time she moves. Her hazel eyes look like they're laughing before she even says anything. Zahra looks amazing, but then again, she always does.

"Yeah, okay." She rolls her eyes at me. "It's not like this year is important."

I groan, knowing exactly where she's going with this.

"Come on, it's senior year. We've got yearbook photos, senior trips, college visits. Basically a million chances to make memories and look good while doing it. If I'm gonna enjoy every bit of it, I need to be on my A-game." The car rolls to a stop at a red light.

"Every single day?" I tease.

She looks at me with the most stoic face she can muster. "I am dead serious, Addie".

I sneer and motion for her to drive.

"Do you plan on going to the kick-off party?" Zahra asks.

My breath catches as the realization hits. The senior party. The one everyone's been hyping up since freshman year, like it's *the* night we'll all remember forever. Just picturing myself walking into that crowd, music thumping, people laughing too loud, flashes from phones going off, makes my lungs squeeze.

I hesitate.

"Um, no, not really. You know how I feel about parties. It's weird. I could just stay home and read a book or watch a movie."

Zahra huffs. "Oh, so you plan to leave me alone? No. Absolutely not. You are coming with me."

"Why did you even ask me then?"

"Because I wanted to be nice and see if you would make the right choice. Anyways, I can swing by your house and we can get ready together. I'll do your makeup if you want," she offers.

Zahra parks the car in the student parking lot. We grab our bags and get out.

"You know how awkward I get with these things," I mumble, more to myself than to Zahra.

"And that's why you have me. What are best friends for?" she says, her smile mischievous but her eyes sharp, like she's daring the world to hurt me before she does. "It's my job to make sure you don't stay home, turning into the cat lady living in the boot." She stops and makes a face. "Is that even the story? She's living in the boot, right?" Zahra waves her hand in a dismissive motion before I can answer.

The halls buzz with kids flashing tan lines from summer trips, already swapping guesses about who'll be homecoming queen. Senior year hoodies, black with neon lettering, dot the crowd like a secret club I haven't joined yet. Friends run to hug each other and cliques begin to regroup after a summer hiatus.

The chorus of laughter drowns out the slam of lockers and everyone seems brighter, louder, like we all know the clock has started ticking on our last first day. Yes, I am nervous, but taking everything in makes me feel more excited than I was before. Zahra sighs and flashes her teeth at me.

I'm grabbing my books from my locker and looking at my schedule. Chemistry first period. *Better to get the hard stuff out of the way,* I think. I finish grabbing my last book and see Zahra's big eyes peeking out at me from her side of the locker.

"Okay, okay. Fine! I'll go. Happy?" I say, though the word scrapes out like a surrender. My insides knots; half at the thought of crowds, half at the thought of what they might see when they look too close.

The only response I get from Zahra is a devious smile.

CHAPTER TWO

Jackson

Sweat slides down my back, but the run doesn't shake off the restless tension under my skin. No matter how far I go, it's still there. A clawing reminder I'll need another fix soon. Back home, I jog straight for the shower, hoping water might rinse it off. It never does.

I haven't been in this town long, but every place has someone willing to sell you a little escape if you know how to ask. My hands don't stop shaking until I feel the small orange bottle in my pocket, its rattle steadier than my heartbeat. In the city, I never had to fake smiles at parties just to score. Here, I play along with people I don't care about for a few pills. Oxy's the only thing that really shuts my head up. Everything else is just noise.

Getting ready for school feels like a bad joke. Teachers barking, kids shouting about summer. I throw on black jeans and a t-shirt, sneaking a glance in the mirror.

Tousled black hair. Green eyes, pupils a little blown. High enough to function. Sobriety? I haven't seen it in a long time.

I climb into my car anyway. The pills whisper I'm fine. The truth? I don't care if I'm not. If the world crashes with me, at least it shuts up for a while. GPS set to my new high school, I'm hoping it's my first and last year here.

Dad and I moved early summer, after Mom died. Suicide. I was the one who found her. Her body twisting from the living room fan, the blades still cutting through the air like nothing had changed. That's the memory I can't outrun. No matter how far I run, no matter how many pills I swallow.

After the funeral, Dad asked for a transfer, like switching zip codes could erase a dead body. He packed boxes instead of talking to me, and I learned quickly that silence was his survival plan. Not that I cared. I didn't want to stay in that house anyway. Every room was a replay of the same memory. Her body hanging, skin purple, eyes bulging, tongue swollen. It ruined everything that used to feel good.

I remember my hands shaking so bad I almost dropped the kitchen knife. I couldn't even see what I was cutting through the tears. I just needed to get her down. That image still sticks. The sound of the rope, the weight in my arms. Dad never saw it, but I think it broke him anyway. He disappeared into work. Stopped speaking. Stopped being there.

I tried waiting for him to come back around. He never did. Guess we both found our ways to cope. He buried himself in his job, and I buried myself in anything that made me feel nothing.

I shake the thought off and pull into student parking, eyes burning from too little sleep. My legs feel heavy, but I kind of like it. Feels like gravity's the only thing still holding me down. Checking my crumpled schedule, I see chemistry first period. Perfect. Nothing like starting senior year with chemical reactions and explosions.

I'm fucked.

Science has never been my thing. I just need enough credits to scrape through senior year and get out. If all goes well, I'll graduate, disappear, and never look back. No one puts GPA on your gravestone.

The plaques on the wall guide me to room 106. I skip the lockers, no point in pretending I'll take notes. I'm a few steps from the door when someone slams into me. The hit makes her bounce off my chest and crash straight into another girl behind her, sending her books flying everywhere.

The first girl starts apologizing a mile a minute, voice tumbling over itself. I tune her out and crouch to help the other one. She's already on the floor, arms full of loose pages, brown hair spilling across her face. When it slips back, I catch a glimpse of flushed cheeks and startled eyes. And for a second, she's all I can see. Not the scars. Not the mess. Just her.

We both reach for the same book, hands brushing before I pass it to her. She whispers a soft thanks I barely catch. The first girl's still talking, loud, nervous, impossible to ignore, until I lift a hand to stop her. She shuts up, eyes flashing like she's not used to being told to.

But I'm not looking at her. My focus drifts back to the quiet one still kneeling on the floor, cheeks pink, trying to pull herself together. There's something about her I can't name. And that's what gets me.

"Don't sweat it," I mutter, brushing past. But even as I head towards room 106, the image of her flushed cheeks won't leave me alone, needling me in a way no pill can quiet.

CHAPTER THREE

Adelina

"Leave it to the first day of school to start in chaos," Zahra mutters, stooping to help me gather the rest of my books. My hands still shake from the collision. "Isn't it called Jerry's Law?" she asks while helping me align the books I'm once again holding in my arms.

"It's Murphy's Law," I say, distracted. "Who was that guy? I don't think I've ever seen him."

"He looks new to me. And he's freakishly tall."

I roll my eyes. "Maybe that's why he bumped into you. Maybe we're too short for him to see us." I keep my tone casual, but the memory of his stare prickles under my skin. He wasn't just looking. He was studying, probably the part of me I always wish people wouldn't notice. At least, that's what it felt like. And yet, even as I tell myself that, all I can see are those green eyes. Sharp, steady, impossible to forget.

"With all due respect, babe, I'm a good three, maybe four, inches taller than you. Eh, give or take a few inches. And the next time you roll your eyes at me, I hope they stay stuck staring at your brain."

With her nose in the air, Zahra turns her head and walks toward her first period class.

I slip into chemistry just as the bell rings, still flustered from dropping my books in the hallway. My hands won't stop shaking, so I slide into an empty seat in the back and pretend to look busy. Mr. Davis walks in right after, diving straight into his intro speech about safety goggles and lab rules.

I open my notebook, scribble today's date, and try to look like I'm paying attention. I'm not. My brain drifts. Same classmates as last year, half of them already bored out of their minds. The front row's empty, obviously. Sitting there is basically a social killer. I like the back anyway, less eyes on me, better view of the board.

My gaze wanders to the wall where all the lab equipment hangs. Goggles, gloves, aprons, the whole safety ensemble. The sharper stuff's locked behind glass, neat and organized. Then my eyes flick to the right and stop.

Four seats away, the new guy slouches in his chair like he owns the air around him. I suck in a sharp breath, heat crawling up my neck. I whip my eyes back to the board, heart hammering loud enough to drown out Mr. Davis. Goodness, please don't let him catch me staring.

When he helped me in the hallway, his eyes lingered too long. It's not like I'm not used to people staring. It's just the *way* he did. Like he was trying to figure me out. Or maybe he was just looking at the scar.

I was born with a cleft lip. Years of surgeries, endless checkups, summers spent healing instead of swimming or going out. Mami found the best doctors she could, and they did their magic, but still. The scars are there. Some days it feels like the only thing people see.

They tell me it's barely noticeable now. Maybe they're right. But when I catch my reflection, I see every stitch it took to get here. Every version of me I had to outgrow just to look normal.

Zahra has been one of my biggest supporters ever since meeting in second grade. A boy sneered "pig nose" and stomped on my hand while I was sitting on the classroom rug reading a book. Before I could cry, Zahra smacked him on the back of the head and planted herself at my side.

"Pick on someone your own size. Call her that again and you'll be picking a fight with me." It was ironic that she said that because she was noticeably smaller than the boy herself, barely reaching his chin.

When the boy stomped away, Zahra extended her arm out towards me. Hesitantly, I grabbed it and she hauled me off the floor. She put her hands on her hips and leaned into her right leg, giving me a curt nod.

"My name is Zahra. What's yours?"

"Adelina." I paused. "Thank you," I then whispered shyly.

"I'm going to call you Addie. Remember, my name is Zahra." She emphasized her name and then blinked at me with those big hazel eyes. She's been by my side ever since.

The bell shrieks overhead, snapping me back to reality. I flinch a little. Everyone starts packing up, chairs scraping against tile, the sound grating in my ears. I take my time, pretending to fix the papers in my notebook, because the new guy's sitting right by the door and I really don't want to walk past him.

If I wait long enough, maybe he'll just leave.

Out of the corner of my eye, I see him stand, slinging his backpack over one shoulder. His desk is completely clear, no notebook, no pen. Like he didn't even bother trying. He runs a hand through his dark hair and walks out without a glance back.

I let out the breath that had lodged itself in my throat and grab my stuff, heart still doing that weird fluttery thing. It's stupid, really. He probably didn't think twice about me. But I can't stop replaying the way he looked at me, like he was trying to read every scar on my face.

I shove the thought away and head to my next class, hoping my cheeks aren't as red as they feel.

***

The day goes on and by the time the last period bell rings, I have all of my syllabi and textbooks stowed away in my locker. I click my lock in place and walk out to the student parking lot. Zahra is waiting for me in her car.

My body isn't even in the vehicle when Zahra starts rattling about the day.

"I don't have not one damn class with you! This is horrible," she says, looking appalled. I close the passenger door and Zahra drives away.

"It isn't so bad. We still have lunch at the same time," I respond.

"Yes. And speaking of, where the hell were you? I looked for you everywhere and didn't see you. I sat with Yoona, Liam, and Matthew. Yoona looked stressed about AP exams already, and Liam kept complaining about math. They asked about you."

"I'm sorry! I went over to the library because I needed a class text for AP English. Ms. Bricker sporadically added it to the class readings at the last minute. Completely inconsiderate." The annoyance I felt then comes back to me now.

"Ah, okay! Well, tomorrow then. The gang isn't the same without you."

"Yeah, tomorrow," I agree.

"So..." Zahra starts.

"What?"

"So, like, are we going to talk about that guy in the morning or are we going to pretend it didn't happen?"

"He bumped into us. No big deal. Why talk about him?"

"Well, I did some digging."

I try to keep my face aloof and uninterested, but on the inside, I am dying to know what gossip Zahra has found.

"And?" I prompt.

"And nothing! *Nada.* No one really knows him. I guess he's, like, *new* new."

"Really?" Now, I'm intrigued. "This town is really small. You should have heard something. No one's seen him around?"

"Nope."

The car comes to a stop in front of my house. I grab my bag and open the door.

"Thanks for the ride," I tell her. "Ride's on me tomorrow morning?"

"Yeah! Swing by around 7:30. I should be ready by then."

"Sounds good." I close the door and walk up to my front door.

"Hey!" I hear Zahra yell out. I turn. She's rolled her window down. "We may not know much about him, but the new guy was looking at you pretty hard this morning!"

"No, he wasn't!" I yell back. "Probably just looking at the thing," I say, jabbing at my face with a laugh too sharp to sound natural. Zahra's curls sway as she shakes her head, her silence louder than anything she could've said.

He was probably staring at my scars. Typical. I'm cool, funny, a solid friend. Guys always say that. Translation: "I'm not into you, but I don't want to hurt your feelings." That could be the title of my nonexistent love life.

"Whatever girl, he was looking!"

My eyes trail her car as it disappears down the road.

CHAPTER FOUR

Jackson

Jay hooked me up with new gear today, but not enough. Just knowing the pills are in my car makes my skin crawl, like my veins are already reaching for them. He swears he'll have more by the weekend.

Oxy used to knock me out cold, but now the nightmares slip right through, like they've learned my weak spots. She's there every time I close my eyes. Lately, I've been thinking about asking Jay for something stronger. I hate myself for even thinking it, but I just want the noise to stop.

School feels pointless, friends feel fake, mornings feel like punishment. What's the point when the demons don't clock out?

Parking my car on the curb, I get out and make my way to the garage. When we moved here, I told my dad I was going to turn the garage into a small apartment loft. He

almost looked relieved when I'd said it. I spent the summer renovating the garage until it felt like my own space.

And now, the garage feels like freedom... No dad, no questions. But also like a cell. I built myself a place no one can find me, and now I'm stuck with the silence. No one to notice me pacing about the living room, trying to avoid sleep. No one to see me slip one pill after the other until I eventually pass out either on the couch or in my bed if I manage to make it up the stairs. And, as of recently, no one to hear my panting breath in the middle of the night when the nightmares come to me.

The nightmares hit not long after mom's funeral, back before we even moved here. I was messing around with this girl, and we happened to be sleeping together when the first one hit. I jerked awake so fast I scared the crap out of Diana.

"What, what?!" Diana's voice called out in alarm.

I was gasping for air and sweating profusely, the sheet sticking to my chest. I rubbed my eyes vigorously, trying to erase the image of my mother's face, bloated and purple, eyes vacant. Every time I closed mine, I saw her hanging there, and I awoke choking on the same air that killed her.

"Fuck," I said in desperation, still rubbing my eyes. Diana's hands wrapped around mine in an attempt to pry them off my face.

"Jax, Jax! Stop it! Jax, you're clawing your face! Stop!"

She managed to pull my hands away and I opened my eyes. Her face floated in front of me, flushed with life, a sharp relief from the cold, dead one haunting my sleep. Slowly letting go, she reached out to cup my face and kissed me. Enveloping her in a tight embrace, Diana climbed onto my lap and wrapped her legs around me.

"It's okay," she soothed. I could feel the heat of her body pressing into mine. Welcoming the distraction, I rolled over, pinned her down on the bed, and tried to fuck the nightmare out of my system.

When we finished, the sun was coming up, casting a warm glow in Diana's room.

"I should go," I said. "Your parents will be home soon, right?"

"No. They won't be back for another day." A long silence stretched between us before Diana asked, "What was that, Jax?"

"I don't know," I exhaled.

"A nightmare?"

"Yeah, I guess it was."

She tilted her head up to look at me. "What happened?"

I hesitated, not sure whether I should tell her. I'm not exactly a fan of divulging my emotions to others. It's just not something I do, but given she already knew something was wrong, I told Diana a shorter, nicer version of the nightmare, purposefully avoiding the truth behind my mother's death. That truth stays between me and my father. Diana remained on my chest, listening. When I was done, another silence passed between us.

"Sometimes, I get nightmares too," Diana whispered to me, getting up from the bed and walking over to her dresser. "Not as bad as yours, but they come and go."

She tossed me an orange bottle like it was candy, like sharing was no big deal. Maybe to her, it was just something to take the edge off. To me, it was about to become a lifeline. The bottle was bare, a medical label conspicuously missing.

"What's this?" I asked.

"A way to quiet things down," she said casually and continued. "Sometimes, I feel myself getting antsy. My anxiety is usually a good warning that I won't be able to sleep much." Diana points to the bottle. "I pop one of those before going to bed," she finishes, sitting back down on the bed.

"So, what exactly is in this?" I rattle the bottle in my hand.

"Oxycodone. It was prescribed to me after I tore my ACL in soccer practice last year. The pills minimized my pain, but when I found that they dulled my thoughts, I wanted more. My cousin is a dealer, so now I get the gear from him. You can keep what's left in there if you want. I'll just get some more from him later."

"You sure?"

"Yup," Diana responded. "Just be easy. You don't want to overdo it. You could like, you know, die." I hesitated, my fingers twitching around the bottle, but she didn't look worried. My gut told me to pause, but if Diana was cool with it, maybe it wasn't as dangerous as it felt in my head. If she did it and walked away fine, how bad could it be?

I nodded, reached over the side of the bed for my jeans, and shoved the bottle in one of the pockets.

It was already late and the sun was long gone when I sat out on my balcony for a while, holding the pill bottle in my hands. The lights from the city's skyline were twinkling away in the distance. Left and right, I shifted the bottle in my palms.

Take it?

Don't take it?

The bottle rattled in my hand.

Take it?

Don't take it?

My brain kept hitting repeat, like it was stuck in a loop. I told myself I could throw it away tomorrow. I told myself it was just once.

"Fuck it," I whispered, and swallowed two pills.

It didn't hit right away. But in the shower my arms got heavy, eyelids sagging like weights. I cut it short, barely dried off, and collapsed on my bed naked. Next thing I knew, it was morning.

By noon my skin was slick with sweat, hands trembling so bad I dropped my phone twice. Every noise felt like a knife. I wanted to scream, crawl out of my own skin. Diana confirmed it. Withdrawal. She sent me her cousin's number. Said he could hook me up.

I swore I was done with those pills and left her on read. A few days later the hell eased up. I told myself I was lucky, symptoms were minor. Told myself I wouldn't touch them again. But the bottle sat on my desk, yellow plastic glowing like a dare. Not because I wanted it. Because I was too mad, too exhausted, to throw it out.

Then came the nightmares. Over and over. Some nights I'd wake up punching the bed, furious that sleep had turned into a horror movie. Mom's body kept flashing behind my eyelids. Her face. Her eyes.

One night, shaking, I reached for the bottle. Five pills left. I downed two with a gulp of water. When sleep finally came, it was heavy and black. No dreams. No screams.

Since then, Oxy's been my only friend. My worst enemy. My go-to when everything else fails. Diana's cousin had been steady, clean, transactional. Jay's late, sloppy, but he delivers. And when the nightmares come, that's all that matters.

Looking down into my hands, I see Jay only gave me enough to get me to Friday. Shooting him a text, I ask when would be a good time to score more. He texts back and lets me know that I can meet with him Friday night. I agree and put my phone down on the kitchen table.

Before I have the time to walk away, my phone goes off again. It's another text from Jay.

I'll be at a party though. If you're cool with that, meet me there. I'll text you the address in a sec.

I respond to his text.

Fine by me.

CHAPTER FIVE
Adelina

The first week back is chaos: new schedules, tons of homework, everyone dragging. By Friday, the halls are whirring like we've all been waiting for tonight. The senior party Zahra's guilted me into going. I keep telling myself I don't care. Every nerve in me disagrees.

In class, I sneak quick peeks at *him* whenever Mr. Davis isn't looking. Just a flash over the edge of my notebook. He leans back, legs stretched, bouncing one foot like he can't stay still. Shoulder rolls, blank stare, zero care in the world. Trouble, all over. And I can't stop looking. Today he doesn't even bother with a notebook.

Our eyes catch.

My neck heats up. I pretend to underline nonsense, praying he doesn't notice. Total idiot moment.

The bell rings and everyone rushes out. I grab my things, heart pounding as I pass him for the first time. All I want is a locker to hide in until the day ends. Instead, I shuffle to second period, trying to shake off the embarrassment. But my mind keeps drifting to tonight, to the party. Everyone's hyped, but all I can feel is this twisting knot of nerves. And somewhere beneath it, that pull towards the boy I can't stop sneaking glances for.

By lunch, I've mostly calmed down and head to the cafeteria. The crew's at our usual spot. Liam is staring intently down at his school work. Yoona sketches tiny frames in the corner of her napkin and Matthew keeps glancing at Zahra like he's trying not to.

When I sit, Liam rakes a hand through his fiery, red hair and flips a math worksheet facedown. "Later," he mumbles to himself.

"Thank goodness it's Friday!" Matthew exclaims almost at the same time. He pats his soccer gear next to him, causing Yoona to raise an eyebrow at him.

"I thought soccer season doesn't start for a few more weeks."

"Yeah, but this moron wants to believe he'll get better if he trains. He needs to accept the fact that I'll always be better than him," Liam jokes, all signs of stress erased from his face.

Matthew punches Liam in the arm and then makes to swat him in the back of the head, but Liam ducks it.

Matthew and Liam have been best friends since soccer camp, but you'd never mistake one for the other. Liam's pale skin and bright green eyes contrast sharply with Matthew's deep brown eyes and rich, dark skin. Matthew's mid-back locks, usually pulled into a loose tie, give him this effortless vibe, while Liam's shorter hair keeps him looking sharp. Despite the differences, they share the same tall, athletic build.

"Try again," Liam smirks.

"On the field, anytime," Matthew shoots back.

"Cease fire," Yoona says, not looking up from the napkin sketch. As always, Yoona is the calm one, radiating tranquility wherever she goes. She's the tallest of the girls and is known for changing her hair as often as the weather. This week, her hair's blonde and shoulder-length. Round glasses frame perfectly lined eyes despite her fleeting complaints about the smooth curve of them.

Yoona is still calling for peace when Zahra raises a questioning eyebrow and looks in my direction. I place my arms up, protesting my innocence. "No idea what's going on here," I say, which makes everyone at the table laugh. When the laughter dies down, Matthew asks what our plans for the weekend are.

"Nothing much. I was planning on doing some abstract painting on Saturday, but that's about it," Yoona shares.

"Still trying to apply to that fancy art university?" Liam asks.

"Yeah, I am. I have to complete my portfolio before the submission deadline rolls around."

"What about you, Addie?" Mathew asks.

"Well, Mami is going out of town for a work meeting," I disclose.

"In other words, nothing." Yoona laughs.

"Hold on," Zahra huffs. "You didn't tell me your mom was going out of town."

Mami's latest text stings my memory:

Cuídate, mi amor. No trasnoches.

I told her I wouldn't, thumbs moving faster than my brain. But the words feel sour now, knowing I'd already said yes to the party even though it was under "best friend duress". Technically I didn't lie. I just... didn't tell her everything.

"That's perfect!" Zahra squeals.

"What's perfect? I'm confused." I can tell she's scheming by the glint in her eyes.

"Yeah, me too," Liam backs me up.

Zahra gives him a sharp look. "Tonight is the senior party!"

Senior. Party.

Just hearing it makes my body tense up. Part of me wants to do more this year, to be more, but I don't know where to start. Senior year's supposed to be epic: parties, last chances, zero regrets. Maybe this party is exactly where it begins.

Exhaling in defeat, I say "Crap, you're right... Sounds like you still want me to go?"

"Yes!" she exclaims. "Actually, why don't we all go?"

"Is it some sort of open invite or something?" Matthew asks.

"Yeah, last I heard," Zahra replies.

Matthew turns to Liam. "Yo, Liam, want to go?"

"Yeah, count me in. Why not? I've got nothing better to do."

"And you?" Matthew directs his question at Yoona.

"As long as I leave before midnight. I really want to start on my painting. But I guess I'll go," Yoona agrees.

Triumphantly, Zahra looks at me. It's *the* look. The 'you're not getting out of this' look.

"Fine!" I surrender. "Whose house are we meeting at?"

"Yours? Won't it be empty?" Yoona points out.

"Sounds cool to me," Liam says.

"Yeah, I can be there around 8:30. Maybe 9-ish," Matthew adds.

"8:30 sounds good. Gives us enough time to party," Yoona reasons.

"Guess it's settled. Addie's house at 8:30," Zahra smiles.

"But," I try to say when the bell rings. Everyone immediately gets up and begins walking away from the table. "But wait," I try again, yet no one is listening, all busy gathering their belongings before heading over to their next class.

"See you all later," Matthew says and Liam waves.

"See ya!" Yoona calls out over her shoulder, already walking towards the exit, Zahra at her side. I begrudgingly pick up my backpack and make my way to fifth period.

What did I get myself into?

***

Immediately after school, I haul myself home and start rifling through my closet like it's going to solve my life. It's still early, but my thoughts are already twisting with anxiety. Parties aren't my thing. I hate them. If there's ever a place I don't belong, it's a room full of loud music, fake smiles, and people I barely know.

Why did Zahra even convince me to go? I flip through shirts and jeans, muttering under my breath, "Nothing. Nothing. Ugh, why is nothing good enough?"

I have a few outfits on my bed when my doorbell rings. I'm half walking-half jogging downstairs and the doorbell rings again. "*Ya voy*," I call out. When I open the door, I find Zahra standing there, two big bags in each hand.

"What are those?" I point to the bags, eyes suspiciously squinted.

"Clothes!" She pushes past me and hurries up to my room. Scrambling after her, I hear her suck her teeth the moment she enters.

"You're seriously not thinking of wearing *those*, right?" She points to the strewn clothes on my bed.

Flustered, I say, "I don't know. I can't make up my mind."

"Well, it's because you're doing it all wrong. Your hair and makeup come first. Then you choose the outfit."

"Right. Yeah. That makes *perfect* sense."

"Don't worry. Just leave it up to me."

An hour later, I'm staring at myself in the mirror. Zahra kept the makeup light. Just a hint of gold shadow, a swipe of mascara, and a tiny wing. She holds up two lipsticks. "Pink is sweet," she says. "Burgundy makes your lips pop on camera." I pick burgundy. Not to hide anything. Just because I like it.

My hair spills down my back, some curls brushing my shoulders. A strapless corset tucks into high-waisted bell-bottoms, flaring over block heels. I tug at the corset, trying to cover the cleavage it creates. Zahra smacks my hand away.

"Leave it alone, you look great!"

"I look like… not me." I don't look like school Addie. I look like an Addie who might actually walk into a party and stay.

"Well, you're not supposed to look like boring, old Addie." Zahra moves until she's standing next to me in the mirror. "You're supposed to look glamorous. And, if I do say so myself, I've done an amazing job."

I glance up from my reflection at Zahra. She's rocking a deep green spaghetti strap top paired with a black skirt that teases a split along one leg. Her curls are half up in two Bantu knots, the rest tumbling freely. She looks amazing. The outfit hugs her curves just right, and she owns it.

As Zahra completes her finishing touches, my doorbell rings. Opening the door for the second time tonight, Yoona comes in with Matthew and Liam at her back.

"These two knuckle-heads found me waiting for the bus, so they gave me a lift. You, by the way, look stunning!"

"Yeah, you look great!" Matthew said.

Liam does a mock bow. "I'm speechless."

I laugh and grab at the corset shyly. "I feel so weird."

"No one will care about your feelings tonight. They'll only be looking at you," Zahra's voice rings out from the top of the stairs. "Also, you're all late!" Making it to the bottom of the stairs, Zahra gives a playful twirl. Matthew's grin lights his face a second too long. When her heel wobbles, his hand shoots out before she can stumble.

Glancing at her phone, Yoona claps her hands together. "Alright, let's head out. I'm on Cinderella time." Her heels click as she saunters to the front door. She's wearing high-rise skinny jeans with a white cropped tube top and white heels. Her hair is tied up in a messy bun, a few wisps sticking out and hanging on the sides of her glasses. Matthew and Liam, deliberately matching with black jeans with a black t-shirt, follow her out.

"We'll take my car," Zahra says to me. I nod. Yoona, Matthew and Liam climb into Liam's car as Zahra and I get into hers.

"Code word?" I ask.

"Pineapple," Zahra says. "You text it, we bounce. No questions."

Despite the corset, I breathe a little easier.

"Got the GPS ready! Follow us?" Liam calls from his car, red hair sticking out of his window. Zahra's response is a simple thumbs up.

"What the hell did you get me into?" I ask Zahra.

Excitement finally activates. I catch myself in the rearview mirror and don't flinch. Maybe tonight isn't about being someone else. Maybe it's about being a little more me.

Laughing, Zahra says "What have I gotten you into? The craziest fucking night of your life."

For some reason, I have a feeling she's right.

CHAPTER SIX

Jackson

The bass rings out into the night before I reach the block, a steady thud that syncs with the itch under my skin. I didn't come for the party. I came to make the noise in my head stop. On the front lawn are people standing in small groups, red cups in hand.

Parking sucks, so I circle the block and snag a spot a few houses down. Summer's still hanging around, warm air sticking to my black ripped jeans, white tee, and leather jacket. Snap-back on, I head to the porch, the door already open.

Inside, the air's thick with weed, booze, and sweat. Bodies move to the music. Hot. Too hot. I do a quick sweep: kitchen left, back door right. Escape routes matter.

A few familiar faces, mostly strangers. Gossip eyes on me, the new kid. I push through, aim for the kitchen, and spot the keg. My mouth tips up. High school party rules: underage drinking mandatory. Jay's there, leaning on the counter, a girl pressed between his legs. He catches my eye, takes a swig.

"Yo, Jax!" he calls out and moves the girl from between his legs, placing her next to him. I walk over. "Didn't think you would make it, man." We shake hands and pat each other's back.

"I'm used to the party scene," I lie.

The girl, a cup in her hand, is eyeing me. Jay gives her a slight push and she sashays off, heading back into, what I would guess to be, the now furniture-less living room/dance floor.

Hands reaching for his pocket, Jay asks, "The usual, right? Just ten?"

"You have twenty with you?" I ask.

"Twenty?" Jay blinks.

I nod.

He looks pleased, not worried. That tells me everything.

"Sleep's been breaking through the seams. I need more just to get back to zero." I force a lazy smile onto my face, but I feel my eyes narrow. "And I have the money for it."

"Alright, if you say so. Just be careful with this shit. The dose is high and it hits hard."

Finished with his counting, Jay hands me a small bag, pills securely tied in. "Double the usual price then." I give Jay the money. He counts it, places the wad of bills into his pocket, and extends his hand. "Pleasure doing business with you." Another lame thing Diana's cousin never did with me, but I shake his hand anyways, just to keep the peace.

Jay and I snag drinks before splitting as I ask about the bathroom. "Upstairs," he nods. I take a long pull from my cup, skipping every other step like I'm racing myself.

There's a line. No surprise. When it's finally my turn, I lock the door and drop the act. A couple of pills and a swig later, I exhale a shaky breath. About time.

The bag's still in my hand, eighteen now, not twenty. I stare at it, brain blank, body moving on autopilot. Another pill goes down. Maybe that's what it takes to keep her out.

Then Diana's voice creeps in, how she'd do it to make the kick hit harder. My fingers are already pulling open the cabinet, looking for something flat. Pills scatter across the sink like tiny teeth. I lean forward, steady breath. The burn lights my nose, chemicals down my throat.

Something in me says stop. I don't.

Wiping my nose, I look in the mirror. Some stranger stares back. I don't even care. A hard knock at the door snaps me out of it. I unlock, step out, leave the mess behind.

Back downstairs, I swap my empty cup for another drink. The room's thicker now, more bodies, a couple grinding in a corner. The third drink hits my hand. My skin's on fire, face hot. Focus? Gone.

The music dulls like it's underwater. Faces smear into streaks of color. The heat keeps rising against my skin while my brain floats free, untethered.

The kitchen drains into hot bodies and loud bass.

A girl's laugh is suddenly too close.

A bedroom I don't remember choosing.

I can hear the music, but the stifling smell of sweat is gone. There's that same laugh again. She leans in. I can't track my own thoughts.

"Wait," I manage, palms up. "I'm not okay," I mumble.

I need air. I need to get the fuck out of here.

I ease her aside and step back. "I'm sorry."

A wind blows in from a partially opened window and I look down at my body. *When did my shirt vanish?* The crumpled heap on the floor feels like someone else's skin. I don't recognize the body I'm in anymore.

Clumsily putting on my shirt, the room starts spinning. Fast. The girl is talking. I think she sounds angry, but I'm not listening. My jacket is nowhere to be found.

"Fuck this," I mutter to myself and stumble out of the room, leaving the girl alone. The need for air is overwhelming me, constricting my ribcage.

Black spots cloud my vision. I miraculously manage to find the backyard and slump down on the steps. Thankfully the backyard isn't as packed as the front lawn. Inhaling deeply, I squint my eyes. Through the blur, I catch the shape of a girl. Her voice cuts clean through the static. Sharp, musical, familiar from class. Or maybe I'm hallucinating.

The girl hangs up, turns around, sees me, and yelps, the phone dropping from her hand. I feel the black spots grow wider, my vision growing darker and darker with each inhalation. I'm not sure what I say to her, but I manage to throw my car keys onto the ground before I collapse forward, welcoming the darkness without an ounce of regret.

CHAPTER SEVEN
Adelina

My anxiety tightens as we circle the block for parking. The bass from the house rumbles through me. Matthew jokes about a speedy getaway, but my mind is already planning one. It takes a long time for us to finally find parking, so after seeing a few spots clear up, both Zahra and Liam speed into their respective spots.

"Ready?" Zahra asks before opening her door.

I can see Matthew already walking over to us. He opens the car door for Zahra and offers his hand. Zahra takes it and steps out of the car, Matthew closing the door behind her.

"Someone take a picture of me!" Zahra calls to the crew.

I take a moment to steel myself and then step out of the car. Yoona, with her artistic eye, begins snapping pictures of Zahra.

"Now it's your turn!" Zahra chirps, dragging me forward. Yoona calls out poses like a director while I try not to trip on my heels.

"Okay hand on your hip! No, the other hand. Good... Now face me. Swipe your hair onto your right shoulder. Let it fall... like that. Now hold it!"

When she finishes, Zahra starts sifting through the pictures. "Oh, these are definitely social worthy," she says.

"Girls, let's go!" Matthew yells with impatience.

Liam motions to his watch. "Time's ticking."

"Yoona, don't you want a picture?" Zahra asks.

"Nah, I took some before I left my place. Took them with the pro-cam for my portfolio," she explains. "Don't think I got this glamorous just for you all."

"Great! Now, *let's go*," Matthew implores, walking towards the house with Liam at his side. Yoona, Zahra and I hurry after them.

Heat, bass, weed, sweat, every sense on high volume. Matthew shouts something about cops and I cling to that like a lifeline. "This is why we need to keep the cars close! The last thing we need is to get caught." Since the five of us aren't of drinking age, I'm filled with relief that Matthew has already considered that.

There are bodies everywhere, pressed together, dancing, sweating. The bass hits harder inside, slamming against me like it's trying to rip me apart. We weave through the crowd, calling out hellos to anyone we know. Zahra finds a decent spot, and we circle up.

Liam and Matthew whisper about sneaking drinks. Yoona's in, no worries about driving. Zahra shakes her head. She's the responsible one tonight, but gives Liam a look that says, *I feel you.* Then she surprises me: she insists they bring me a drink. And I actually say yes. For once, I go along with it. They all freeze. I can feel their shock, but honestly... I kind of like it.

"Come again?" Yoona puts her hand to her ear and leans in.

I surprise even myself. "Yes." It feels like a dare, like maybe becoming more starts with a sip.

Zahra, who is as dumbfounded as everyone else, jokes, "Well, that was easy!"

"Liam, close your mouth," I snap. "You too Matthew. Unless you want me to change my mind."

"No!" everyone yells.

Zahra and Yoona push the guys away and they disappear into the crowd of people. Coming back a few moments later, Liam passes Yoona her drink and Matthew mine. Yoona proposes a toast, holding her cup in the air.

"Senior year!"

Matthew and I tap our cups against hers and cheers, Liam and Zahra toasting with us, despite their lack of drinks.

One of Zahra's favorite songs hits, and she's moving like the beat is stitched into her bones. Yoona joins, laughing with every step, and suddenly I'm pulled in too. The bass continues to course through me, each beat echoing through the house, and for a second, nothing else exists. I barely notice the tap on my shoulder until Zahra shakes me back to reality.

We split up. Liam dances with a few girls, Yoona disappears to her art friends, Zahra and Matthew grab water, and I head for the bathroom. The crowd's bigger than I expected, definitely more college students than high schoolers. That explains the chaos, the endless booze, and the heat crushing down on me.

Halfway up the stairs, my phone lights up.

Mami.

Panic spikes. She has no idea I'm here. My nerves make me stumble, nearly sending me tumbling down the steps. I catch myself, detour to the kitchen, and let the call go to voicemail. Quick, nervous texts to my friends, a fake excuse, and I tuck my phone away.

When I glance up, a guy's leaning against the sink, also glued to his phone. I clear my throat. He looks up.

"Do you know where the backyard is? I don't want to pass through all those people again if I can help it," I say and gesture towards the dance floor.

"Yeah, just make a left when you leave the kitchen and you'll see the screen door."

"Thanks!" I turn to leave.

"Hold up," he calls out.

I freeze. "Yeah?"

"Weed? E? Coke?" he grins. His eyes slide down my outfit. "It'll make your night special."

My pulse jumps higher. "No thanks."

Attempting to make a fast getaway, I begin walking, with purpose, out of the kitchen to the backyard.

"Just ask for Jay if you ever need anything," he calls out behind me.

Thankfully, the backyard is not as packed as I expected it to be. There are clusters of people standing about, a few hidden away in the dark shadows. Sending a quick prayer to every God that exists, I walk to a semi-empty spot in the backyard, away from the house and the music, and call my mother back.

"*Hola*, Addie. I tried calling you," she answers.

"*Hola* Mami," I say softly, turning my back on the party. The music pounds behind me, English lyrics mixing with her Spanish questions. "I was in the shower. How are you? How was your flight?"

"I'm okay, *gracias a Dios*. The flight went well. It was quick, but there was a long line at baggage claim." She pauses. "What's that noise in the background?"

"Oh, I have the music station playing on the tv." The lie slides awkwardly off my tongue. "Do you meet with the other psychologists tomorrow for the conference or is that on Sunday?"

Mami falls for the distraction. "Yes, it's going to be a long day, but I'm excited to present our findings." Then she says, "Okay, I'll let you go. I'm ordering wine from room service. There's sancocho in the freezer. Heat it up, maybe add some buttered toast. I also left rice, beans, and *pollo guisado*. Can you manage until I get back?"

"*Sí* Mami, I'll manage."

"Okay Addie, it was good to hear your voice. I miss you already. Call me if you need anything, okay?"

"*Sí* Mami," I say again, with a tone that let's her know she's nagging a bit.

"I love you," she says.

I say it back and hang up.

Having gotten away with lying to my mom, my anxiety is subsiding. I check my messages and see one from Zahra.

Babes, we're all back. Where are you???

Turning around to go back to the party, I text her back.

Be right there. :)

I'm about to put my phone away, but then I scream, the sound coming out before I even know why, and the phone hits the floor hard.

***

"Holy shit!" I yell and grab my heart, scared half to death.

Sitting on the steps is the absolute last person I expect to see. Hair's a mess, collar smeared red. I blink, trying to match this to the boy from chemistry. Nope. Brain's on strike. After a second, I grab my phone, shove it in my purse, and force myself to walk over.

"Hey." His deep voice is sluggish and heavy.

"Hey?"

He looks at me, eyes glassy-bright. Greener than I've ever seen them, like neon under water. For a instant I just stare, frozen, because what do you even do? His eyelids start to sag, heavy, like the whole world's slipping out from under him.

"Hey!" I snap my fingers in his face. This time, I'm a bit more forceful. "Are you okay?"

"You should know. Because I'm probably going to die," he slurs.

"What? What are you talking about?"

The new kid reaches into his pocket and throws his keys at me. *What the heck?* He sways a bit even though he's sitting.

"My car. I think it's down the block." There's a pause. "Not sure."

With that, his upper body leans forward, his head landing between his knees.

I run over to him in a panic, lift his head up and smack his cheeks a few times. No response.

"You have got to be freaking kidding me," I mumble. "There's no way you're *that* drunk."

I pace the patio, scanning for anyone who looks remotely useful. No one. Everyone's wrapped up in their own world and I can't scream over the music. I drop to my knees and lean close to his face. He's breathing. Pulse is there. Alive. I stand and pace again. "Crap, crap, crap," I whisper, because say it enough and maybe it'll stop feeling unreal.

I grab his keys, remembering he said his car was down the block, and try to haul him up. He's dead weight. One step, then I'm stuck. I'm about to flag down some guy when he bends over and vomits on the grass. Gross. I bail out the side door and sprint down the street clicking the key fob like a maniac.

A car beeps a few houses down. I run, high heels slapping the pavement, start the engine and pull it close to the driveway. The backyard's thinning out now; a few stragglers. He's still slumped on the steps.

"Hey, new kid, work with me," I tell him. He mumbles. "I'm going to lift you, but you have to help." Somehow he does, a slurred stumble, and we make it to the side exit.

Two boys step out, smokers, I think. I call, desperate, "He passed out. Drank too much. Can you help me get him in his car?" They look at each other, shrug, then take him from me. They haul him to the back seat like he's nothing and shove him inside. I say thanks and refuse their offer to stay. No idea why I do that.

I'm sweating. My feet are sprouting fresh blisters from my heels and my hands shake. I yank my shoes off, tie my hair up, breathe. Call 911? *No! I don't want to be the girl who ruins the party.* I grip his keys. "Don't make me do this alone," I whisper, staring at his limp form in the mirror.

I text the group:

Hey, I need you guys to come out front.

No answer.

Helloooooooooo????

Pineapple.

Silence. Voicemails when I call Zahra, Yoona, Liam, Matthew. Figures. I'm solo.

I dig through his pockets, find a wallet, pull his license. Jackson Hurst. Eighteen. New York. There's a post-it with an address. Close enough. I shove the wallet back, start the car, and drive like my life depends on it.

A few blocks out, he gags. Vomit floods his lap like a sick waterfall. I skid to the curb, throw the door open, clamber into the back, and shake him. "Jackson! Jackson, wake up!" The smell hits me hard, but he's alive. Thank God he's alive.

This is past my skill level. This is emergency-level. I roll every window down, change route, and gun it to the ER. At the ramp I jam my shoes on, fling the door, and bolt into triage, leaving the car idling because I don't care about the keys. I'm sprinting, breath burning, heart hammering, yelling for help the second I hit the sliding doors.

Nurses move. Somebody yanks a gurney. I can't stop shaking. I keep repeating his name until someone takes over and tells me to step back.

They take him. I hover, stupid and breathless, until a nurse looks at me like I'm the only one who matters. "You did the right thing," she says, and the words land like a soft rock in my chest. I slump onto a bench and finally let the air out, the panic draining one shaky breath at a time.

One of the doctors approach me. "Do you know what he had to drink tonight? Any drugs?"

"No! I don't know. He just passed out, then he started vomiting, so I brought him here." My response is nowhere near as calm as his questions.

"Are you sure? The more we know, the quicker we can help him," he presses.

"No, no, I'm sorry!"

"Rivera!" one of the nurses yells. The doctor glances up, and I follow his eyes. The nurse beside Jackson mentions finding a small bag in his pocket. The doctor just goes "tsk" and shakes his head. They start rolling him toward the ER. I didn't see any bag when I rifled through his wallet. What the heck did he get into tonight?

Dr. Rivera returns his attention to me. "Are you related to him?"

I should tell the truth. I should tell him that I don't know Jackson. That I just found him like this. I should call my friends again and go home. There are many things I should do. Instead, I lie. Again. The words taste bitter, but I swallow them anyway.

"I'm his sister."

Dr. Rivera nods for me to follow. "Roll him into intensive care," he orders, then pauses at the desk. "He's probably taken more than his body can handle. We'll start with charcoal, try to avoid pumping his stomach. He's still breathing. A good sign." He sees my face and softens. "You did the right thing bringing him here."

He shakes my hand and walks off, leaving me to sign in and head upstairs. The eighth-floor waiting room is nearly empty, just the steady sound of vending machines filling the silence. I drop into a chair, head against the wall. I keep telling myself I should've left, but I didn't. I'm still here. Watching a stranger's undoing like it's my own brother's.

Opening my eyes, I check my phone to see the blur of missed calls and unanswered texts from my friends. For the umpteenth time this night, the lies flow out of me: taxi ride home, Mother Nature dropping in unannounced. Classic. Predictable. Liam, Matthew, and Yoona take the bait. Zahra, on the other hand, isn't as easily convinced.

BS. WTH is going on Addie? You texted Pineapples.

Of course, Zahra would be the one to question me. I prepare to text her back, but I'm interrupted. A nurse calls out for the Hurst family and it takes me a minute before I realize I'm the one she's looking for. I call back to her and she beckons me over.

"We've got him stabilized and he's on an IV for fluids. For now, he's holding up well and we were able to avoid pumping his stomach," she informs as we walk out of the waiting room. We stop at a door at the end of the hallway and I follow the nurse inside.

"Should he wake up, just hit this button right here and one of us will be in to check on him. Do you need anything before I go?"

"No," I respond. "I'm okay. Thank you."

When the nurse leaves, I sit in the reclining chair positioned next to Jackson's bed. He almost looks peaceful except for all of the wires connected to his arms. Not wanting to disturb him, I recline the chair back and take a moment to reply to Zahra.

I'm ok. I just came home. Too much going on @ the party. Anyways, I'm going to sleep now. Text you in the morning. <3

She responds.

Sighing, I put my phone on silent and slip it into my purse. In one way, I guess Zahra was right. This has been the craziest night of my life.

CHAPTER EIGHT
Jackson

It's dark when I enter my house. I set my keys down on the foyer table and begin removing my shoes. Doesn't seem like anyone is home yet. Dropping my shoes beside my book bag, I head over to the kitchen. Having spent a few hours on the track field with my team, my stomach has been nagging me for hours, rumbling for food.

I'm passing the living room, almost making it to the kitchen, when I see something from the corner of my eye. I still haven't bothered to turn on any lights. I step into the living room and flip the switch, bright lights coming on.

My breath catches in my throat and I freeze. She's just hanging there. Swaying. I'm confused. I'm not exactly sure what I'm seeing. And then, reality begins to sink in. My heart plummets and I scream.

I open my eyes and try to calm my breathing.

Just another fucking dream, I tell myself.

I sit up, disoriented, IV in my arm, dim light bleeding in from the hallway. A nurse rushes past. Rubbing crust from my eyes, I spot a pitcher of water on the table and grab it like I'm dying of thirst.

Then I notice her, curled in a chair beside me, hair spilling across her face, chest rising and falling under a blanket. Chemistry class girl. Why the hell is she here? Hell, why am I here?

Piecing last night together is brutal. Jay, the score, the pills, loud music, maybe a hookup... my leather jacket's gone. Everything else is a blur, and somehow, I'm in a hospital.

She stirs, opens her eyes slowly, still looking as muddled as I feel.

"Hey," I gently call out to her, not wanting to scare her. She looks my way, groans, and then smiles.

"Hey," she whispers back, arching her back. The blanket has fallen from her upper body exposing not just her arms, but her chest.

"You're from my chemistry class, right?"

"Yeah," she shifts her gaze to the floor.

"Think you can tell me how the fuck this happened?" I ask her, circling my index finger around the room.

"So, I'm not exactly sure," she begins. She shifts the chair upright, blanket pooled across her lap, legs tucked under. Her fingers worry at the edge of the fabric, eyes flicking between me and the floor. In small, halting bursts she explains. The senior party, backyard, finding me slumped and barely breathing. My keys in her hand. Her panic. The rush to get me here.

When she finally meets my eyes again, her bottom lip trembles. The word "overdose" hangs unspoken in the space between us. She tucks a strand of hair behind her ear, almost shy, and says that she told the hospital she was my sister. No reason, she mutters, she just did.

I regard her for a long moment and she seems uncomfortable under my gaze. "So, does my hero have a name?"

"Um, Adelina, but everyone calls me Addie. You're Jackson, right?"

"Jax. No one has ever called me by my full name except for—" I cut my sentence short. Truth is, the only person who called me by my full name was my mother.

"Just call me Jax"

"Jax," she repeats. "It has a nice ring to it."

A nurse hustles in, relieved I'm awake, chattering softly while checking my vitals. Quick questions, a hospital menu handed over. I stick to plain pancakes and eggs. She winks at Addie, slipping her a promise of one too.

Once we're alone, Addie stretches and heads to the bathroom, hair falling like a dark curtain down her back. Something about her shifts in my head. Her lip curves just a little differently, almost like a secret signature. It tugs at me.

Back in the chair, she scrolls her phone, lashes thick and long. I can't stop staring. When she looks up, cheeks flushed, hair framing her face, I notice the faint line of her scars, barely there, but somehow making her more real. Different. And I can't look away.

When I call to her, she responds "Yeah?", putting her phone down beside her.

"Can you help me get to the bathroom?" I ask her, point up. "I don't want to fuck the wires up."

Addie nods, and I haul myself out of the bed, limbs heavy and sore. She untangles me from the wires, and we shuffle to the bathroom, me leaning on her shoulder, one hand on the IV. She steadies me, but even now, part of me still aches for what nearly killed me.

Alone, I hit the bathroom, relieve myself, splash water on my face, brush my teeth. My throat burns, alcohol still clinging. I glance in the mirror; trashed doesn't even cover it. I manage a quick wash, careful with the wires, but every movement drags at my muscles. By the time I tie the gown, my hands are shaking, like my body is still screaming at me.

***

Feeling a nudge on my shoulder, I wake up, Addie's face above mine. "Breakfast is here," she says.

I sit up and begin unpacking the food, Addie doing the same on her chair. We eat in silence. I'm halfway done with mine when a doctor enters the room.

"Good morning. I'm Dr. Rivera. How are you feeling?" he asks.

"I'm fine," I lie.

I can feel my body's weakness, in desperate need of recovery. Or maybe another fix, I'm not exactly sure I can discern the difference at this very moment.

"Well, you seem to be in better shape than yesterday. Your heartbeat has come up, back to normal. You might feel sore for a few days though." Dr. Rivera looks between me and Addie, his eyes slightly softer than before as they land on mine. "I recommended a few treatment programs available for youths in your discharge papers. Everything will be ready for you tomorrow morning when you're checked out. Any questions?"

"Tomorrow? I can't leave today?"

"I don't recommend you leave today. We still want to keep an eye on your vitals," he explains.

"I think I'll do just fine at home," I say.

Dr. Rivera gives me a look before turning back to my chart. "You're of legal age. I recommend you stay, but it is ultimately your decision." Then he turns to Addie and says, "Maybe you can convince him otherwise," and she nods, giving him a small smile. "When you make your decision, call one of the nurses over. Good luck," he says, signing my chart and then placing it at the foot of the bed before walking out.

"Are you sure you want to leave?" Addie asks doubtfully.

"Yes. I can do the same exact thing from the comfort of my own bed."

"Okay," she says, but I can tell she disapproves.

I shove the rest of my breakfast aside and slowly get dressed, wincing at every sharp ache. Addie's face goes bright red, and she looks away to give me some privacy. Once I'm done, I call her over, and we head to the main desk. A few minutes of insurance talk and forms later, Addie is leading me out to my car.

"I'll catch a ride or something," she says.

I raise an eyebrow. "I can't drive," I tell her flatly. "My vision isn't exactly steady right now."

"You want me to drive you home?" she blurts out.

"Unless you want to find me dead in a ditch somewhere, that would be nice. You can get a ride from there."

We get into my car and Addie drives out of the parking lot. I set the car's GPS to 'Home' and the directions light up on the dashboard. The drive is silent, Addie seeming to be deep in her thoughts. In my own thoughts, I look out the passenger window and observe the scenery.

When we get to the front of the house, I direct Addie to drive around back. Getting out of the car, Addie follows me to the garage. She's silently looking around, taking in her surroundings, but her eyes come away confused as though asking why we're walking into the garage and not the house.

"I like having my own space, so the garage is kind of like my own apartment now. You'll see when we go in," I explain to her.

I dig through my pockets and nothing. My gear's gone. Panic spikes until Addie taps my shoulder, holding my keys. *She needed those to drive, moron.* I thank her, grip what's left of my dignity, and unlock the door.

CHAPTER NINE
Adelina

If Friday night was insane, being alone with Jax here tops it. I could order a ride, call Zahra, or just leave, but I follow him. His "garage" is nothing like I expected: a loft with spiral stairs and trophies lining the walls, proof he once ran toward wins, not escapes. I exhale, letting the quiet wash over me.

Jax is bent down in front of me, placing his shoes in the shoe holder, when he glances over his shoulder and asks, "What?"

"Nothing. It's just that it's really nice!"

"It took me a good part of the summer to put it all together, but I'm pretty happy with my man cave," he says with a laugh.

Surprised, my eyebrows shoot up. "You did this all by yourself?"

He gets up and motions for me to take off my shoes. As I do, he responds "Yeah, though the couch was a pain in the ass to get through the door. Should have brought it in before getting rid of the garage door. Not my smartest moment."

Jax walks over to the living room, me in tow, and sits down on the couch. Walking to the opposite side of the couch, I sit, silence enveloping once more. I look over to see Jax rubbing his face.

"You must be tired," I say. "I can order myself a ride now. I feel like I'm intruding." I can hear myself rambling, my nerves taking over.

"Addie, you're not intruding, but I'm sure your parents are wondering where you've been."

I pause. "No." His eyebrows slightly raise, as if surprised. "My mom is out of town." I have no idea why I just told him that.

"That would explain why you were able to play super hero last night," Jax jokes. His smile doesn't reach his eyes and I feel the joke land heavy.

"Something like that," I respond, reaching for my phone. "What about your parents? Isn't the hospital going to call them or something?"

When he doesn't answer, I look over to him. His face is devoid of emotion and I worry I said something I shouldn't have. Just as I'm about to begin nervous rambling, Jax speaks.

"Being 18 has its perks. No calls."

"That's right," I say quietly. Opening my phone to order a ride, Jax places a hand over the screen.

"If no one's expecting you, let me drive you home later. It's the least I could do."

A dozen rules flash through my head, the ones Mami trusts me to follow while she's away. But I don't move. My eyes find Jax. Dark circles under his eyes, exhaustion hanging like a shadow. He's joking, trying to lighten it all, but maybe leaving him would be the "right" choice. Maybe. Then I catch that look in his eyes, and suddenly all the "should's" vanish. I do the one thing I shouldn't. I stay.

"Ok," I nod. "I could use a bit of water if that's ok."

Jax gets up, long legs carrying him to the kitchen quickly. He returns with two glasses and, this time, sits next to me. I take in the contours of his face, the strong bridge of his nose, the perfectly shaped cupid's bow above his parted lips. Now my palms begin to sweat. *Why is he making me so nervous?*

I can't look away as Jax meets my gaze. "I make you nervous."

My eyes snap to his. It's a statement, not a question. As if he can read my every thought.

I take in a sharp breath and lower my gaze to my lap, picking at my nails. "Yeah, you do," I confess. "This entire weekend has been crazy. I'm completely out of my element. I haven't showered. I'm still wearing this ridiculous outfit." The words spill out of me as I release frustrations I didn't even know I was carrying.

"For one, you don't look ridiculous. You look nice. But I do agree on the shower part. You still smell like party. Come," he tells me and walks me over to the bathroom. Opening up a cabinet, he hands me a spare towel. "You can shower here." He pauses, sizing me up, and then smirks.

"I'll bring you some sweats and a t-shirt. You want a toothbrush?" I nod and he rummages in the cabinet until he finds one. "Toothpaste is there by the sink," he points. "Use whatever you can find in there," he points in a circular motion to the tub, "and I'll leave the clothes out by the door for you."

I thank him quietly, clutching the towel to my chest. The moment the door closes, I smell my hair, then try to sniff my armpits. Jax is right. Embarrassment floods through me. Putting the towel on a hook, I strip and, after a bit of tinkering, successfully get the water to the right temperature before stepping in.

The water runs through my hair, down my face and body, and it feels amazing to finally wash off last night's grime. I search for shampoo and sigh. Of course Jax only has one of those two-in-one bottles I can't stand. Still, I lather up, and by the second rinse my annoyance is gone, replaced with gratitude for just being able to shower. I grab his body wash next, earthy sandalwood, and scrub until the water at my feet runs murky. Gross, but not surprising. Hours of sweat will do that.

I shut off the water and step out, wrapping a towel around me. Cracking the door, I find a pile of clothes waiting, grey sweats, socks, and a white t-shirt. I pull them inside and close the door fast. They smell faintly of sandalwood, same as his body wash, and for a second I wonder if that's what Jax actually smells like. The thought makes me dizzy, and I shove it away.

I slip into the socks and sweats, then hesitate with the t-shirt. No bra. Panic flickers, but there's nothing I can do. I pull it on anyway, tuck it into the waistband, tie the drawstring tight, and let a few damp strands of hair fall forward across my collarbone, hoping it hides enough.

Back in the living room, I flop onto the couch, phone in hand. Jax's footsteps echo upstairs, and I ignore the string of missed calls and texts from Zahra. I answer Mami's instead, keeping one lifeline sane.

Scrolling through my socials, I freeze. Zahra posted a picture from last night. *Is that me?* The smile, the twinkle in my eyes, the silhouette outlined in Liam's white car behind me. Triple-digit likes with comments like "Is that Addie?!" and "Wow, who would've thought?"

I shut the phone off.

I *should* feel happy. But that girl in the photo? She's not me. She's built with makeup and the "right" outfit. She's someone who is not defined by the lines, the scars, the part of me I try to vanish. By Monday, I'll be back to boring old Addie, unnoticed and invisible.

I tuck my feet under me, head against the armrest. The shower runs in the distance. My eyes grow heavy. Zahra's picture lingers in my mind, a fraud hiding behind artificial beauty.

CHAPTER TEN

Jackson

Walking down to the living room, I find Addie curled up at the edge of the couch, asleep. Not wanting to wake her, I place a blanket over her and dim the lights as I head out of the living room and back up to my bedroom.

Skeptically walking over to one of my drawers, I reach towards the back, and after rummaging for a few seconds, I feel it. Hidden and tucked away for moments exactly like this one. Sighing, I bring my arm out. I mouth a silent thank you to myself, then catch my reflection. Addie's downstairs, and here I am upstairs, still choosing poison.

I know I should give my body a break, but the shakes are back, sweat slick on my forehead. Withdrawals creeping in like a bad dream. *What do you even have left to lose?* The voice in my head taunts. And honestly? Nothing. So I pop a pill anyway, praying it'll shut the noise up. The darkness doesn't argue.

***

Hours slip by. The sun sinks low, casting the room in a wash of warm orange light that stretches through the window and softens the edges of everything. When I stand up, I've got a mellow high which makes me feel sluggish, but my hands are back to normal.

Jogging down the steps, I raise the living room lights slightly and am a bit surprised to see Addie still asleep. I look at my watch and count how many hours she's been out cold. Hunger pangs hit me and I wake her up this time around.

I crouch down in front of her and rock her shoulder gently. Addie mumbles something and slowly opens her eyes. When her eyes settle onto mine, they widen and she shrinks back a bit. I take my hand away from her shoulder and stand, giving her some space.

"How long have I been asleep?" she asks grogily.

"Enough to figure out what we're having for dinner."

"Dinner?!" Addie's eyes grow wide and she reaches for her phone. When she sees the time, she groans. "Jax, I'm so sorry. I should leave. I didn't mean to fall asleep." She's reaching for the rest of her things.

I lay a hand on one of hers and she freezes, looking up at me. I offer dinner and a movie. Truth is, I just don't want the silence back yet. "Or I could just drop you off now if you want. I'm indifferent, all up to you," I add.

I leave Addie on the couch and check the kitchen. Fridge's empty. Pantry's worse. Just sad little cans. Food hasn't exactly been my priority lately; most of my allowance goes to pills, not groceries. I frown and turn around. Addie's perched on a stool at the island, watching me like she's trying to figure me out.

"So, what's for dinner?" Addie asks, one of her shy smiles coming out.

Not thinking she would actually accept my offer, I smile back at her, noting how small she looks in my clothes.

"I mean, I don't mind putting together a struggle meal. I was thinking sloppy joes." Addie cringes. "Yeah, that's what I thought. We can do take-out?"

"Take-out sounds better. Have you ever eaten from *Mamitas*?"

"I've passed it, but no, I haven't eaten there."

"Well," she starts, "it's Latin cuisine. They have huge portions for a really good price. And they serve good side dishes. Also, their desserts are to die for."

"You had me at huge portions," I joke and she gives me a bigger smile.

Thirty minutes later, we are sitting on the kitchen island, plates spread between us. After a few bites, Addie squints her eyes and wags her spoon at me. "How'd you end up here?"

The question is unexpected, but I follow her lead and ask "What do you mean 'how did I end up here'?"

"Like, here. In this town," Addie clarifies. "Your ID says you're from New York and I'd never seen you around until the first day of school."

"The first day of school?"

"You know, when you ran into my best friend and I dropped my books."

Now it's my turn to bunch up my face. "You're the girl who dropped her books?"

"Yeah," she says. In a smaller voice, she adds, "You don't remember?"

"Not really, I wasn't really paying attention. I didn't know that was you on the first day. But I do remember how hard that girl was blushing." I tease. "Kind of like you are now."

Addie looks down at her plate and clears her throat. When she looks back up at me, I answer her question.

"I was born and raised in New York. My father ended up getting a promotion right before the summer and that's how we ended up here." It's a lie, but it's better than the truth. "It's a big difference, but life is a lot calmer here. What about you?" I divert the attention back to her. "Have you always lived here?"

"Yeah. Mami was born over there though. She came with her parents from the Dominican Republic who worked their butts off so she could get an education. She became a psychologist and even has her own practice in town."

"And your father?"

Addie pauses and drops her gaze again, picking at her fingers.

"He passed away a few years ago," she says slowly.

"I'm sorry to hear that," I respond earnestly. I don't ask anything further knowing all too well what it's like to not want to talk about the dead that haunt us.

Surprisingly, Addie continues. "It was a rare form of cancer. Stage four when they found it." She sighs at the last part and then laughs. "He taught me how to fight."

"Fight?" I raise my eyebrows at the unexpected turn in the conversation.

"He was worried kids would bully me because of my condition. So, he trained me in boxing."

"Now that's impressive."

"No, no," she quickly adds. "It's not like I've ever actually had to fight. People here are generally nice. It could be worse, you know?"

I study her carefully and avoid asking her about her condition even though I'm curious to know what it is. Instead, I take a drink from my cup and ask "What's this one again?" pointing to a container that seems to have a very liquidy cake in it.

"*Tres leches*," she says, drawing out the syllables.

"Three... milks?" I repeat, grinning when she nods.

"Exactly," she laughs, "Try it."

She watches me take a bite, her face lighting up, and I realize it's the first time in forever she's given me something that isn't just survival. A few feet away, her scent drifts over, mingling with mine. I shouldn't notice it this much. But I do.

"Here," she says, passing me the spoon. I lean in and open my mouth instead of grabbing it. Her words catch mid-air, pink spreading across her cheeks. My motion started playful, but seeing her blush makes it almost unbearable.

Addie holds my gaze for the first time. Her brown eyes catch the kitchen lights, turning golden. I open my mouth, and she slowly feeds me the cake. Without thinking, I cover her hand with mine, guiding the spoon back to the table.

"So?" she whispers.

"It's good," I murmur.

Heat coils through me, my body wanting her, every scar, every inch. I stand, pulling her close, hand on her lower back. Realizing there's nothing under her t-shirt, desire spikes. I lean in... then stop. She closes her eyes but doesn't move closer. I brush her hair back and feel myself trembling. *What the hell am I doing?*

A phone rings and Addie steps away.

Almost as if coming out of a daze, she clears her throat, blinks a few times, and quickly walks away into the living room to answer her phone.

Where the hell did it come from? I've been with plenty of girls, but this... this burns in a way I've never known.

Tidying up in the kitchen, I overhear Addie on the phone, speaking in Spanish. By the time I finish up and go over to the living room, she is in the process of putting it away, an awkward, tangible tension cleaved between us. Addie places a lock of hair behind her ear.

"That was my mom," she says, filling in the silence.

"Everything good?"

"Yup, all good."

Trying to cut the tension, I ask Addie if she wants to watch a movie. I don't even care about movies, but I need something to keep my brain from spiraling over her. *Why the hell did I ask her to stay?* Internally, I kick myself.

She nods, and I head to the cabinet under the TV. *Because you totally wrecked her weekend, that's why.* I pull out a stack of DVDs, hoping one of them can distract both of us, or at least distract me from staring at her.

"I don't have much of a selection. Just comedies, horrors and action. No romance or chick flicks or whatever," I tell her, bringing the stack over to the couch.

"I *hate* romance anyways," she states, emphasizing the word 'hate'.

I study her again. "Okay. So, what would you like then?"

"Can we do an action movie?"

"Sure, pick."

Addie picks a superhero movie, and I set it up, lights off as I return to the couch. I leave space between us like distance can fix anything. She's glued to the screen; I'm glued to her.

What is it about this girl? The way she fits in my hands, soft skin, those big brown eyes that cut through me, scars and all. Her lips look soft enough to taste. For a second, I want to lean in and ruin everything.

But I don't. I can't. The kitchen was a stupid move. She's the only clean thing I've touched in months, and I'm poison. She deserves to stay untouched by it.

So when the credits roll, I'm up fast, voice flat. "I'll take you home." It sounds like I'm pushing her away, because I am. She mentions changing back into her clothes and I toss her a hoodie instead, hanging on to the thin thread of control left in me.

By the time we're in the car, she's gone quiet, staring out at the dark, walls built up again. I see it in her eyes, the same walls I've had my whole life. It kills me.

Then the itch starts crawling back in, whispering to me from my emergency stash at home. My hands tighten on the wheel, forcing myself to keep driving straight. She's right next to me, but I already feel myself slipping.

CHAPTER ELEVEN
Adelina

Once my address is plugged in, Jax starts the car without a word. The gentle rumble of the engine fills the space where his warmth used to be. I slump into my seat, arms crossed, wishing I could just blink and disappear before either of us has to say something awkward.

He's quiet too, eyes locked on the road like I'm not even there, but every time we hit a red light, I feel his gaze flicker over me. Quick. Unreadable. Nothing like the guy from a few hours ago.

The air gets colder with every mile, like we're both slowly turning back into the versions of ourselves from school. Him, distant, untouchable. Me, small and invisible. Fifteen minutes drag by before the car slows in front of my house, and the silence between us feels heavier than the night outside.

I go to open the door when I hear Jax say, "Hey, hold up a sec."

I let go of the door handle and look at him. Not wanting to meet his eyes, I look past him.

"Yeah?"

"Thanks again. For everything."

"You're welcome. It was no big deal."

"It kind of was though."

I need to get out of the car. I need to get away from him and the mix of feelings he creates within me. It's a whirlwind of emotions that I can't keep up with. Nodding, I open the door and step out of the car. When I close the door, he rolls the window down. I turn around.

"Dinner was nice, Addie."

My face immediately grows hot, cheeks and nose turning a deep shade of red and betraying the poker face I'm trying to maintain. Not knowing what to say, I turn away from him and walk to my front door. I don't hear his car drive off until I've closed the door behind me.

I know he's bad news. Drugs, danger. Everything I should run from. And yet, my body doesn't listen. It pulls me toward Jax like gravity, ignoring all the warning bells going off. Whatever this is, I've never felt it with anyone else.

I've always kept my distance, scared rejection would hurt more than never trying. I flash back to a sixth-grade birthday party. Spin the Bottle. The bottle landed on me. The boy froze, shook his head, and mouthed he didn't want to kiss my lips. Heat burned my cheeks as I ran to the bathroom, holding back tears. When I came back, everyone had moved on.

I never wanted to feel that again. But right now, I do. Rejected, embarrassed, and, worst of all, wanting him.

I wanted him close, his scent spinning my head. If Mami hadn't called, who knows what might've happened.

He looked everywhere but at me, and it stung worse than words. Maybe he was scared. Maybe it wasn't all rejection.

I bury the thought fast. By the time I collapse into bed, tears are already streaming. I should've never stayed. Mami always said I skipped the rebellion phase, but this isn't how I pictured it. Out of my depth, hurt, and crying, I shut my eyes, regret pulsing through me.

***

On Sunday, I contemplate burning the outfit I wore, instead choosing the safe option of hiding it in the back of my closet, never to be seen again. Monday comes. Tuesday too. By Friday, chemistry's first period feels emptier than the back row. Then, two weeks slide by.

In that time, I had to answer a lot of questions from Zahra who was, and still is, convinced that I am lying, which I am. Keeping to my newly acquired skill, I continuously tell Zahra the same story over and over. Eventually, Zahra let me off the hook and we went back to business as usual.

I can't lie. A part of me still looks forward to seeing Jax. I try to push him out of my head, but it's impossible. His touch lingers, his voice echoes, his smile and scent tangled in every thought. He haunts me in ways I'll never admit.

But he hasn't been at school for days. His chemistry chair stays empty, and every time someone walks in late, I hope it's him, then realize it's not.

It should feel like a relief, but it doesn't. Forgetting him takes every ounce of energy, and even then, his memory claws back.

To escape, I throw my book bag in the car and drive to the soccer field. Liam and Matthew are walking together; I honk and wave, they wave back. A few minutes later, Zahra and Yoona spill out of the gym. I honk again. Zahra spots me, and they head over.

Getting in, Zahra is talking about how gruesome it is to still have gym class as a senior.

"I could be doing other things with my time. Like writing my personal statements for my college applications," Zahra complains.

Yoona sucks her teeth at Zahra, but says nothing.

"That's what you have study hall for, Zahra," I counter. To this, Yoona responds.

"That's what I've been telling her this entire period. She's not the only one. I'm stuck in gym too and I also have personal statements to write."

"Well sorry for being so whiny! I also hate sweating. Not everyone is like Addie here, who decided, voluntarily may I add, to take gym during Period Zero when no one in the world is awake yet. How many years did you even do that for?" Zahra asks me.

I take a moment to think. "Two years. Maybe two and a half years. I just wanted to receive the credits quickly and make room for other classes."

"Like chem and psych," Yoona chimes in.

Zahra sharply turns to me. "You're taking Psych 101? But that's a college level course."

"I wanted to get ahead," I say and shrug my shoulders. "Anyways, are we going to the café or not? We could stay here and argue about classes too if that seems more fun."

"Drive," commands Yoona, her index finger pointed out to the road in front of us.

We get there quickly and easily find parking. Entering the café, the three of us place our orders, sitting at a table in the back right-hand corner of the room. It is a small and cozy café, with wooden benches covered with pillows and comfortable chairs to sit in. On the table are little bowls with bits and pieces of chocolate espresso beans. I take a few and chew on them, leaning back into one of the benches.

In the midst of small talk, the waiter brings our food over and, after having a few bites, Zahra puts her spoon down. Yoona is sipping her tea and I'm stirring chocolate espresso beans into my coffee.

"We have serious business to talk about ladies," Zahra declares.

"Spit it out then," Yoona says, rather calmly.

"This is senior year!" she begins excitedly. "There is so much we need to do." I begin to protest about wanting a calm year by remaining under the radar, but she shoots me a stare so deadly that I shrink back. Huffing, she holds her hand up. "First, we kicked off the year with an awesome party." She folds her thumb in. "Then, there's college letters." Down goes her index finger.

Yoona bunches her eyebrows and says, "I'm confused. This is what was so important?" She laughs. "This isn't that serious. One has already happened and the other will happen. You made it seem like the end of the world is coming."

"You didn't let me get to three." Zahra looks at Yoona, deadpan.

"Three?" I ask her.

"Prom."

I groan. This is what she wanted to talk about all along!

"Oh no," Zahra snaps. "We have to talk about it."

"I'd be more than happy to help the both of you, but I'm not going," I explain.

"Why not?" Yoona asks with genuine curiosity.

"It's just too much trouble. Dresses, hair, makeup. Finding a date. Planning the night. I get anxiety just thinking about it," I tell them.

"Addie, you know very well your mother can afford whatever dress you decide to pick. Everything else will fall into place," Zahra states.

"Oh, and you just expect a date to fall into my lap?" I ask.

"You'll get a date, Addie. Besides Zahra, there's still months left until prom. I'm sure guys aren't thinking about prom dates yet." I can tell Yoona is trying to play the mediator.

"See? Addie won't get a date with that attitude," Zahra says.

"Zahra," Yoona cautions.

"What?" I ask.

"It's just that you're so negative any time we talk about prom. I was hoping you'd be open to it after the senior party, but you're even more uptight than usual," Zahra hisses.

Yoona is busy cutting at her bagel and is avoiding making eye contact with anyone, clearly sensing that this is an issue between me and Zahra.

"I'm not negative," I counter. "I'm realistic. Zahra, when has a guy ever actually wanted to talk to me? Any time we go out, they always go for you or Yoona, and I'm left in the background. I'd like to save myself the embarrassment for once."

"That's because you never let them in," Zahra argues back.

"Because you don't know what it's like to live my life, to walk in my shoes. You have no idea how people look at me." My tone is sharp and I'm beginning to lose my patience.

"Lower your voices," Yoona urges. "And calm down."

Ignoring Yoona, Zahra continues. "Yeah, I may not have your face, but people look at me differently because of my skin color. Like it's a sin to be black."

"Your skin color doesn't stop guys from wanting to be with you!" I flinch as soon as I say it.

Zahra tilts her chin, hurt under the heat. "People look at my skin before my face," she says, voice tight. "It is not the win you think." Zahra inhales, in an attempt to compose herself. "I wish you could see what we see," her frustration seeps out despite her attempt. "You survived a lot and you are still here. Stop letting middle school boys live rent free in your head."

Then, she says the thing best friends aren't supposed to say. "Maybe if you loved yourself more, people wouldn't get away with calling you ugly."

And the truth lands like a deafening blow.

I take in a sharp breath. Yoona stops cutting her food and freezes. Everyone else in the café is staring over at our table.

Astonished, I look at Zahra. "Look whose true colors are coming out." I turn around to grab my phone and wallet from the bench.

"I didn't... Addie, that's not how I meant it," Zahra stammers.

"Yes, it is," I say before storming out.

I try to hold my head up, but tears are falling as I reach my car. Zahra's right. I shut people out. Always afraid of getting hurt, of being rejected. Alone feels safer than judged.

But part of me doesn't want to believe her. *Why me?* I just want normal. My face makes that impossible. Nothing about me is normal, and maybe it never will be.

My phone lights up and it's a text from Yoona.

```
I'm sorry about what happened. I'm sure
Zahra is too. Call me if you need me xoxo
```

I place my phone into the cup holder and drive. I don't know where I'm driving to exactly, but I'm not ready to go home yet. Cursing myself and the tears that still stream down my face, I drive over to a quiet place at the edge of town.

CHAPTER TWELVE
Jackson

The alarm bleats. I thumb it quiet. By noon the room smells like stale air and I still have not brushed my teeth. I count the cracks in the ceiling because it feels like the only thing I can finish. Being away from Addie feels like a weight lifted. Every time I see her, my emotions betray reason. Distance is the only way to keep her safe.

Something dark has gripped me since then, nameless but suffocating. The nightmares have dulled, yet the days feel like quicksand. Getting out of bed drains me, I eat only when hunger hurts, and even running has slipped away. A heavy fog clouds my mind.

Each morning the alarm drags me up and I wish I could stay asleep, sometimes even wish I wouldn't wake at all. That thought scares me. I know some part of me still wants to live, but it feels buried too deep to outshine the darkness.

On cue with the enveloping darkness, another thought arrives like a shortcut. One pill. Quiet for an hour. I picture the ER wristband, the image fleeting, not lingering long enough for the consequences to settle in. I take the pill anyway, hating myself in the same motion.

Only ever leaving my place to meet up with Jay, I count my pills and the number is not to my liking. I'm running low again, so I set up a time to meet with him later today.

Dragging myself out of bed, I head for a run. The air hits my lungs, and for a second, the fog in my head lifts. My legs loosen, my body feels almost human again. I start slow, taking in the trees, clouds, and hidden animals along the trail.

I pick up speed, sweat dripping, and for a little while, it feels like I'm okay, like me again. Two hours later, I finally drag myself home, make a late lunch, and take a long, hot shower. Clean and dressed in jeans, a hoodie, and a cap, I look fine. But the feeling doesn't last.

Arriving at the dorm, the RA desk makes me sign a visitor sheet. My hand shakes and I mess up my own name, the dopamine of the morning's run being short lived. Upstairs, a stranger opens the door, and I feel fifteen again, caught and small.

"Yo Jay! Your friend is here," the stranger announces. Then he walks away into the kitchen and leaves me alone at the entrance.

"Back here!" Jay calls out and I follow his voice. His door is open and I enter his room. "What's up Jax?" he greets me.

"Hey," I say.

"What can I do for you?"

What I want to say is, 'My order is the same as always, you dumb fuck', but instead I bite my tongue and say, "Just ten."

"You got it, bro."

Jay gets up and saunters over to his computer desk. After counting and placing the pills into a plastic bag, he comes back to me and places them in my palm while our free hands simultaneously exchange a wad of bills. Transaction complete, he counts the bills and then nods.

"Pleasure doing business with you," he tells me and I walk out of his room, ignoring him.

I show myself out and, when I'm back in my car, I swallow my second pill of the day with some water. I can't bring myself to head home. Trying to escape the threat of silence hidden between four walls, I wander the town instead, past the high school, through the square, down streets I've never explored.

Time passes, and a slow tide of warmth washes over me, softening the ache in my body. Usually, I can drive while high, but the initial kick always takes me a few moments to get used to.

I spot a wide clearing and park, realizing I've driven straight to a pier. The water sprawls before me, catching the sun's fading glow, sparkling molten gold. I breathe until my heartbeat evens, the high settling over me like a heavy, familiar blanket. I would give anything in the world to be able to carry this calmness with me everyday of my life.

Piercing through the peace, I hear gravel churning and when I turn, I see another car enter the space. Taking it as my cue to leave, I get back in my car. As I'm getting ready to reverse out of the clearing, a small body steps out of the car and climbs onto the hood, sitting cross-legged. Her silhouette looks familiar to me, long hair flowing in the wind. A hand reaches up and places a lock of hair behind her ear. Looking out into the horizon, those long, black lashes blink.

Recognition hits me and the voice in my head urges me to leave. I know I should leave. I want to leave. *Why can't I leave?* I start the car and her head turns in my direction and then back down to her lap. I don't think she recognizes me. *Leave now,* the voice says.

Instead, I do the exact opposite.

I kill the engine and climb out, my body moving like it belongs to someone else. Heavy, fuzzy feet walk me across the space to her car. Up close, her face comes into focus, eyes red, sleeve dragging away tears.

A sob escapes Addie just as I lower myself next to her. Feeling the dip of the car, she turns and we look at each other. Confusion covers her face and then sadness. She returns her gaze to the horizon. The sun, now a dark blue shade in the distance, lingers above the water. Wiping her tears with her sleeves again, I maintain the silence.

It takes a moment, but eventually the tears slow, her breathing becoming constant, steady, uninterrupted. The evening has quickly grown brisk with the setting sun, a sharp wind flowing about. The sky, clear of clouds, is dotted with bright stars that help the moon lighten the darkness of night.

My thoughts are completely silent, a calm serenity hugging me. We sit there for a long time, coexisting with one another. Me riding my high while Addie rides the edges of her own thoughts.

When a particularly cold wind passes, she shivers beside me and I take off my hoodie. Without a word, she slips it on, the loose fabric folding around her like a shield.

"Thanks," she mumbles.

"Yeah," I respond and the corners of her mouth turn up.

"Are we bumping into each other now in times of crisis?" she jokes, though her voice is low, barely above a whisper.

"I guess so." Glancing in her direction, a single tear spills down and, without thinking, I wipe it away with a now steady thumb. "Pretty girls shouldn't cry."

"I'm not a pretty girl," Addie tells me.

"What do you mean?"

"I'm not a pretty girl," she repeats. "I hate living like this." Addie pulls her knees up in front of her and places her chin there, arms curled around her legs.

"You do not have to earn softness," I say, meaning every word. "You are kind and thoughtful and smarter than me on my best day. That counts more than faces ever will."

"Yeah right. You're only saying that to make me feel better, Jax. I know what guys make of me. Good body, good friend, not pretty enough for them."

I sit, wrestling my scattered mind into obedience, praying she won't notice the haze clinging to me. Before it can come up with an answer, she hits the hood of the car with a closed fist.

"Zahra was right. This is exactly what she was talking about. I'm my biggest enemy. But I know the truth."

"I'm not sure who Zahra is, but I still stand by what I said," I tell her.

"Yeah, a scarred up nose and a busted lip," she gives me a thumbs up and sarcastically says, "Yeah, great girlfriend material."

The words leave my mouth before I can stop them, gentle and real, unlike anything I've ever said to a girl. "If a guy is only judging you by the outside, then they're a dumb ass. You have a bigger heart than you care to accept." She remains silent for a moment.

"You haven't been in school." It's a swift change of subject.

"You're good at that."

"At what?"

"Changing the subject."

Addie smiles. "It's my way of getting out of uncomfortable conversations."

"I can see that. And yeah," I take my cap off and brush my hair back before putting it back on. "I haven't really felt like going."

"Aren't you afraid of falling behind? Failing?"

"No. I'm probably too far behind to catch up now. Anyways, I've never exactly been the brightest one in class." I point a finger to my head. "School has always been tough for me." Even worse now, but I don't speak the truth out loud.

"I'm sorry to hear that." She's playing idly with her shoelaces as she says it.

"It's all good. It's not like I plan on going to college or anything. I just need to pass senior year and that will be good enough for me."

"If you want, I can help you," Addie tells me.

"With school, you mean? Nah, Addie. Thank you, but you'd be wasting your time on me," I respond.

"Sounds like you're also your biggest enemy then."

"Ouch. Couldn't have said it better my damn self."

Addie removes her cell phone from her pocket and glances at the time.

"I should go," she says. Pushing myself off from the hood of her car, I pull myself to stand upright.

Fuck it, I think and gently take her phone from her hands. Typing my information into her contact list, I throw the phone back to her and she catches it.

"If you want to try this studying thing, text me a day and a time. If you don't want to waste your time on me, no pressure. I can handle failing on my own," I explain.

Seemingly at a loss for words, she nods then puts her phone away. Stepping away from her car, she gets into the driver's seat. I watch her drive away and get into my own car when hers is no longer visible.

When I begin the engine, I roll my window down and feel a slight chill. I look down and smirk to myself. Addie drove away with my hoodie. With that thought in mind, the voice in my head is silent and I drive back home.

CHAPTER THIRTEEN

Adelina

I give us a week to cool off, setting a reminder: "Call Zahra Monday," with three safe sentences I can actually say. It stings that she's right. I push people away, especially boys, to dodge rejection, and I can't stop wondering if things could've been different. Pride keeps me from answering her messages... for now.

At lunchtime, I hole up in the library, pretending I'm working on college essays. I clean the same smudge, copy the same sentence, and finally slam my notebook shut, frustrated but trying to pass it off as nerves.

Home at last, I reach for my bathrobe, but something falls. Jax's hoodie. I stand there, frozen, the weight of Zahra's words louder than ever. And suddenly, I want to prove her wrong.

With determination, I walk over to my phone and search for Jax's contact. Finding it, I send a text.

Hey, it is Addie. I have your hoodie. If you want to grab it, we can meet in the morning at my place or the Square. Your call.

Nervous, anxious, I throw my phone on my bed and begin undressing. While I'm securing my bathrobe around me, my phone screen lights up and my heart skips a beat.

I reach for it with ever so anxious fingers, afraid it isn't him. The anxiety forms to a giddy warmth that settles within when I see his name on my screen.

Hey. Was wondering when you would text me. Does the hoodie not live up to your standards anymore?

I smile down at my phone, matching his playful tone with my own.

It does. I'd keep it, except it fits me more like a dress.

I'm clutching my phone, but he doesn't respond. Nervous that I may begin overthinking our conversation, I put my phone down on my computer desk and go take a shower. When I return, I actively avoid looking at my phone, worried that I will be disappointed to not find a text message.

Without checking, I start my nighttime skincare routine, however I keep looking from the mirror to my phone and back again. With nothing else left to do, I take my phone into my hand. I close my eyes and hit the home button.

When I finally look, I see messages from Jax. My heart flutters. I swipe and our chat opens.

Too bad, guess I'll have to get it back.

I can meet at your place. When is a good day
for you?

Saturday?

I think for a moment. Mami is usually away Saturday
mornings until late in the evenings, it being her busiest
day in the office. Feeling more emboldened than before, I
respond.

Saturday works. Come by at eleven thirty.
Two hours max. We study first, food second.

I see that he's typing back to me and then stops. He
begins typing again and a second later, I get his message.

Why?

I respond quickly, not wanting to back out of
something I have already started.

Don't think I forgot. We are going to get
you to graduation. So be ready :)

He responds much quicker than I anticipate.

I'm ready for the challenge. See you Saturday
Ms. Addie

I let out a small, quiet laugh and respond.

Good night Jax.

I set my phone aside, still smiling, as if his warmth
tonight could erase all the times he's iced me out.

* * *

Determined, I spend the rest of the school week truly
studying in the library. Though I miss her, the conflict with

Zahra has slipped entirely from my mind and my focus is solely dedicated to writing my personal statements. I print the statement and grimace at line three. Fifteen minutes of tweaking later, it reads clean. I drop the final version into my advisor's mailbox, standing a little straighter on my way out.

I exit the school building, using the closest exit to the student parking lot. It's a short walk to my car and I'm reaching for the door handle when I feel my phone vibrate. My hand retracts from the handle and I take my phone out of my back pocket. Though preparing to set, the sun is still pretty strong at this time of day.

I turn away from its glare and look down at my phone. It's a message from Jax.

I feel a pang of immediate dread in my gut and assume he's messaging me to cancel our plans. Wanting to get the rejection over with, I have to read his message a few times before I'm able to comprehend what he is asking.

```
Hey, what's your address? It didn't save on
my GPS.
```

```
Also, what should I bring?
```

It isn't a rejection.

His text is the furthest thing from a rejection.

That giddy feeling finds me again and just as I'm about to respond, someone calls my name. I look up and see Liam's red hair in the distance. Waving at him, he walks over, using his long legs to close the distance between us rather quickly.

Embracing me in a hug, Liam greets me. "What's up Addie?"

"Hey! Nothing much."

I take a step back just to look up at his face, allowing Liam to look down to look at me. A secret smile tugs at my lips; I do the same with Jax, always looking up at him because of *his* height.

"What are you smiling about?" Liam taunts.

Brought back to reality, I say, "Nothing, just a good day." Then I ask, "What are you doing here so late on a Friday?"

He lets out a sigh. "I'm failing Algebra again, so I have to stay for some after-school credit recovery program. I don't know what language I have to speak in for them to understand that math and I do not click! Ever."

I cringe and express how sorry I am that he has to go through that.

"It's bullshit," he says, "because I won't graduate without some kind of math credit." Liam throws his hands up in the air then uses one to brush his hair back. "If I could do math as good as I play soccer, I'd be set," he says, finishing his rant.

"I thought my mom helped you and your parents get the education plan, no?" I ask him.

Back in freshman year, I offered to tutor him, and he spent every other weekend at my house for months. Mami, still wary of leaving me alone with boys at the time, always hovered nearby. Thankfully, she never embarrassed me, just slipping in now and then to offer food.

Until one day, Mami asked him to set a clock and he couldn't. One phone call to his parents, a referral, and an evaluation later determined Liam has dyscalculia. The plan that followed gave him extra time on assessments and tools to help him succeed.

"Yeah, which has been a huge help," Liam continues "but I still need some basic math credits if I plan on going to college. If I'm scouted by the state and accepted on their soccer team, I could get a full scholarship. Not having that math credit is really messing me up Addie. My parents can't afford state college. That soccer scholarship is my only chance of getting in."

"I'm sure you'll get through this Liam. You've gotten through most of it. This is just the final game," I reassure.

"Thanks," he says, running his hand through his hair again.

"Do you need a ride?" I offer.

"Nah, my car is parked by the soccer field. Matthew and I are gonna do a few drills. He's probably already mad that I'm late, but he can't stay mad when he finds out you're my excuse," Liam laughs.

"Get going then!" I urge. "Tell Matthew I said hi!"

"Yeah, for sure." He begins to walk away, but abruptly spins back to face me again.

"Okay," he states, "not my business at all, but whatever happened between you and Zahra needs to get fixed. She's not happy and she's been really snappy lately and you're not hanging with us at lunch. Yoona is all mopey and Matthew and I would love for everything to go back to normal. Again, not my business... see ya!"

Speeding away nervously, Liam heads off and I sigh. He's right. Determination fills me as I remind myself of my plan to mend things with Zahra. Turning around to reach for my door handle, I get into my car and place my phone into my cup holder.

Oh crap! I think as I wake my phone and shoot Jax my address. A grin lingers after I hit send. Logic tries to flare in the back of my mind, but elation drowns it out. Driving home with the windows down, I sing softly into the wind, my favorite song carrying me away.

CHAPTER FOURTEEN
Jackson

I'm slumped in the living room on a dead school night, mid-game, when my phone chimes. It's Megan, some girl I hooked up with at the senior party, telling me she's coming over. The problem? I can hardly remember her, and I have no idea how she even got my number.

That still didn't stop me from responding to her first text, teasing and flirtatious, clearly hinting she wanted more than friendship. I didn't see the harm in inviting her over. I still don't.

I get up and turn off my gaming console. Wrapping the charging cord, I place both the controller and the cord back in the cabinet underneath the tv. After a quick shower, I throw on a pair of basic sweats and a shirt, not really caring what I look like. My hair is messy, but I can't work up the energy to fix it. Moments later, I hear a knock on my door and go to open it.

Standing there is a girl with short, loose blonde hair, piercing blue eyes, and a nervous tap of her sneaker against the step. None of that, however, is what catches my attention. Draped over her small frame is my leather jacket. I catch a flicker of memory, her laugh from the party maybe, but nothing I can pin down. Smiling, her eyes roam past me and I take her hint. Stepping aside, I motion for her to come in.

She enters, slipping off her white sneakers along with *my* leather jacket, and offers empty compliments about my place as I guide her to the living room. Settling on the couch, Megan sits noticeably close to me, close enough for me to smell her shampoo and the overwhelmingly sweet scent of perfume coming off her pale, smooth skin.

"You really don't remember me, do you?" she asks in her high-pitched voice.

"I think I might, but I was too wasted to remember much of anything," I respond, wanting to get the banter over with.

Megan bites her bottom lip. "I couldn't tell." Scooting closer to me, her thigh is now resting on top of mine. "I have a confession to make."

I shift my body more towards her direction. "Spit it out."

"Promise not to be mad though," Megan says, pouting.

I nod.

"So, you didn't exactly give me your number. We hooked up for a bit and you were actually a jerk, come to think of it." She rolls her eyes. "I thought we were going to do more, but you just walked out on me. I tried to put that night behind me, but I couldn't forget your kiss or how your strong hands held me down on your lap."

Megan traces a manicured finger up and down my arm. "I saw you in the kitchen with Jay earlier that night, so I asked him for your number. I hope you're not mad about that."

Smiling tightly, I say, "Nah, I'm not mad." I lean closer into her and feel the warmth of her body, warmer than mine. She tilts her head, waiting.

I lean in, my mind three steps behind my body.

Slipping into the version of me I know so well, I scoop her up and place her on my lap. At first she's caught by surprise, but quickly settles, her legs softening around me. Leaning forward, Megan plants a wet kiss on my neck, followed by another, and another, until they come down with feverish intent.

I pull her back.

"Megan, you have to know, I'm not into relationships."

She leans in and kisses my neck again. I feel her teeth and a light nip.

"Neither am I," she says, her hips rocking back and forth on my lap.

"Positive?" The final question before I fully lock myself into the version of me that only exists here.

Megan starts kissing my chest and I can feel myself growing hot, stiff. When her lips sigh consent against my skin, I grab her by the waist and flip her over to the couch. Our clothes land in piles. My body keeps moving, but my mind stays hollow.

There is a moment of calm when we finish and I relish it. Megan pulls away from me, her blue eyes still glazed over. She asks where the bathroom is and I point her in the right direction, not wanting to get up yet.

When she disappears, my phone chimes. I grasp the phone from the inside of one of my jean pockets and read. Her message lights the screen, sharp and ordinary, cutting through the haze of sickly sweet perfume and sweat.

Addie.

The surprise is short lived, my response coming in fast, initiating a playful exchange with her. I feel the pull of my mouth wanting to form a smile until I hear my bathroom door open. The corners drop, and my lips go flat.

Before I'm able to respond to Addie's latest text, Megan saunters over.

"That was amazing," she tells me in a satisfied tone. Then, clearly aware of what "no strings attached" means, Megan grabs her purse and makes her way over to the door, thankfully sparing me of any awkward conversations.

"I hope we can do this again soon," she says, putting her shoes back on.

"Yeah." I give her a charming yet very fake smile, deliberately refraining from handing her the very same leather jacket she entered with.

Megan opens the front door like she owns the night and steps out, tossing a quick "I'll text you" over her shoulder. I shut the door behind me and stand there for a second.

Megan isn't like the others. Most girls catch feelings, and I'm good at ending things before it gets messy. But Megan, she's direct, knows what she wants, and somehow makes it work.

My phone buzzes and I'm yanked back to reality. Addie. We text about Saturday morning, studying together. I let the smallest smile slip, the first one in a while that doesn't feel forced. Even alone, it hits me how much she lingers in my head, the way her voice, her laugh, her eyes pull me back no matter how much I try to push it away.

Then the itch hits. The one that never really leaves. Sharp, nagging, impossible to ignore. Freedom's a joke. I reach for a pill, pop it, and lie back, restless and trapped by choices that aren't really mine. My thoughts drift, dark and heavy, and for a second the world feels quieter only because I've numbed it.

But the pull of Addie, the pull of control, and the pull of the next high. They're all tangled together, and I don't know which one will win.

***

I'm up before my alarm rings, unable to find any restful sleep last night. Turning it off, I sit on my bedside, palming the bottle. I think about pocketing it, then set it down. *Just one day clean*, I tell myself. I don't believe it. I take one anyway.

After a shower, I pull on dark blue jeans and a black shirt, sleeves snug around my biceps, and throw on my black leather jacket. I consider a snap-back but skip it. My hair isn't too crazy today.

Jogging down the stairs, I lace my sneakers, grab my backpack from the trunk, where it's been untouched for weeks, and text Addie before heading out in the car.

`Good morning, on my way`

Backing out of my driveway, I make it there faster than expected, not exactly driving at the speed limit on this morning's exceedingly empty roads, and park in Addie's driveway. Book bag wrapped around one shoulder, I walk to Addie's front door.

The grass is trimmed sharp, the pillars steady. My shoes feel too dirty to touch the stones. Ringing the doorbell, it takes a moment before Addie opens. She welcomes me in and I follow.

I take in the grand chandelier that hangs in the entryway, winding stairs leading upstairs, and hardwood floors that complement warm, neutral decor. When I finally take in Addie, she's in light blue skinny jeans and a tucked-

119

in baby pink long-sleeve that matches her fuzzy pink socks. Her curves and strong legs are obvious, but I stop myself. *Why am I thinking that?* Instead, I focus on her socks and smirk, finding them charming.

"We're going up to the study room," she says, breaking me out of my thoughts. "Mami and I use it when we want some silence. I've been in there already today, working on some homework. Please excuse the mess."

Reaching the top of the stairs, we make a turn until we come up to a door which Addie opens. I take a step in, eyes widening. Tall bookcases climb the walls, a brick chimney anchors the room, and sunlight spills through a huge window facing the backyard.

A reclining chair with a rumpled blanket hints at where Addie was moments ago; on the other side, a long wooden table holds textbooks, a laptop, a notebook, pens, and a half-finished mug of coffee. Shadows linger in the corners, adding quiet contrast to the warm, serene space.

Addie leads me to the table and pulls out a chair. I sit, letting out a low whistle as she slides into the one beside me.

"Who the hell are your parents? Are they rich surgeons or something?" I ask her.

"What? No," she laughs. "Mami makes good money as a psychologist and is on the state board. Dad ran the engineering department at the state college. They built this house together. Dad handled construction and Mami did the decor. All before I was even born."

"Okay, not surgeons, but clearly wealthy," I sum up.

She shrugs with indifference, "Yeah, I guess so," she says, then adds, "Not many people come here. Just a few of my childhood friends. Guess I'm not used to having new people here. I don't know what to say."

"You don't have to say anything. This is just impressive."

Addie flashes a smile and moves her laptop over. "Alright, let's see what classes you're taking."

"Chemistry, Algebra II, World History, AP English, and Gym," I tell her.

"That's good," she mumbles, thoughts already spinning. "I'm assuming you don't need help with gym class, right?"

"No. I'm sure I'll have to make up some credits though. Missing a few weeks couldn't have done me any good."

"Sports give you added credits. I know soccer tryouts are happening soon," she informs me. "Any good at that?"

"Yeah, I'm actually pretty good at it."

Addie makes a dismissive gesture and says, "Problem solved. I'll ask Liam and Matthew when they start and I'll text you the info."

"Who are Liam and Matthew?"

"A few of my best friends and they do nothing except soccer. They're on track for college scholarships. Anyways, they'll know."

"Alright, sounds good."

Grabbing my textbooks, Addie continues speaking with a confidence and authority I've never heard before. I let her pull me into hours of studying, with brief coffee and snack breaks in between. It's the most I've ever studied, but she's an excellent teacher—clear, patient, and engaging, like the material itself is coming alive. I don't feel ashamed to ask questions or slow her down.

If school had always been like this, I might've actually cared.

***

Two hours of studying and one very much needed secret pill later, we're taking a short break when I dare ask, "When are we going to stop?"

"I'm not trying to overwhelm you. We'll do another thirty minutes and then we're done." Addie's response sounds reasonable and, more importantly, doable.

In the middle of me asking her another question, her doorbell rings. She looks puzzled as she picks up her phone and checks the time. "I'm not expecting anyone," she mutters and walks out of the study room. I follow her out to the stairs, but remain at the top, leaning on the handrail.

Addie descends quickly and the bell rings again. When she opens the door, a girl pushes past Addie.

"So, you don't respond to my texts and you don't answer my calls!"

"Zahra!" Addie's voice pitches up in surprise. "Uh, what are you doing here?" She angles her body in a failed attempt to block the doorway, but the girl pushes past her with an air of familiarity.

"How many times do I have to apologize? I've been feeling horrible about the things I said and I've missed you like hell," the girl blurts out.

"Zahra, I know, but right now isn't—"

The girl cuts her off.

"What. Is. *He.* Doing. Here?" she asks, looking up and pointing a very sharp, very accusatory, finger at me. I give her an awkward wave and she snickers. "Addie, what's going on?"

"Zahra, relax. That's Jax. I'm helping him with school stuff." Addie's voice is carefully casual, as if to say it's no big deal.

"Oh, so now we have secret boys that we don't tell our best friends about?!"

Addie's patience finally snaps, the way it only does with someone you're closest to. "Oh my goodness, you're so dramatic. I'll text you later. Go home!"

"Like hell I will! Dramatic my ass."

Addie starts pushing her out the door while Zahra keeps mouthing off. The scene is chaotic, but Addie remains calm, every movement deliberate. I watch her reenter the house, and for the first time, I realize how effortlessly she commands a room. It's impossible not to respect her control, even as tension lingers in the air.

Coming up the stairs, she walks right past me and motions for me to join her in the study. I follow and sit as Addie paces the room.

"So, Zahra is my best friend. We had a fight last week and I've been avoiding her. I planned to message her tomorrow to try to patch things up soon, but, as you can see, she's annoyingly impatient." Addie sighs. "I love her, but this is the longest we've gone without talking."

I sit and listen to her. Addie explains that no one else knows about what happened between us at the senior party, not even her close friends. "That creates a bit of a problem," she ends.

"Why?" I ask, but secretly, I'm thankful. Thankful that for the first time, someone knows this part of me. That my secret isn't mine alone anymore.

"Well, I don't exactly have many male friends except for Liam and Matthew." She fidgets with her fingers before adding, "And I'm not even sure if you're a friend or just a study buddy."

"Sounds like you're in a bind." I chuckle, trying to keep it light, but she shoots me a look that dares me not to.

The smile slips from my face. I stand, shifting toward her before I can second-guess it.

"Friend," I say, meaning for it to sound steady, certain.

Her big brown eyes lock on mine, searching. "What?"

I want to explain, to ease the storm in her expression, but the words don't come. Instead, my arms move on their own, pulling her in. I tell myself it's just to comfort her, to let her know she's not alone. But the second her body stiffens against me, I realize how much more I want it to be.

Then, slowly, she softens. Her arms circle my waist, her head tipping against my chest. I hold her closer than I should, my chin settling on her hair.

"Friend," I repeat, though the word feels heavier in my mouth, less true.

Her palms press against my shoulders, a gentle push, not enough to break the closeness. Vanilla drifts up from her skin, intoxicating. I breathe it in, betraying myself.

"Don't do that," she whispers, eyes on the floor.

"I'm sorry," I answer quickly, though I don't even know what part of me I'm apologizing for. The hug, the closeness, or the truth it uncovered.

I see Addie close her eyes and her eyebrows bunch up. Lifting her chin up at me, she opens her eyes. I'm mesmerized once more by the dark brown color of them, reminding me of deep, amber warmth. Addie blinks and her lips part.

"You confuse me, Jax," she breathes, a slight hurt in her eyes. Unsure of what she wants from me, I stand there, silent, watching, waiting.

Then a thought flashes through my mind.

Yesterday.

Yesterday?

Megan.

Remorse floods my face before I can mask it, and Addie sees it. I don't need to say a word. Her eyes narrow, reading me like an open page. She takes a few steps back, as if my guilt itself might stain her.

The truth cuts deeper than I'd admit: Megan is easy, reckless enough that I don't mind dragging her into my mess. But Addie? She's untouched, bright in a way I know I'll only darken. Standing here, I can already feel the damage I'd do to her, the poison I can't help but carry.

"I'm no good for you, Addie. Seriously. I'm messed up with more crap going on than I can even handle. You don't deserve to get dragged into my mess. I don't wanna do that to you."

"You can't just play with my emotions. You think I don't know there's something dark about you? I don't want to feel like this, but you make it hard for me."

"You're right," I acknowledge. "What I'm doing isn't fair to you."

"Jax... do you even like me? Am I just a random girl to you?"

"To be honest, I don't know, Addie."

There's a silence.

"Thanks," she finally says and I hear a slight tremor in her voice.

"For what?"

Addie turns to face me. "For at least being honest with me. Come," she beckons and we both sit back down. Regardless of everything, she gives me a warm and beautiful smile. A smile I don't necessarily deserve right now. "Let's just keep studying, okay? A friend doesn't let another friend fail."

"I'm okay with that," I concede.

Addie jumps back into tutor mode, academics her version of a distraction, but I am completely absent-minded and incapable of paying attention. The thirty minutes fly by and I'm soon gathering my things to leave. Addie walks me outside.

"Do you want to keep doing this? We can meet again next Saturday. Maybe at the library next time?" she asks before adding, "As friends."

I hesitate a beat, but not enough for Addie to notice. "Yeah, that sounds good," I agree.

We say our goodbyes, actively avoiding a hug or any other form of physical contact. I'm still in my thoughts by the time I get home, not being able to get Addie out of my mind. As usual, the room is quiet, but the guilt presses against me like a weight I can't lift.

CHAPTER FIFTEEN
Adelina

Zahra called me shortly after Jax left, insisting I go to her house the following day, which is where I'm currently headed. I park, and my hands stay on the steering wheel too long. I check my reflection only because I don't want to check the door. Too lazy to fix my hair after I showered, I'm wearing a baseball cap with a long-sleeve shirt tucked into some sweats. I've looked crappier. I think.

Steeling myself with a quick sip of coffee, I get out of the car and ring Zahra's front bell. The door swings open and Zahra's mom welcomes me in.

"Addie! It's so nice to see you!" She greets me with her thick West African accent as I remove my shoes. Embracing me, Mrs. Obasi's hug lingers, familiar, loving, warm, and, for a second, I forget why I'm here. When she lets go, we walk into the living room where Mr. Obasi is watching the morning news.

"Good morning Mr. Obasi," I greet him.

He peers at me, his glasses sitting on the tip of his nose, and then gives me a big grin. "Eh, Addie, is that you? How are you?" he asks with a thicker accent than his wife.

"I'm alright, thanks! Zahra told me you all travelled back to Nigeria over the summer. How was it?"

"It was magnificent. Very lovely to see the family again," he responds.

"Yes, and the food was fantastic. I was finally able to go to the market and buy some proper items. It just isn't the same over here," Mrs. Obasi tsks.

When Zahra jogs down the stairs, she looks as wrecked as I feel, hair messy, eyes puffy, like sleep barely touched her. The sight of her cracks something in me, and all I can manage is a shaky smile. She pulls me into a hug. Quick, but enough, and I cling for that extra second, needing it more than I'll admit.

"Mama, Papa, Addie doesn't want to hear about our boring vacation," Zahra protests.

Nathaniel, Zahra's older brother, who enters the house from the backyard, puts his soccer ball down in the kitchen. Sweat slicks his temples, darkening the edges of his shirt. He grabs a glass and fills it to the brim, the water catching the light as it sloshes. Between greedy gulps, his eyes lift, catching mine over the rim.

"Ah, Addie. From the window I thought I was seeing a ghost," Nathaniel jokes. Mrs. Obasi hits him on the back of the head and tells him to apologize. "Okay, Mama, sorry. It was a joke." He laughs.

I shake my head at him and say, "Not a ghost. I might be pale, but I've got plenty of flavor," I shoot back. "And you love me anyway."

"We all love you," Mr. Obasi adds.

"Now, that's the truth," Nathaniel agrees, pointing a finger at me.

"Okay, I'm taking Addie up to my room now. And Nat, don't be so obnoxious."

Zahra laces her fingers through mine and tugs me upstairs toward her room, leaving the rest of her family behind. From below, Nathaniel's voice drifts up, already pestering his parents about what's for dinner.

Finally alone in her room, door closed, Zahra and I go sit out on her balcony. It's a warm day even with the fall season being well underway, and we have to shift our chairs to avoid the sun. Zahra closes the balcony door behind us and everything is silent except for the rustling of leaves and the birds creating their morning song. I twist my coffee mug between sweaty palms, letting Zahra break the silence.

"You know I don't like being ignored," she says, hurt and betrayal coating her voice.

"I know." I sigh. "I wanted to message you sooner, but I got busy with writing my personal statements. I had it on my phone to text you on Sunday so that we could talk on Monday."

"A week? You really expected me to wait an entire week, plus three extra days, might I add, to speak to you?" Zahra looks at me bewildered. "Like, seriously?"

"I'm sorry, but we're here now." I let out a weak, shaky smile.

"Yeah, after I go all the way to your house and find you with a random guy that you didn't even think to tell me about!"

"I wasn't ready to speak to you yet because I was still deep in thought. A lot of what you said cut deep, Zahra. Mostly because I know it's true." The end leaves my lips like a whisper.

"But you know I didn't mean to say it like that," she implores. "I just wish you would allow yourself to live a little sometimes. You shelter yourself so much. What are you afraid of?"

"Rejection," I say, the word landing like the bottle spin years ago.

"Addie, we all face rejection in our lives."

"Me more than others."

There's a silence.

I continue, "Look, I know you want me to live this life where I can be popular and party and have boyfriends. That isn't me. My reality is different from yours. Yes, I know I'm not exactly low in the social hierarchy, but that's because I have you, Yoona, Liam, and Matthew. It's like being popular by default. When boys come over, it's to talk to you and Yoona. I'm their last resort. And though I love cheering on the two of you, I wish you were more mindful of how these situations may make me feel."

I let out a laugh because Zahra is giving me one of her signature eyebrow stares.

"I'm not saying you have to reject boys," I continue. "All I'm asking for is understanding, compassion, and for you to stop pressuring me into doing things that make me uncomfortable. That said, I will admit that I do need to get out of my comfort zone more."

Zahra gives me a musing frown. She shrugs her shoulders and rolls her eyes. "Looks like you have the boyfriend part covered without any help. So... what's up with that?"

A pause hangs, then Zahra grins. I know we are okay, at least for now. Grinning back, I give her a light nudge. She motions to an invisible watch as if to say *I'm waiting.*

I feel the lie sour in my throat, but I swallow it and speak anyway. "It was that guy that bumped into us and made my books go flying. Remember?" I pause and when her eyes widen in recognition, I continue. "He recognized me from the first day of school and introduced himself. After a few days, he mentioned he was struggling in class and I offered to tutor."

I keep the information light, knowing that Zahra would combust with BFF overprotective judgment if I actually said "Oh yeah, I think he overdosed, I took him to the hospital, and we've been friends ever since." Perhaps, one day, I'll tell her everything. But for today, this is the version I decide to give her.

Unconvinced, Zahra squints at me. "Eh, just like that? He tells you he needs help and you offer to tutor him? No strings?"

"Yeah, just like that." I snap my fingers.

"How long have you been tutoring him?"

"Actually, that was the first time."

Zahra lets out a breath. "Well, I'm going to believe this crazy story for now. On the bright side, you're pretty much studying with the hottest guy in school."

"I don't know about that..." I manage, too embarrassed to admit how attractive I find him.

"Jax, right? That's what you said his name was?"

I nod. The following words cut sharper than I wanted to admit. My face stays still, but my stomach drops.

"At dance practice, Megan won't shut up about some new guy. Girl, she's got a new dude every other week. My guess? They're probably together. That's why I totally freaked when I saw him at your house. Those pieces clicked, and I got that sinking feeling."

"Well, good thing Jax and I are only friends then," I say coldly.

An icy chill runs through me as I steel my emotions. I promised Zahra I'd be more open, but this is exactly why I'm always guarded. Sooner or later, I'll get hurt. I tell myself Jax is just a friend I'm studying with. No matter what's happened before.

Zahra's information leaves me with no doubts or confusions, so I'll tuck his hoodies deeper into the closet, as if that will tuck him out of my head.

Plastering on a poker face and eager to change the subject, I ask Zahra how her college application process is going and we spend a long time talking about it. Zahra tells me how difficult it's been for her to write her personal statement since she doesn't find anything personal worth writing about.

After tossing around a few ideas, Zahra invites me to our favorite café Friday. I agree once she promises no fighting. We pick a time and loop the rest of the crew through the group chat. They're all in.

With that settled, we head downstairs to Zahra's bustling family lunch, a sharp contrast to my quiet dinners with Mami. Later, we talk on her balcony for a few more hours before I leave, feeling good about where we stand. We say our goodbyes and promise to meet tomorrow at lunch.

***

I kill the engine and tell myself today will cooperate. Parking my car, I hurry over to the building and settle in for chemistry class. I'm taking my notebook and pen out of my book bag when I feel someone take a seat in the chair next to mine. *That's odd. No one ever sits there.*

Jax drops into the empty seat. My fingers forget the pen and it pings under his shoe. I take it from his hand when he passes it over.

"Hey," he breathes out. "I'm not too late, right?"

I blink, open my mouth, but nothing comes out. Saving me, Mr. Davis greets the class as he sets up the board.

"Guess not."

The only response I give him is a nod.

His body wash cuts through dry erase markers and old paper. His leg bounces with that familiar rhythm, both soothing and unsettling. Summoning every ounce of willpower, I force myself not to look in his direction.

He shifts. Clean cedar slips across my focus again. Unable to avoid it, I feel something coil inside of me. Doing what I know best, I throw myself into today's lesson, trying to ignore Jax's presence as much as possible.

Halfway through the period, Mr. Davis asks us to pair up with someone for a partner activity just as he directs us to grab microscopes from the front of the room. I nudge my chair forward before Jax can speak, smiling as I say, "I'll go with you," determined to keep things friendly in spite of the pull I feel.

Walking up to the front of the room, I'm giving myself a pep talk in my head. *Do the work, Adelina.* I should want to sit next to him, even as a friend, but the thought of him with Megan claws at me. It's unsettling how much it gets under my skin, pathetic really, since we both swore we were keeping things strictly "friendship." And now, with him actually trying, I can't stop overanalyzing every little move.

I take a deep breath in and the voice in my head returns. *That's it. Finish the work. Don't think about him. You got this. Easy.*

Not entirely convinced, I return to the back of the room and spread the materials across the desk. I slide Jax's materials over and start setting up the microscope. I roll the coarse knob until the grid blurs, then tick the fine focus until cell walls snap sharp.

I'm examining the cell when I hear Jax asking me what I'm doing. Looking up into his green eyes and tying my hair, I explain.

"Well, we have two slides. Both slides are onion epidermis. One grew in plain water, the other in a nutrient solution. We note cell size, turgor, and membrane visibility, then guess which is which. Make sense?"

"Yeah, I think so," Jax slowly responds.

He gets up and walks over to where I'm seated. When he reaches me, I'm painfully aware of how close he is. Cedar slips down my throat. I swallow too loud.

"What were you just doing? Looking at one of the cells?"

"No, I was setting up the focus. Here, look." Jax bends over until he is looking into the microscope. "Looks clear?" I ask. He makes a noise of approval and then I move the focus knob. "How about now?" I ask again.

"Oh," he breathes, almost a whisper, eyes still on the lens.

Standing up to his full height again, I lean over and refocus the lens.

"I'll look into it first and tell you what I see. You can take notes in my notebook and then we'll switch. We can do that for both cells and then we'll make our hypothesis. Are you okay with that?"

"Yes, Ms. Addie." The nickname lands warm and annoying at the same time.

We spend the remainder of the period working together until the bell rings. Mr. Davis tells us to leave the materials on the desks for the next class, so Jax and I grab our bags and exit the room together.

"Thanks for working with me." I'm sincere, even as I force myself to sound like we're just friends. "Which way are you headed now?"

"I don't know what good I was to you, Addie," he jokes. "You did most of the work in there." Shrugging, he points his index finger towards the stairwell down the hall. "My next class is upstairs." Then, with a smile, he says "See you tomorrow," and walks away, fixing his baseball cap as he does.

I abruptly turn away and rush to my next class. I force myself not to turn back. Something about him fixing his hair sends a rush through me.

As I near my next class, a fleeting thought crosses my mind. *Does Jax have any classes with Meyun?* I shake my head vigorously, almost as though I'm trying to literally shake the thought out of my mind. Forcing myself to think about something else, anything else, I enter my next class, quickly putting chemistry behind me.

***

"Finally!" Matthew exclaims as he reaches our lunch table. I'm the first to arrive, my food already placed neatly in front of me. "I thought it would never end." Spotting Liam, he waves his arms and yells, "Liam, look!"

Liam holds his heart and runs over. Scooping me up for a bear hug, he fakes crying. "Matthew, we are whole again!"

"Okay, okay. Let me go! I've missed you too," I tell them. Zahra and Yoona join us moments later and the weighted blanket that was placed over us lifts.

We dive into raucous conversation filled with jokes made by Liam and Matthew. I laugh until my stomach hurts, tears streaming down my face.

"You two need to stop," I plead. "I can't eat my food!"

"Yes, please!" Yoona's face is red from laughter.

"I need water. I can't do this." Zahra joins me and we walk over to the hydration station and refill our water bottles before walking back, regaining our composure.

We are a few paces away from the table when Zahra sucks her teeth. Oblivious to what's happening, I follow her gaze and then I understand. Coming down the hall to our right is Jax. We lock eyes and he smiles at me. I hate myself for giving him a shy smile back.

"Hey again," he says to me.

"Hey," I say back. Zahra taps her nail against the bottle, our code for behave. "Jax, this is my best friend, Zahra. Zahra, this is Jax." Zahra gives Jax a tight smirk and walks away, leaving me alone with him.

"She's still mad at you?" he asks, his eyes following her back to our table.

"Oh that? No, that's just Zahra being Zahra. Anyways," I turn my body, "I have to go back to my friends." Friends who, by the way, are openly staring at us.

I notice his smile slip. "Sounds good," he responds cooly and continues walking past the cafeteria. I almost call after him. An invitation sitting on the tip of my tongue. I cap my water instead.

Back with my friends, I'm not laughing as hard. My thoughts drift to Jax... Am I being too harsh? Could I be friends with him without all the formality? If only my feelings weren't so tangled, maybe I could be like I am with Liam or Matthew. But then again, I've never kissed either of them.

With the lunch period almost ending, we throw out our garbage and start grabbing our bags. Exiting the cafeteria, we all say our goodbyes, and I walk away with Yoona, heading in the same direction for our next class. On our way to the second floor, Megan's laugh pierces the stairwell and my shoulders climb to my ears. *Nope*, I think, *definitely not being too harsh.*

***

The bell outside the café door keeps chiming in the wind. I warm my fingers on the mug. The weather has begun to shift, fall suddenly taking hold, forcing us all to wear thick sweaters. Yoona, Zahra, Matthew, and Liam are each sipping on their choice of warm beverage.

"I'm thinking about doing a movie night at my place for Halloween. A way to decompress after all this college application stress," Yoona announces.

"Oh right, Halloween is next week," Matthew remembers. "Damn, time goes by quick. Have we really been in school that long already?"

Brushing his hair back, Liam responds, "Speak for yourself. I've been drilling math into my head for two painful months and I'm ready to explode!"

"Yes, but you're going to pass your exams," Zahra encourages. "It sucks now, but you'll be done with it soon."

"Yeah, I get that," Liam sulks.

"So... warm, cozy movie night at my place then?" Yoona suggests again.

"I'm in," I answer. I'm not ready to dive headfirst into another party just yet, but I promised Zahra I'd push myself and I intend to. Even if it scares me, I need to stretch beyond my comfort zone and actually feel my senior year. College applications loom, stressing every thought, but she's right: this year won't wait for me to be ready. It's transformative, fragile, fleeting. Who knows where we'll even be after graduation?

"Same! What time?" Matthew adds.

"I'm thinking 7:00pm? My parents will be out of town for the weekend and you're all more than welcome to crash. Halloween falls on a weekend this year."

"Can I bring my onesie?" Liam's question makes us all laugh.

"Only if it still fits," I say, and Liam clutches his chest like I have wounded him.

Yoona laughs. "Knock yourself out."

"Are we making this a onesie movie night then?" Matthew probes suspiciously.

"I guess so?" Zahra's eyebrows bunch together in question, eyes jumping to each of us in search of an answer.

Matthew, baffled and slightly embarrassed to be friends with us, responds "I don't have a stupid onesie."

I raise my hand. "I don't have one either. Want to shop with me?"

"Are you serious?" he asks, face void of any humor.

"Yeah, why not?"

"Matthew, stop being so fussy and just buy one with Addie," Zahra whines.

Looking away, Matthew mumbles something under his breath and scowls. Liam puts a hand on Matthew's shoulder and says, "Don't worry. I promise not to take any pictures of you, Mr. Cool." Matthew glares back at Liam, who is trying to do his best impression of Matthew.

"I hate you," Matthew says and Liam stands up triumphantly.

"He's in!" Liam yells.

The barista turns his head in our direction and Liam sits back down. "He's in," he whispers, looking around the café.

My pocket vibrates and I fish out my phone. Yoona is scrolling through movie options, but I barely register her words. Jax's name flashes across the screen, and my heart flips, the butterflies I thought had settled now thrash wildly.

I stare at it in disbelief, heart hammering, completely tuning out Yoona as the world narrows to him.

Still on for tomorrow?

Studying. I think it through and then respond.

Yeah, if you want.

My phone buzzes again and he responds.

Library?

Looking around, I get an idea.

Do you like cafés?

He texts back.

Cafés are chill

I send him the address and tell him to meet me tomorrow morning.

Sounds good.

I slip my phone away and catch up with my friends, who've moved on from Yoona's movie night. We stay long enough for two more rounds of drinks and pastries. As the sun sets, we ask for the check, and before leaving, I drop a pin on the map and close the app. Tomorrow at ten, no excuses.

CHAPTER SIXTEEN

Jackson

I catch up on enough missed work to barely stay in the clear. Without Addie drilling me last week, I'd be lost. I hate owing her, but I owe her. She notices when I'm lost and explains before I even ask. But as the week goes on, she grows distant, speaking only about school in class. In the hallways, she smiles and moves on, always surrounded by friends, making it hard to connect outside class.

Initially, I accept it, thinking that this is the way things should be between us. The more she pulls away, the more I just wish she'd open up. My brain and ego are at war, leaving me unsure about us, but some things are constant: the darkness I hide, the shaking hands I beg she won't notice, the nights with Megan that don't mean anything but won't stop happening.

I try so hard to forget her, to scrub Addie out of my head. The softness of her hair, those big amber eyes, the curves I can't stop remembering, her vanilla scent, the way her lips part when I'm near... it all sticks. When we're alone, I'm not me. I'm someone else entirely. Someone better.

The turmoil that lives within me simmers down and is replaced by a yearning flame. Even with the high coursing through my mind, her face keeps pushing through. She infiltrates every thought as I surrender to darkness within. I am a moth yearning to get close to a flame that is dimming for me.

Megan's become my escape, letting me shove all my Addie feelings as far down as I can. I see her almost every day after school, picking her up before dance. We never even make it back to my place, she can't wait, and honestly, neither can I. The car steams up quick. No names, no promises, just a mess to forget Addie by.

Today being one of those days, I'm parked in my car with her. She has just crawled off my lap and is in the passenger seat, putting her shirt back on. I crack a window, letting the nice, crisp, fall air carry any fleshly aromas from the car. Leaning over and reaching for my leather jacket in the backseat, my eyes pass over the rear-view mirror and I stop. Twisting my body back to normal in my seat, I crane my head to the left and see marks on my neck. *Hickies.* My eyes narrow.

I grab the mirror, jaw tight. "Not on my neck," I snap. "I don't want questions." The words come out like cold steel.

She looks over to me, an intentional smile growing. "That's nothing. They'll fade quickly."

"I don't give a fuck how quickly they fade. Don't do it again."

My hand comes down and I unlock my car.

"Oh, don't be like that." She rolls her eyes. When I don't respond to her, she says, "Fine. I won't do it again," and stomps out of the car.

Slamming the door behind her, I don't even wait for her to step away. I push my foot hard on the gas and my car speeds off.

I wear a black hoodie the following day in an attempt to cover my neck. I'm angry at myself for not realizing she was leaving marks, but there's nothing I can do about it now. I do my best to sit to Addie's left in chemistry class, not wanting her to see my neck. Mr. Davis doesn't have us work as partners, so I'm able to keep to myself. Addie and I go on as we have been the entire week, doing our best to seem aloof.

When I get to Algebra class, our teacher announces the date for the unit exam. Knowing that I'm not fully prepared, I say more profane words than I should in my head. When class is over, I try going to the library for the first time ever during study hall. Sitting down at an empty table by the window, I take out my math textbook and do my best to solve a few problems.

At first, I'm able to solve the simple ones, but get completely stuck when I have to shift and use a different formula to solve the second set of problems. The numbers blur until I want to rip the page out. My hand twitches for the pill bottle.

After failing to solve the problems, frustration coils in me. The bell rings, the day drags on, and I'm finally heading home. I drop my bag by the door, hang up my hoodie, and retreat to my room. I pop a pill, my hands jittery, feet restless, a well of agitation simmering under my skin.

Unable to find the source of my agitation, I go for a run. An hour later, I'm back home, still as agitated as I was before I left. I undress and go shower, letting the hot scalding water run over me. Clenching and unclenching my fists, I try to take a few deep breaths, determined to mellow myself out. It works slightly.

After I get dressed, I search for my phone, wanting to order some takeout for dinner. Remembering that I left it in my hoodie, I walk over to grab it. My eyes fall to the floor and pause when they catch my book bag. My fingers hover over the phone.

Caring feels weak. I type her name anyway.

Knowing full well that I won't be able to pass Monday's exam without her help, we agree to meet again. Addie chooses a local café as our meet-up spot and sends me the address, which I save onto my phone. If I'm going to attempt to be in school, I might as well actually try.

***

I make it to the café before Addie arrives and order myself a coffee. I slide into the corner table, back to the wall. Old habits. Safer that way. Attempting to work through the formula that's confusing me the most, I sip my coffee and do my best to concentrate.

To my advantage, the café is mostly empty and silent, the few other customers silently working away on other things. The high I'm already on keeps me calm, but the anticipation of seeing Addie still breaks through it, eyes nervously glancing to the door every time the bell chimes open.

Finally, Addie walks in, coming to sit in front of me after waving her over. She swings her book bag off and places it on the floor next to her chair. Leaning over, she takes out her own books.

"Hey, Jax," she says, still deep in her bag. "Sorry I'm late. Had a bit of a late night with my friends."

She's wearing a white v-neck and simple blue jeans with black knee-high boots. There's a black sweater tied around her hips and she has a black cap on, her thick waves loose beneath it. To my surprise, she's wearing glasses.

I catch myself staring. "Didn't know you wore glasses." I sound like an idiot, but she laughs.

"I usually wear contacts, but I was too lazy to put them in this morning. These are my last resort."

I stay quiet, offering a simple smile. She's so damn cute, but I can't let it show.

"I'm going to get some coffee. Want a refill?" She stands and points to my mug.

"Yeah, milk and sugar. Thanks."

Addie walks away and is back within minutes. Handing me my cup, she sits with her hands wrapped tightly around her own mug.

"What are you up to?"

Sighing, I explain. "I have a unit test on Monday. I can do this basic formula," I point to it in my notebook, "but I can't do this one at all."

"Let me see." She grabs my notebook and studies it. "Yeah, that formula is hard to understand if you don't know how to label your Xs and Ys."

I make a face and lean forward. "But there's four points on the graph. How am I supposed to label them?"

"Each set of points has one X and one Y intercept. You're getting it wrong because you're labeling them wrong." She fixes my error and then pushes the notebook my way. "Here, look."

"You're joking right?" Running a hand through my hair, I give her a baffled look.

"Nope. You're doing the actual math correct, just labeling your numbers wrong. Try it again."

It takes me a couple minutes, but for once, the answer makes sense. The rush feels almost better than a hit. "That was easier than I thought it would be," I tell her, bringing the mug to my lips and taking a sip of the now lukewarm drink.

"Yeah, you'll need to remember your labels. Soon, we'll be doing equations in chemistry," she responds, picking up her own mug.

I choke on my drink and put it down. "Come again?"

Laughing at my reaction, Addie says, "Chemistry isn't just looking at cells. Eventually we'll be working with compounds and having to use formulas to understand their composition. When we begin doing reactions, we'll have to understand what caused the reaction and why."

"Fuck me," I groan.

Addie laughs again and I give her a tight look. She relents and apologizes, trying to convince me that my reaction was too comical not to laugh. Her grin slowly makes my tight face melt away and, before I know it, I'm laughing along with her. The sound of her laugh is music to my ears and I love that I'm the sole cause of it.

When we're finally able to compose ourselves, I offer to buy Addie breakfast. Agreeing only if she's able to buy the next round of drinks, I get up and order us two breakfast platters.

When the food arrives, I pause, excusing myself to the bathroom. Part of me doesn't want to, I'm enjoying this too much, but my leg won't stop bouncing, my hands won't stay still. I can't let her see.

I slip one anyway, forcing my body to calm before I head back. Clearing the table of books, we start eating. After a bite, I tell Addie I'm impressed with her food picks, and we drift into a lighthearted conversation about the town, its fun spots, and the not-so-fun ones.

It's like a weight has lifted from both of us. This is what I've wanted with her. Her smile, her laugh, the way she leans in when she talks, the soft vanilla scent she leaves behind. Her eyes when she explains something, the way she licks her lips thinking... with her, time stops. I'm numb in all the right ways. No pain, no haunting memories. Just her. And being haunted by her is better than any high I've ever had.

After we finish eating, we huddle closer together, working through a problem when Addie's eyes freeze on my skin. The mark on my neck throbs hotter under her stare.

And just like that, my high runs icy cold.

I'd completely forgotten about the hickey on my neck. My sweater is off, leaving me in just a black long-sleeve that does nothing to hide it.

"It's nothing," I tell her, pushing myself away.

Addie gives me a hard look, but it disappears as quickly as it comes, a calm look replacing it. Her eyes betray her emotion, however.

"You don't have to hide it." There's an edge to her voice.

"Hide what?"

"That it was Megan."

"How do you know that?" The perfect morning turns bitter, and a harder version of me takes root, ready to defend myself, even as guilt gnaws at me, even as I sense her pain.

"Who doesn't know about you and Megan? She can't exactly keep her mouth shut, you know. The entire dance team knows about you two and word travels fast here."

I place my hands behind my head and lean into my chair, keeping my eyes steady on Addie.

It's unfair. She doesn't deserve it. Still, the words slip out. "So what if it was her?"

"Are you dating her?" Addie asks with a slight edge, dodging my own question.

"That's my business."

"Right."

Tension ripples in the air between us. Addie is leaning into her own chair now, looking down at her notebook. I place my hands on the table and lean in.

"You agreed to be friends." The accusation escapes my lips harshly.

Addie meets my eyes. "Yeah, you're right."

The resignation in her voice is clear. But I don't want resignation. I want a fight. I want the truth and I want her to say it. I *need* her to admit that she feels what I feel. That she feels this pull that keeps bringing us together even if it's wrong. Even if we shouldn't. Even if *I* shouldn't.

"So, what's the problem?" I challenge.

"Nothing. Seems like you're getting along well."

"Oh, cut the bullshit, Addie." I can feel myself growing angry and try to reign it in.

"You're the one who said you're not good for me, Jax. I'm following your lead."

"What do you want me to do? Lie to you? I don't do relationships." Indeed, I lie. The selfish part of me craves her admission. I am broken and full of darkness, but she is the light at the end of my tunnel. She is pure and I don't have it in me to corrupt her even if my desire for her boils my blood.

"But you can do *her*." The words land sharp. My whole body stiffens like she has struck me.

"Don't go there." I check my temper. "You can't like me, Addie," I caution.

"You can't like me either and yet you do."

Silence.

"I don't want to like you and yet I do," she continues with a sigh. "I try to push you out of my head and I can't. You're like a plague." And just like that, I got my admission. It just doesn't feel the way I thought it would.

"I know the feeling," I admit back.

"I should go," Addie says, getting up from her chair.

My hand moves quickly and I reach out to grab hers.

"Don't," I say.

She looks down at my hand and slowly pulls out of my grasp. Grabbing her things, she swings her bag over her shoulder and exits the café. I let her go, watching her back as she leaves, feeling like I keep stacking one disappointment on top of another.

Done with studying, I shove my stuff away but stay seated, that dark mood creeping in. The voice in my head snickers. *You know how to fix this.* My thumb hovers over Jay's name before I cave. One text later, his reply is instant. I grab my things and head out of the café.

CHAPTER SEVENTEEN
Adelina

The moment the question escaped my mouth, I couldn't hold myself back...the words spilled too fast, like pages ripped from a diary. The irrational anger within kept rising, a flame threatening to combust. At some point, rational thought tried to reign in the anger and the flame dwindled. Preventing my anger from amplifying once more, I did the only reasonable thing and left.

I replay what transpired between me and Jax over and over in my head, a jumble of emotions coursing through me. I was disappointed in myself, stung by Megan, confused by Jax, and angry that I'd let it all show.

I jam my earbuds in until the sound drowns thought with rhythm.

The next time I open my eyes, the sun is shining bright through my window and the earbuds that were once in my ears lay in random spots on my bed. I stretch and slowly stand up, allowing my body to wake. Garlic and sofrito curl through the hallway. My stomach growls loud. I freshen up in the bathroom before walking down into the kitchen where I find Mami sitting on a barstool, sipping her morning coffee.

"*Hola amor,*" she greets me.

"*Bendición,*" I respond.

"There's a plate of breakfast in the microwave for you. I didn't want it to get cold. The coffee's still hot though," she smiles.

"Thanks, Mami," I say and walk over to retrieve my plate. Settling next to her, I glance over in her direction.

"What?" she asks.

Quickly, I say, "Nothing," and continue eating, but what I'm actually thinking about is how Jax would likely marvel at the spices drifting through the air. I let out a big internal sigh, knowing full well that my heart won't rest easy until I make amends. Finishing my breakfast, I thank Mami again and return back to my room. Unplugging my phone from its charger, I sit on my bed and pull up Jax's number.

`Sorry about yesterday. Can we talk?`

I hit send and close my eyes, letting out a physical sigh this time. Not expecting him to respond so early in the morning, I walk over and set my phone down to charge once more. Turning away from the nightstand, I hear a notification go off. I pivot and grab my phone, heart skipping. My thumb hesitates over the screen before I finally check. Jax's reply is already there.

`Yeah, sure`

Suddenly nervous that he has agreed, I respond back.

His response is immediate.

I turn my screen off and walk over to my closet, throwing on a similar outfit as the day before. It takes me a while to find my glasses, having misplaced them before going to bed. I finally locate them on the bathroom sink and put them on, completing my look.

Grabbing my car keys from my desk, I go downstairs to tell Mami I'm leaving. This time she's in the living room, sitting on the couch with her feet tucked beneath her, a laptop on her lap.

Mami raises an eyebrow at me. "Don't forget you have school tomorrow."

"Yes, I know. I won't be home late. I promise."

"Do you have your phone on you?"

"*Sí*," I reply.

Mami gives me a nod and I exit the house, walking to my car. It's a bit of a drive to get there, so I blast my K-pop playlist, the same one Yoona made me memorize, drumming my fingers against the wheel. This is the only way I know to help control my nerves and soon, I'm attempting to sing along.

I smile, remembering when Yoona first introduced me to K-pop. I'd never heard it until that day in her remodeled basement art studio. I'd brought the supplies she asked for. She was dancing and I was yelling to get her attention. With the music still blasting, she finally looked at me and smiled.

"This is one of my favorite songs," she said over the music.

Already bobbing my head, I yelled back. "Yeah, it's really good! What is it?"

"It's K-pop! This new group is my current favorite. I'll send you their album."

"Yeah, Zahra would probably like it too!" I suggested, handing her the bag of supplies.

"Oh, heck yeah! The groups all do their own choreography. Zahra is going to lose it when she hears the song."

The song ended and Yoona lowered the volume. I helped her set up her next project, and she soon put the music back on. Ever since, I've been hooked. We even hit a few concerts in the city last summer, with her insisting I learn the Korean lyrics first, which I appreciated. Now I can, mostly, sing and dance along with her.

Seeing my exit, I steer my car to the right and drive a few more minutes before reaching the pier. It's a calm Sunday, the sun high in the sky. The weather is chilly, but comfortable if you have a sweater. At this time of year, the pier is usually empty, so I park in one of the many empty spots and wait. Moments later, I see Jax's car pull up next to mine and he gets out. He motions for me to do the same. I turn off my engine and meet him halfway.

"Let's walk along the water." I nod to him and he takes the lead, his long legs bringing us closer to the ocean.

Finding a spot to sit alongside the shoreline, the smell of sea salt envelops us. Gulls cut across the sky, and the planks creak under us as we dangle our feet.

Taking a deep breath in, I start apologizing for my behavior the day before. "I shouldn't have said the things I said. I had no right."

Jax's gaze is far away. "It's my fault for leading you on."

"Were you leading me on for nothing?" I ask hesitantly, bracing myself for the worst.

"No," he answers and rolls his shoulders back. "No, Addie, it wasn't for nothing. But we can't give in to those emotions. We won't be good for each other. At least, I won't be good for you."

"I understand. I'm used to guys not wanting to be with me." I swing my legs and look down into my lap. "I'm not Megan. No blonde hair, no perfect skin. Just me. Why choose me?" This time, I'm somber, not angry, and I mean every word I say.

"It's not like that. Addie... you're beautiful. Being around you is nothing like I've felt before. You quiet the chaos in my head. I can... breathe. Even now." His hand cups my chin, tilting my head up, those green eyes locked on mine. "You have no idea how much you mess with my emotions. I promised myself I'd never be in a relationship... I'm broken, Addie."

"Broken how?" I ask him.

Jax lets go of my chin and stretches both hands out behind him, leaning back, his eyes staring off into the water.

"I'm always chasing a high. Stop, and I shake. Keep going, and I burn."

"That explains the overdose the night of the party."

"Yes, that explains the overdose," Jax repeats after me. "Usually, I don't do *that* much," his voice trails off.

"Why do it at all?" My tone is more curious than judgmental.

"It isn't something I talk about. We all have demons and mine all lead to addiction. I can't shake the habit even if I wanted to." He pauses and then continues. "Listen, I've been with my fair share of girls and you don't strike me as one who should be with someone like me."

I resist asking him more about his demons. "So... you're trying to protect me by pushing me away?"

Jax exhales. "Pretty much."

"What if I don't want to be pushed away?"

Jax makes a grunting noise and I shift to face him. "I'm serious, Jax. You have no idea how you make me feel. You're like a magnet that I can't avoid. I try to keep my distance from you, but one way or another, we connect again. It's tiring, the back and forth."

"You would willingly be with someone as broken as me?"

"I don't think it's up to me at this point. Like you, logic tells me to run, but I can't. I've been so afraid to be around boys, so afraid of rejection, that I've pushed them all away. Then you come along..."

"Addie, you're a beautiful, smart girl. There's no reason for you to be afraid."

I snort. "Yeah, okay."

Jax turns and we're both facing each other. "Why can't you see what I see?" His question comes out low and soft.

He reaches with his hand and brushes my cheek. His touch lights a flame within me that I've never felt before. I lean into his palm, not wanting to fight it anymore, and relish the warmth of his fingers on my face.

"Look up," he gently orders and I do. "You have beautiful eyes." I can feel my face flush and I give him a shy smile. His thumb crosses over my bottom lip and when he goes for my top lip, I try to coil away involuntarily, but his hand holds me there.

"Every part of you is beautiful, Addie. Your scars feel like constellations to me." He traces my upper lip, my nose, my eyebrows.

My breath gets caught in my throat and I'm mesmerized by him. How can someone be so broken yet so gentle?

Jax finishes tracing the contours of my face before cupping the back of my head. His eyes search mine, almost as if asking permission, and my body answers, not needing any words. I feel his hand in my hair as his lips come down to meet mine.

The flame within me ignites further, burning hotter than I ever thought possible. I kiss him back, savoring the soft touch of his lips against mine. Finally giving in to each other, our kiss transforms into something that steals the breath out of both of us. Momentarily coming up for air, our lips come together once more, hungry for each other's touch. Suddenly, the kiss turns soft and delicate before Jax pulls away from me.

"What's wrong?" I ask timidly.

Jax smiles down at me. "Nothing, trust me. You are perfect." He leans over and gives me a soft kiss. "I just don't want this to be how it is with other girls. You deserve better than that."

"This?"

"Yeah, whatever this is. I won't lie though, I come with a lot of baggage. You need to understand that," he tells me.

"I know," I say and he shakes his head, looking out over the water. "It doesn't hurt to try, Jax."

"No, it doesn't hurt... not yet." And still, his fingers curl around mine, a mix of promise and worry.

CHAPTER EIGHTEEN

Jackson

Monday comes quickly and I'm trying to study a bit before my math exam. Sitting in my chemistry seat, my head is deep in my notebook until I hear Addie sit next to me. I look up and she flashes a bright smile before placing her own notebook on the desk. We still have a few minutes before class begins, so I opt to spend the remaining time trying to relax my thoughts.

"I hate math," I say, sighing to Addie. She brushes her fingers against mine, just long enough to anchor me.

"Don't stress it. It'll come to you. Just give your brain a break."

I sink into my chair and fix my cap, black strands of hair resting on the back of my neck. Looking over at Addie, I see her absently twirling her hair between her fingers.

I lean in close to her and whisper, "I've always thought you have beautiful hair."

Blushing, she rolls her eyes at me and points to the front of the room. Looking over, I see Mr. Davis has already arrived, preparing to start the lesson. I shift so that I'm sitting comfortably in my seat and do my best to pay attention, even with my anxious thoughts.

Exiting together when the bell rings, Addie asks, "When's your test?", over the chatter in the hallway.

"Third period."

"I'll be sending you some luck."

"Thanks."

Addie begins to walk away in the other direction and then stops.

"Um... do you want to sit with me at lunch?" Her voice dips low, like she regrets saying it out loud.

I'm a bit stunned, but I accept her offer. Smiling, she instructs me to wait for her outside of the entrance. I nod, then head to my next class.

Too soon, there's an exam on my desk, staring me in the face. I open the booklet, read the first question, then close it. Letting out a disgruntled sigh, I open it again and begin taking the test with seriousness. I'm able to finish the last question right as the bell rings and I hand my booklet to the teacher as I exit the room. Swearing that I bombed the test, I'm just glad to have gotten it over with.

The hallway is filled with bodies and I try to maneuver my way down to the lunchroom. Taking the back staircase, I'm able to mostly avoid the traffic jam that tends to occur during transition. I reach the ground floor and, as I exit the staircase, I bump into someone. My feet take a reflexive step back and I hear a high-pitched laugh fill the air. Megan stands there with two shadows at her side. The sight that used to thrill me now grates.

"Hey Jax," she greets me and moves to give me a hug. I take another step back, avoiding it. Megan's friends give each other a look.

"Hey, I'm late for something," I quickly explain, hoping to shake them off.

"Is everything okay?" Megan purrs. "I've been texting you since Saturday and you haven't responded."

Truthfully, I had been ignoring her texts all weekend, her existence slipping my mind after spending time with Addie at the pier. Narrowing my eyes, I say, "Yeah, I've been busy," and walk past her and her friends. Her face says she doesn't like it, but I don't care.

Addie is waiting for me by the entrance of the cafeteria when I arrive. I bend and kiss her forehead before I think it through. Heads turn. She tugs me inside fast.

"That wasn't awkward at all," she complains.

"Don't pay them any mind."

She brushes me off with a "Yeah, yeah, yeah," and then waves to a table of people. Two boys, one with messy red hair and one with long, tied up locks, wave back. I see the girl who's always hanging with Addie along with another girl with bright, platinum hair, attracting any eyes that look her way.

"Those are my friends," Addie says to me, head tilted in the direction of their table. "Are you sure you want to eat with us? If it's too much, you don't have to."

"Addie, let's go. I'm hungry." I speak quickly before I lose my nerve. Truth be told, this is completely out of my comfort zone, but if it makes Addie happy, then I'm willing to do it.

"Wait, aren't you in my math class?" the boy with red hair asks.

The recognition is instant because he's one of the few that sits in the backrow like I do. "If you have Algebra II, then I guess so," I respond, taking my seat at the table with Addie.

"That test was crazy. I'm pretty sure I failed," he says.

"Yeah same." I laugh out.

"My name is Liam, by the way. This is Matthew." He points to the boy with the locks, who nods to me. "That's Yoona and that's Zahra."

I look over to the girls and nod their way, but they're busy having a hushed conversation with Addie.

Clearing his throat, Matthew asks me, "You're new this year, right?"

"Yeah, I moved here before the summer started."

Liam wiggles his fork at me and Addie. "How do you two know each other?" His tone is suspicious, but there's a slight humor attached to it.

"We're in chemistry together," I explain. "So, are you all close friends or something?" I deflect.

"Yeah, we all came together freshman year, but some of us go way back. Liam and I have been friends since we were three, and the girls met before high school. When we got here, we just clicked," Matthew says, crossing his fingers for emphasis.

"These two are the biggest knuckleheads of the group. Please tell me you're here to mellow them out," Yoona tells me, the girls returning to our conversation.

"I'll try," I say. "But I'm not a miracle worker."

Liam makes a shushing gesture to Yoona, who returns a crude gesture of her own and I can't help but laugh. Suddenly, Liam's eyes open wide and he whispers something in Matthew's ear. Matthew's own eyes grow wide and he gives Liam a noise of approval.

"So Yoona," Liam begins, trying to use a professional voice. "The boys were talking and we've decided that we're tired of being outnumbered. I vote for Jax to join us this weekend."

"I concur," Matthew chimes in.

Yoona opens her mouth then closes it again. "I don't mind," she finally stammers. "As long as Addie's okay with it," she adds.

"Would you like to join us?" Addie asks me shyly.

"Join you for what?"

"Yoona is having a Halloween movie night at her place this weekend," she tells me.

"But you have to wear a onesie," adds Liam.

I give Addie an apprehensive look and Matthew pipes up. "See?! I'm not wearing no goddamn onesie. I'm with the new guy."

"I'll go, but I'm skipping the onesie," I tell them.

"Whatever, I'm still wearing mine," Liam says indignantly.

"Matthew, you're insufferable," Zahra finally adds.

The bell rings and Matthew stands up, Liam following. Swinging his bag over his shoulder, Matthew gives Zahra a wink and she averts her eyes. The rest of us clear the table and get up, ready for our next period classes.

"I'm off to study hall," Liam complains.

"Same," I say.

Walking over to me, he unexpectedly puts his arm around my shoulders and looks down at Addie. "I'm stealing him," he tells her and Addie smiles her approval. Liam laughs and lets go of me, walking over to Matthew. I fix my cap and look at Addie.

"Your friends are nice," I tell her privately, making our way to the exit. I'm not used to anyone claiming me so quickly. "Guess I'm spending study hall with Liam."

"Yeah, that went smoother than I thought." She gives me a quick hug before running off to make her next class. Having finished saying his goodbyes, Liam comes back and we walk to the library together.

I quickly learn that Liam is talkative, which makes study hall fly by. He acts like he's known me forever, but when we finally settle to work, my thoughts drift. Since losing my mom, I've avoided social life, preferring to be alone. Still, I can't deny I enjoyed lunch. It's been a while since I genuinely smiled with someone, and it reminds me of the happiness I've been missing.

I'm scared to let myself be happy. It always disappears. Everything good vanished the day I held her cold hand in the hospital. Since then, I've sunk into a black hole of drugs, sex, and solitude I can't escape. Addie doesn't know it, but she's been pulling me out, piece by piece, and that terrifies me. I'm not sure I'm ready to tear down the walls I've built, but she's already cracking them.

Refocusing me, Liam taps me on the shoulder and lets me know the period is over. We walk out of the library and he starts telling me about his personal statement, asking me if I'll be submitting my college applications in November.

"Nah man," I tell him, pulling on my black leather jacket before swinging my bag onto my shoulder.

"How come?" he wonders.

"Not sure. Not my thing I guess."

"Honestly, I don't think I'll make the November deadline. I'm trying to get a soccer scholarship, but I need to pass math to qualify and math isn't exactly my strong suit," Liam explains.

Remembering what Addie told me about gym credits, I ask Liam about tryouts. "Addie told me you and Matthew play a lot of soccer. When are tryouts?"

"A lot is an understatement," he huffs. "We basically live soccer. Tryouts are on Wednesday, actually. Do you play?"

"A bit. I just need to make up some gym credits."

"Swing by then. Do you know where the field is?"

I nod.

"Then meet us there on Wednesday after school. Wear your soccer gear if you have some," he advises.

"Sounds good."

Reaching the end of the hall, we part and go our separate ways. My remaining classes pass quickly, and I leave the building, walking over to my car. Taking out my phone, I text Addie, asking her to meet me in the parking lot, and she does.

When she finds me, I pull her into my arms. "Today was... different."

"Different good or different bad?"

"Different good."

"Good," she smiles, "I'm glad. How did it go with Liam?"

"Chill," I tell her. "He told me tryouts are on Wednesday."

Addie slaps her forehead and begins apologizing. "I totally forgot to tell you about that," she groans.

"No, it's fine. What matters is that I know about it now," I say, leaning into my car, bringing her with me.

We hear a shout in the background and Addie peers over my shoulder and then buries her face in my jacket.

"Oh goodness," she whispers, clearly embarrassed.

"What?" I ask.

"Turn around."

I do. Zahra and Yoona are waving madly behind us and I hear Zahra say, "Hurry up and get over here already!"

"I have to go," Addie tells me. "We made plans to hang out at Yoona's house today."

"Don't let me hold you up then," I say. Addie pushes herself away from me and as I lean in to kiss her, she stops me.

"Not yet, Jax. Yesterday was great, but I don't want to rush into things. Is that cool?"

I take a pause, letting her words register. "Yeah, I get it."

Addie sighs a breath of relief and smiles, leaving me to go with her friends. Getting into my car, I sit and look down at my hands. They've been shaking for over an hour now and my cap is the only thing hiding the sweat that has been forming on my forehead. Texting Jay and loathing my pathetic weakness, I drive to his dorm and pick up more pills.

***

The morning before tryouts, I wake up drenched in sweat, having had another nightmare. I can still see my mother's decomposed face in my mind moments after I wake up. It's been a while since my last bad dream and my nerves are in overdrive. Contemplating skipping school, I pick up my phone to shut off my alarm and see a text from Addie.

I know I'll see you later BUT... Good luck today! :) I'm sure you'll make the team.

168

I shoot her a thank you text and drag myself out of bed. My mood is dark and grim, past memories now haunting me. Three pills lined on the counter. Too many. I swallow anyways.

I walk into chemistry in the same foul mood I woke up in. Addie leans over with concern and asks if I'm alright. I nod without looking at her, keeping my attention on the front board. The pills are kicking in hard. I feel my body relax in my chair, eyes slightly heavier. I lean my head back against the wall, and sink lower, extending my legs. Addie keeps glancing over my way, but I ignore her.

After class, I walk out of the room in a daze. A hand reaches out and grabs me by the shoulder, whipping my body around.

"What is wrong with you?" Addie demands, searching my face.

"Really bad morning," I tell her.

Her brown eyes settle on mine intently. "Are you high?" she whispers, but her hand recoils as if I'd burned her.

I don't lie. "Yes."

Addie closes her eyes and takes a shaky breath in. "Okay," she says, opening her eyes again. "Will you be okay?"

"Yeah."

"And tryouts?"

"I'll be fine," I snap, immediately regretting my tone.

"Fine," she snaps back and walks away.

I daze through the rest of my morning classes and skip lunch, choosing to spend it in the library, where I nap for two consecutive periods. When I wake up, I'm much more alert than I was in the morning, my body having recharged. The sluggish pull from earlier is gone, replaced with the usual haze I'm so used to. I make an effort to apologize, but Addie is nowhere to be found after school.

I change and head to the field where Liam and Matthew are already running drills. They jog over as soon as they see me, filling me in on everything I've missed before we split off to warm up. Passing, shooting, joking around. It feels natural, like we've been doing this for years. My body remembers what to do, and the easy vibe between the three of us keeps me loose.

Soon the coaches round everyone up, have us call out positions, and split us into groups. I claim striker, which earns me an impressed look from Matthew, and then we're off. The drills flow into scrimmages of two twenty-minute games where I manage to score twice. Liam and Matthew control the midfield, feeding me perfect setups, and together we bury three more goals.

By the end, I'm drenched in sweat, grinning despite myself, and the coaches thank us before saying the roster will be posted by the gym. Lifting my shirt to wipe the sweat from my face, I hear Matthew and Liam begin talking.

"The three of us make a good team," Matthew comments, still trying to catch his breath

"Yeah, who knew Jax could play like that?" Liam manages to say between his own unsteady breaths.

"It's been a while since I've played," I tell them. Thankfully, the high from this morning has mellowed out to a tolerable haze, ensuring I didn't screw up on the field.

"Sure didn't look like it," Matthew responds.

We grab our bags from the sidelines and begin walking to the student parking lot together, making small talk about the tryouts. Once there, we agree to look at the listing together on Friday before leaving.

***

The first thing I do when I get home is take a long shower. Even though I crushed it on the field, my mood's still dark, and that familiar fog is creeping back in. I can't find a shred of happiness or calm. Just this heavy, sinking feeling that won't quit.

Stepping out of the shower and drying myself, I walk up to my room and have only put on my boxers when my phone rings.

Addie's name lights up and I answer. "Hey," I say warmly, trying to mask my brooding emotions.

"Hey," her warm voice comes through. "How are you?"

"I'm... okay," I lie this time.

"Okay, that's good. I just wanted to check in on you."

"Thanks."

"Are you sure you're okay? You don't sound okay."

"I'm just going through some stuff," I say, trying to keep it brief.

"I'm guessing you don't want to talk about it?"

"No."

"Chocolate fudge ice cream. My peace offering and my question in disguise."

Curiosity and intrigue cut through me. "What?"

"Look outside your window."

I do and there she is. Leaning against her car, using one hand to hold the phone to her ear and the other is balancing two pints of ice cream. A genuine smile stretches across my face and I hang up. I jog to the front door and Addie is already there. I scoop her up, embracing her in a hug.

"What are you doing here?" I ask after putting her back down.

She shrugs and wags the ice cream pints in the air. "I don't know. I just know ice cream helps me feel better. Thought you could use some. Also, go put some pants on!"

Walking in, she goes directly to the kitchen and takes out two bowls. I enter the kitchen after putting some sweats on and take a seat. I watch her serve two bowls of ice cream, one bowl slightly larger than the other. She hands me the bigger one and takes a seat across from me.

Her eyes linger on my chest and she swallows. "You're not planning on putting a shirt on?"

"Oh shit," I swear. "I forgot. Do you mind if I stay like this? I don't want to go back upstairs."

"You're good. I'm just messing with you a bit. Though pants are a must, so thanks for that one." She laughs nervously and avoids meeting my eyes.

We eat our ice cream in silence. Finishing first, I wait for her, then carry both bowls to the sink. Addie gestures for the couch, and we each take an end, facing each other. It's simple, but it lifts the fog a little, reminding me how good she is for me, so different from the pills I chase when life feels heavy.

"Explain it to me," Addie starts, seemingly resolved to have this conversation. "The drugs, I mean. How often do you do them?"

"I don't think you want to know," I warn.

"I do, Jax, or else I wouldn't be asking you." She inhales shakily. "I don't agree with it all, but I want to try to understand you."

Sighing, I begin explaining. "I try to keep it to a few pills a day. Morning, noon, night. Sometimes I take more. When I take less, I get withdrawals."

"What do you feel when you're high?"

"Um," I place my hands behind my head, "I'm pretty used to it by now. I get a mellow feeling, my limbs feel heavy."

"And if you take more?"

"If I have enough in me, then I might actually feel high."

"What happens when you withdraw?"

"Cold sweats. Shaky hands. I don't know what happens after that. I don't let it get any worse than that."

Addie takes a pause. "How many times have you overdosed?"

"Just once," I answer honestly. "I didn't mean to. It just sort of happened."

"I don't think anyone means to, Jax."

I nod and remain silent.

"Why do you do it?" she asks quietly.

"I told you, I come with a lot of baggage."

"I know," she agrees, "I'm just really trying to understand you."

"Why I do it is not something I talk about."

"Okay, I'll respect that. Do you ever think about stopping?"

"Sometimes. And then I'm reminded of why I take them and then I keep going. It's a vicious cycle."

"Should I always expect to see you high?"

"Addie, I'm never sober. You probably won't often see me as high as I was earlier, but yes."

"Would you stop? If you think you actually could, would you?"

"Maybe," I tell her. *You couldn't even if you did try.* The voice slips in, creeping out from the dark, oily corners of my mind, and I will it away.

She stares down into her lap, head nodding slowly. When Addie's eyes meet mine, she simply gives me one of her many beautiful smiles.

"Okay," she says.

Confused, I ask, "Okay?"

"Maybe isn't a no, so I have faith in you. One day, you will get through all this."

"And you?"

"Me? I'll just be here to help you, Jax."

"Until you grow tired of me," I comment.

"No. The true Jax will be out before that happens."

I stare at her. Without expecting it, Addie comes closer and gives me a hug, her chin resting on my shoulder. I inhale her warm scent. Her hands are cool against my bare back. She plants a soft kiss on my shoulder and my hands grab her hips, pulling her in, our restraint snapping.

Addie's kisses trail from my shoulder to my neck. Her hands push me back, lowering me onto the couch. Legs on either side of me, she leans forward and kisses me fervently. I return the kiss with equal intensity, savoring her taste. My body is burning hot. I shift my hips, she tightens her legs around me. Kissing her again, sounds of pleasure escape her lips and I let out my own.

We come up for air. It's clumsy and desperate. Addie kisses my neck and pulls my hair, exposing my neck further. A guttural sound comes out of me. Her nails dig into my back, but my body only registers the pleasure, ignoring the pain. I'm tempted to lift her shirt, stripping it from her body.

I think about the things Addie has told me. Her fears. Her past. Before getting carried away, I slow our movements.

"Wait Addie," I breathe. "Didn't you want to take it slow?"

Beautiful brown eyes looking intently into mine, she nods. "I know. I just... I've never felt like this before. And I've been wanting to do that for a long time."

I don't want to ask, but I have to know.

"Have you ever been with someone?"

Hurt skirts across her face and she leans away from me a little. "Does that matter?"

"No," I answer quickly. "I only ask because I want to respect you. You deserve better than rushed couch sex. I want your first time to matter."

"I've never really thought about the first time," she states. "I never thought I'd ever be in this situation to be completely honest."

"Well, you deserve something better. After that, you can have all the couch sex you want."

Addie's laughter fills the room and she climbs off me. "If you say so," she says between laughs. Slowly getting up, she fixes her hair and does a small stretch. "I should get going. Mami still has me on curfew."

"Sounds like a smart mom," I tell her.

Shooting me a grin, she says, "The smartest and most amazing mom I could ever wish for."

I walk her to the front door and lean down to give her one last kiss, which she sweetly accepts. Stepping out into the night, she asks, "Do you still want to come to Yoona's house this weekend?"

"Yeah, as long as I get to see you in a onesie," I remark.

"There's nothing wrong with onesies," she chastises me. "See you at school tomorrow."

"Wait, before you leave, I have to ask you something."

"Sure."

"When we're in school, you don't want anyone knowing about us?" I ask, thinking about the way she denied a kiss from me in front of her friends.

Addie shuffles her feet before saying, "It's not that. It's more that word has gotten around about you and Megan and I'm not exactly comfortable with people thinking what we have is the same."

Completely understanding where she's coming from, I hug her goodnight and watch her drive off, a smile still fixed to my lips.

CHAPTER NINETEEN

Adelina

"You think Jax made the team?" Yoona looks at me.

I rise on my toes, craning my neck, heart pounding faster than it should. There's a crowd of boys surrounding a small bulletin board, all eager to see if they made the team.

"Well, we know Liam and Matthew made it for sure. They've made it every year," Zahra remarks.

"Let's see." I gesture to Matthew, Liam, and Jax, who are now approaching the bulletin board. Jax hangs back while Matthew and Liam cram their heads together, reading through the names.

Without warning, Matthew drops to his knees, fists clenched, and Liam starts bouncing on the balls of his feet, shouting so loudly my ears ring. Jax takes the opportunity to read through the list. He turns to face us girls and gives us a knowing smile.

"What? What?" Zahra shrieks.

"Looks like Matthew's team captain," Jax informs us and Zahra runs over to give Matthew a hug.

"No way! No one's ever made team captain for three years in a row," Yoona says, completely floored.

"And you come at us for training as much as we do," Liam rebukes.

"How about you two?" I ask, joining everyone else at the bulletin board.

"Liam and Jax both made it," Yoona reads aloud.

I pull all three of them into a tight hug, feeling the heat of their excitement, and wish them luck for the season ahead.

"With this guy's skill," Matthew points his thumb at Jax, "and Liam and me playing midfielders, we're going to obliterate this season!"

"Well, what are we still doing here?" Zahra calls out, already walking towards the exit. "Let's go celebrate!"

The drive over is charged with the thrill of a new possibility. I can't help smiling at the thought that, after all the chaos, Jax finally has something good going for him. For a moment, the weight of everything else, his mess, his secrets, feels a little lighter.

Entering, Matthew's place smells like leather and laundry detergent, nothing like Mami's polished kitchen.

"Matthew, where are your parents?" Zahra asks.

"They won't be home for another few hours."

"And your brother?" I question.

"He won't be back from university until Thanksgiving break."

We follow Matthew down to the basement, which he and his brother, similar to Yonna's setup, have turned into a mini two-bedroom setup. He and Liam shove the couches into a semicircle while we laugh and grab a spot, plopping a round table in the middle for pizza and soda. It already feels like the ultimate hangout spot.

It's the perfect way to spend the afternoon, celebrating the boys and their achievement. Liam and Matthew completely take over, making hilarious jokes that make the rest of us howl with laughter. Even Jax laughs, a sound I haven't heard enough to get used to.

After a few hours and six empty pizza boxes, we call it a night, still planning to hit Yoona's tomorrow for a Halloween movie marathon.

"I'm not wearing a onesie!" Mathew calls out from his door as we're getting into our cars.

"Whatever Matthew!" Yoona and Liam yell at the same time, which sends them each into a fit of laughter.

I hear Jax chuckle next to me and as he puts on his jacket, whispering, "Me neither."

***

Yoona scoops me and Zahra up the next morning and we head straight for the mall. We duck into one of those Halloween pop-up shops, and the second we walk in, we split to hunt down a onesie for me. I'm flipping through racks when Zahra yells my name. I follow her voice and find her and Yoona grinning, holding up something way too racy to even be called a costume.

"There's absolutely no way I'm wearing that," I protest immediately.

"What? Why not?" Yoona pouts.

"Look at it!" I squeal. I came looking for a unicorn. They hand me Mortal Kombat Barbie.

181

"Yeah, it's hot! And you're the only one of us who can actually fight," Zahra reasons.

"But why do I have to be wearing something like this just because I can defend myself? I can still defend myself as a rainbow unicorn!"

"Because you'll be the only one not wearing something hot tonight," Yoona says.

I clear my throat. "What?"

"What did you think Yoona and I were going to wear? Yoona has a sexy cat unitard and I have a sultry bunny one."

"Oh, you have got to be shitting me," I complain and throw my arms up in the air.

Yoona grabs one of my hands and pulls me over to the changing rooms. Pushing me inside, they urge me to try it on. I begrudgingly undress and try to squeeze into the costume. Finally getting it on, Zahra and Yoona help me zip it up. They stand behind me and the three of us look at the image reflected back in a unified daze.

"You look good," Yoona nods.

"Better than good," Zahra coos. "Completely sexy."

"I don't know," I say skeptically, picking and pulling at the fabric. It's so tight that I pinch my own skin in the process, a pang of self-consciousness slivering through me. I'm not used to this. It feels like the kind of outfit that will leave me completely exposed, like everyone in the room will be able to see right through me.

Zahra removes my hair tie and shakes my hair loose, letting it fall down my front and back. "There," she says and Yoona smiles. I groan, but in the mirror I can't quite hide the way my lips twitch up.

After buying the outfit, Yoona drives us to her place with her playlist blasting, me and Zahra dancing like idiots in our seats. We dump our bags in her room, then head downstairs to set up for tonight. Popcorn and candy in big bowls, blankets draped over the couches, lava lamps glowing green. The whole vibe is spooky and perfect. By the time we're done, it feels like a real Halloween hangout spot. With a few hours left before the guys show up, we head back upstairs. Zahra pulls out her bunny costume and lays it next to Yoona's cat one, both of them nodding in approval.

"Tonight should be fun," she says cheerily.

Yoona, who is grabbing her things to go shower, makes a sound of approval as she walks out of the room.

"Do you think Matthew will like it?" Zahra asks me.

"Zahra, the guy likes you either way. I wish you two would just tell each other that."

"It's not that simple. We've been in the friend zone for years and I'm not sure he wants to take me out of that bubble."

From the worried look on her face, I can tell she's overthought this in her head.

"I highly doubt that," I say truthfully. "I've caught him staring at you a few times. And he's really playful with you."

She rolls her eyes. "Yes, but Matthew is naturally goofy. I can't tell if he means it or if he's playing around with me."

"He sure as heck doesn't play with me and Yoona like that. Just going to throw that out there," my voice trails off, waiting for her response.

Contemplatively, she responds. "I guess so. Think he'll like the outfit?"

I laugh. "Zahra, even *I* like your outfit!" She gives me a smile. "I think the brown color will look beautiful on you. I know I could never pull off that color."

Zahra hesitates. "Will you let me do your makeup?"

"Only if you keep it simple," I bargain.

Zahra promises me and Yoona walks back in. I grab my stuff and enter the bathroom, Zahra going after. By the time she's back, I'm drying my hair while Yoona's already on her makeup. Music's blasting as I let Yoona curl my hair, then Zahra joins in to finish my makeup. Once we're all ready, we slip into our costumes, helping each other with the final touches.

"Addie, you look so good!" Yoona compliments.

I look over to her and admire the simplicity of her makeup; a simple wing liner with mascara and a red lip that compliments her black cat outfit. Her hair is styled in a straight bob, this time a grey color.

"You look good yourself," I shoot back.

Having outdone herself, Zahra's hair is parted down the middle, a braid adorned with gold cuffs on either side. The braids stop at the crown of her head, tied off with gold bands. Below them, the rest of her hair hangs loose, curling over her shoulders in big, defined spirals. Instead of a black wing liner, her liner is a soft gold that almost matches the color of her outfit. Wearing a simple brown gloss on her lips, she looks incredible.

I tousle my hair a bit and let it fall down my back. Choosing an array of dark reds and browns, Zahra has given me a soft brown eye, with a small wing barely passing the edge of my lashes. Curled with a deep black mascara, my brown eyes twinkle, looking a shade lighter. She completed the look with a deep wine-red lip. For once, the mirror doesn't feel like an enemy.

"I seriously need to learn how to do my own makeup," I mumble.

"It's easy, but you don't really need much Addie," Zahra responds honestly. "I barely put any color on your eyelids and your lashes are so naturally long that I almost skipped the mascara altogether."

Yoona's doorbell rings, making us all jump in alarm. "Is it time already?" she asks.

Looking down at my phone, I nod and follow her out of the room, Zahra trailing behind me. Liam bursts through the door and scoops Yoona into a hug. I crack up the second I see him. He wasn't kidding about the Charmander onesie. His face sticks out of the open mouth, a tail dragging behind him as he grins like it's the best outfit ever.

"I didn't think he'd actually do it," Matthew says, entering the house far more calmly than Liam did. Unlike Liam's full-on onesie, Matthew keeps it classic. Black jeans, black tee, black jacket. It's his signature, understated but sharp. His locks falls loose around his face tonight, framing his features in a way that makes him look effortlessly put together. He gives each of us a quick greeting before shrugging off his jacket and dropping onto the couch like he owns the space.

Liam is helping Yoona with the drinks when the bell rings a second time. Offering, I get up and answer the door, leaving Zahra and Matthew alone on the couch. Hiding my body behind the door, I open it and smile when I see Jax standing there. Similar to Matthew, he's wearing all black, but has skipped his cap today, his dark, black hair styled neatly.

"Why are you hiding?" he chuckles with a smile.

"Because I look ridiculous. Promise not to laugh too hard," I plead.

Jax promises and I step out, letting him see my outfit. He stands, silently looking down at me and when he doesn't say anything, I ask, "What do you think?"

His voice low and rough, Jax responds. "Ridiculous?" He shakes his head slowly. "Not even close."

"Really?"

He pulls me into a quick hug before guiding me inside, then greets the others. Yoona and Liam are handing out drinks while Zahra and Matthew scroll through movie options. Jax and I take the couch, his hand finding my thigh. Heat spreads through me, and I fight to keep it down. Once we pick a scary movie, Yoona sets up the TV and we all settle in.

I grab one of the blankets and wrap it around myself until Jax gives it a slight tug. Understanding, I take the blanket and place it over the both of us. His hand finds mine under the blanket, intertwining his fingers with mine.

Later in the movie, I notice Yoona's head is leaning on Liam's shoulder and Zahra is curled up tight against Matthew, shielding her eyes from the current scene. Smiling, I give Jax's hand a small squeeze, which he returns.

***

When the movie finishes, Yoona suggests watching another movie, but Matthew interjects.

"Hold up! I just got a text from a friend. Halloween party at his place. Are we down?"

Zahra looks over at Yoona, who looks at me. The first one to answer is Liam.

"Yeah, but I'm going home to change first. Can't party in this," he says and Matthew laughs at him.

"Are you embarrassed bro?"

Liam runs a hand through his hair and denies Matthew's allegations.

"Addie," Zahra calls over to me, "do you want to go?"

"Um," I begin, but Yoona cuts me off.

"We're already dressed up. Might as well," she reasons.

Turning to Jax, I ask for his thoughts.

"I don't really mind either way," he responds.

"Cool, I'll let my friend know we'll swing by for a bit," Matthew announces.

Not having driven to Yoona's house myself, I get into Jax's car, Zahra in Matthew's and Yoona in Liam's. We make a quick stop at Liam's place where he changes into an all black outfit, matching Matthew and Jax. When he's back in his car, Matthew takes off first, Liam and Jax following behind.

Sitting in the passenger seat, I glance over and admire Jax. He's driving smoothly, body relaxed in his seat and eyes focused on the road. Music is softly playing on his radio and his fingers drum absentmindedly on the steering wheel. I put my left hand on his right thigh and his vivid green eyes quickly flicker over to me before returning to the road.

Coming to a red-light moments later, Jax brings my hand to his lips and kisses it.

"You look gorgeous," he tells me and I thank him, feeling my cheeks warm. "Sexy actually." He leans in, brushing a soft kiss against my lips before the light changes.

By the time we pull up, the music is already spilling into the night. Inside, the air is thick with sweat but free of weed and booze, which makes me breathe easier. No surprise cops tonight.

Matthew leads us over to his friend Andrew, who gives us the lay of the land before we hit the dance floor. We find a spot together, and when the next song drops, Jax grabs my hand, pulling me against him. At first I stumble, but soon I'm moving with him, his hands tight on my hips, guiding me. To my left, Zahra and Matthew are just as close, while Yoona and Liam have found their own partners.

The beat slows into *reggaeton*, and the dance between Jax and me turns hot, my hips circling, his body glued to mine. Even when the track ends, we stay wrapped in each other, unwilling to break the spell. Then Jax's head lifts, his gaze hardening at something behind me. Before I can turn, a rough hand shoves my shoulder. I spin and freeze, fury flooding me when I see who it is.

"You're ignoring my messages for *her*?" Megan shoves through the crowd, voice slicing the music in half.

I feel Zahra, Yoona, Liam, and Matthew close ranks beside me as the party stills, the music thumping against a sudden hush. Dancers pull back, creating space. Jax drags a hand down his face, pinching his nose before opening his eyes, now cold, sharp, and furious, a look I'm grateful has never been turned on me.

"What?" he snaps, irritation unmistakable.

Megan takes a threatening step forward. "Of all people," she glares, "I thought you were better than that, Jax."

Matthew steps between Megan and Jax, Liam tugging at Jax to pull him back. Around us, the party has quieted, eyes turning our way. The corner of Jax's lips curls into a snarl, fury flashing in his gaze like I've never seen before.

Sliding her eyes to me, Megan gives me a menacing smile. "Oh look, you've done us the favor of covering your face. You didn't need to though; it would have made a good Halloween mask."

My eyes narrow at her and I do my best to steady my breathing. I ignore her and turn away, Zahra and Yoona turning with me.

"That fucking bitch," I hear Zahra say under her breath.

It seems like Megan heard because she yells. "What did you call me?"

When Megan slaps my shoulder, I snap. Hitting me is different. My dad made sure I learned how to defend myself, "so nobody messes with you," he used to say. I don't waste the lesson.

I lean into her hand, pivot my foot, and snap a hard jab. It lands with a crunch; she stumbles and collapses into a friend, nose bleeding. The music dies. Everyone's frozen. I step closer, watching her hold her face as the room goes completely quiet.

"Don't. Ever. Touch. Me. Again," My voice shakes, but the words hold.

Pissed, I roll my shoulders and head for the front door. Voices begin speaking at once, but, in my current state of fury, I couldn't care less. Walking out into the night, I hear my friends running after me.

Jax approaches me, but I hold my hand out to stop him. "I'm not angry with you, I just need a moment," I warn. Nodding, he walks over to Liam and Matthew, who stand a few feet away from us.

"I don't know what the hell got into her." Zahra's tongue lashes out in anger. She turns to Jax and points a finger at him. "You. What the hell was that about?"

"Calm down," Matthew urges her.

"No," Zahra snaps. "What the fuck just happened?" Zahra's hand comes down as she shoves Jax, and I flinch. He doesn't move, doesn't speak, but his jaw tightens, eyes narrowing, icy and unyielding. The surge of adrenaline goes straight to my head, the music inside fading to a distant hum.

I step forward, planting my feet, aware of my friends' eyes on me. "Zahra, it's done," I snap, not unkindly, but firm. Zahra's arms cross, jaw tight, daring me to falter. My blood pounds in my ears, but I force myself to inhale, steadying the quiver in my hands. The tension in the air is sharp, biting, but I refuse to let it sway me.

I motion at Jax, then toward his car, each step measured, deliberate. Zahra's glare burns against my back, ever my protector, but I don't turn. Jax's gaze follows me, unflinching, unreadable. Sliding into the passenger seat, I let the weight of the moment settle between us. No words are needed. The crowd, the chaos, the anger. It all recedes.

Outside, Yoona climbs into Liam's car while Zahra heads for Matthew's. Luckily, I grabbed my phone and keys, leaving just a small bag of clothes and toiletries at Yoona's. "Take me home," I say, and he drives without a word. I use the ride to sort through my thoughts. When he parks, I turn to him. "Mami's not home. Come on," I say, letting him know I mean it.

We go directly to the back yard where I sit on one of the rocking chairs, facing the lawn and the cluster of trees beyond that. Jax remains standing.

"I'm not seeing her, Addie." Every word seems to cost him, his jaw clenching as he holds back the anger still simmering beneath the surface. I watch him, steady, letting him settle before I push.

I ask about the last time he saw her, and he hesitates, fingers twitching against his thighs. "A few days before the pier", he says, eyes dropping for a beat. He hasn't seen her since. A knot forms in my throat, but I keep my voice level.

Sex. He admits it, quick and almost ashamed. But there's nothing behind it, no strings, he insists, just a mistake fading into nothing. His shoulders are tense, his hands restless, and I catch the flicker of guilt flashing in his eyes.

I think of her texts, the ones he ignored. He shrugs, almost too casually, and mutters a quiet apology. My mind races, sorting through hurt and relief. He hasn't lied. He hasn't tried to hurt me. Not really.

I let out a slow breath, the weight of everything pressing against my ribs easing a fraction. My heart still stutters, but the anger fades. If what he says is true, it isn't on him. I don't like the situation, but it is what it is. And somehow, that feels enough.

We're silent, staring out into the dark night, all of the words that needed to be said tonight already said. When his voice pierces the night, it's light, humorous, needed. "That swing was... solid," Jax said, half-smile breaking through.

A tiny laugh slips out of me. "I've never had to hit anyone before. That was the first time I hit someone and actually meant it. All of the other times were during training."

"Well, it sure paid off," he acknowledges.

"I just don't like people touching me. That's a hard limit. You can say all the mean things you want, just don't ever touch me."

"Heard you loud and clear," he says somberly.

Letting out a sigh, I stand up and stretch. I have no clue what time it is, but my eyes are on fire, so it's definitely late.

"You can crash here," I say to him with a tired smile.

"Where's your Mom?" he asks.

I shrug. "Now that I'm older, she's always gone for work or book tours. Didn't used to be like this, but now... I kinda like having the house to myself." Opening the backyard door, I pause, turning back to Jax. "And no, I don't sneak people in often."

Jax laughs at that. "Often? Have you done this before?"

My face grows serious, honest. "Never."

Feigning shock, Jax brings his hands toward himself. "Does that mean I'm your first?"

"Shut up," I mumble and open the door.

I lead Jax inside and show him to my room, too drained to talk. I let him shower first, handing him a spare towel. He comes back shirtless, hair dripping, and I toss him some shorts left by my cousin a while back. I fold his clothes by the laundry basket and take my own shower. Later, I drag myself back to my room to find him on the small guest couch, phone in hand.

"Come on," I call over sleepily. Jax gives me his phone to charge and then watches me prepare the bed.

"I can sleep on the couch, Addie. I don't have to sleep with you."

I glare at him. It's painfully obvious that the couch is too small for him. "I'm not going to the closet downstairs for extra blankets Jax." I glance over at the clock. "It's three in the damn morning. We're going to sleep."

I don't wait to hear his response. I turn off the light and crawl under the covers. The left side of the bed dips as he settles in beside me, his warmth pressing against my back. I turn slightly toward him, letting him wrap an arm around me, and for the first time all day, I let myself relax.

My body is exhausted, but my self-respect soars, proud of standing up for myself, and even more so knowing he was ready to stand up for me too. Whatever this is between us, it feels real, not just a fling. All I can do now is close my eyes, letting that thought settle over me like a calm, steady weight.

CHAPTER TWENTY

Jackson

In the following weeks, things chill between all of us. The "fight" spread like wildfire at first, but quickly died down, everyone shifting their focus to the fast-approaching college application deadline. I officially cut Megan off the morning after the party. Not because she deserved any courtesy, but because Addie thought it was the right thing to do. Megan wasn't thrilled. Every hallway glance from her feels like a blade, her whispers trailing behind like smoke. So much for "no strings."

While Addie and the others compared college applications, I flipped through my soccer plays, reminding myself I probably didn't belong in their plans. Senior year was finally starting to hit hard. Classes got serious, and Addie didn't let anything distract me in chemistry. Half the math now made my head spin, and I knew falling behind again wasn't an option.

On the day college applications are due, we are all having lunch together except for Liam, who enters the lunchroom toward the end of the period. Liam drops into the seat, shoulders slumped, his food untouched. Even his usual jokes are gone.

I catch Yoona peeking up at him through her glasses and she opens her mouth as though to speak, but no words come out. Thinking better of it, she closes her mouth and goes back to looking over her application. The bell rings and Liam is the first to get up, grabbing his school things with him. Zahra tries to ask him what's the matter, but he ignores her and storms out of the cafeteria.

"Can you check up on Liam?" Addie asks when the others are earshot away.

"Yeah, sure. I'll go see what's up when I catch up to him." Sighing, she gives me a rushed hug, avoiding getting to class late.

Walking to our usual corner in the library, I spot Liam sitting in a chair with his head down, only recognizing him by his red hair.

Patting Liam's shoulder before taking a seat, I ask, "What's up?" in a hushed tone. He lifts his head to look at me and then shifts his weight so that he's leaning back in his chair.

"Sorry, I'm just not in a good mood," he tells me, a hand running through his hair.

"Yeah, I get that," I try to empathize with him.

"It sucks not being able to get the math grade I need. I'm gunning for a soccer scholarship, and if I don't get the credit, that's basically it. My advisor says to wait for the second round, but that's not until March. And by April, acceptance letters are already out. If the state team fills up, I'm screwed."

He flings his hands up, his head hanging low like the walls could swallow him whole. His midterm sits in his lap, the grade staring back at him. He taps it with a finger, lets out a long, heavy sigh, and stares at the floor, as if the numbers alone could decide his fate.

His backpack lies open, books scattered, but he barely notices. Following my eyes, Liam explains "I've got dyscalculia. Numbers don't click the way they should. Forty-five is as far as I go."

Understanding, I show him my exam, the sixty-five glaring up at me. "Passed. Just barely," I mutter, and we both snort, trying not to draw attention. He leans back, shaking his head, and I catch a glimpse of relief in his expression, like he's not alone in barely scraping by. We start comparing notes, pointing out the same questions we messed up, laughing at the ridiculous mistakes we both made.

For a moment, the stress of grades, scholarships, and future plans fades, replaced by something simple. Shared struggle, a quiet understanding. I realize we're actually enjoying this, and that maybe, just maybe, surviving senior year is a little less lonely with someone who gets it.

***

The cold air hits us as we cross the lot, but the smell of roasted coffee in the café chases it away. We drove here quickly and as we walk in, Liam offers to buy the first round of drinks. It's his way of apologizing for his foul mood earlier. Soon, we're sitting together at a round table, warm drinks in hand.

Looking up from her cup, Zahra waits until an appropriate time to get everyone's attention. "So," Zahra begins, a grin spreading across her face, "we all know a certain someone is turning eighteen soon."

Addie freezes mid-drink, her cheeks flushing instantly. Zahra raises her hands like she's unveiling a masterpiece. "Since I'm part of the student committee this year, I got the inside scoop early... The school's senior trip is happening right after the holiday break. And guess what? We're heading to Barcelona!"

Addie's jaw drops. "As in *Spain*?"

"Yup," Zahra says, nodding enthusiastically. "The main thing is all the cultural tours and architecture, but there's more. Think mini-challenges, scavenger hunts, and a few surprise awards for the seniors. Superlative-style stuff. It's going to be epic, and since I know your birthday falls on one of the days, we can make sure it's extra special for you."

I glance at Addie and see the excitement in her eyes, the kind that makes her smile light up the room. Meanwhile, dread grows in my stomach. I swallow hard and try to imagine it: sunny streets of Barcelona, museums, dinners, sight seeing... none of it feels like freedom. It feels like a cage. No pills to quiet the unwanted thoughts in my brain, no shortcuts to numb the constant edge in my veins. I can already feel the itch, the jitter in my hands and legs, the restlessness I can't soothe.

How am I supposed to last that long? How do I keep myself together when every instinct I have is screaming for the escape I won't have? I force a smile, nod along with their excitement, but inside I'm calculating, planning, and already questioning if I can survive a week without falling apart.

Yoona jumps up, clapping her hands. "No way! I'm so in!"

Matthew grins, practically bouncing in his seat. "Same! This is going to be insane."

Liam, on the other hand, furrows his brow, muttering under his breath. "All that sounds amazing… but flights, hotels, food… how much is this going to cost?"

Zahra leans back, smiling as if she's proud of herself. "The student committee worked hard and raised enough money to cover most of the senior dues this year. Families would normally have to chip in for the rest, but my parents insisted on covering everything for us. Flights, hotels, meal vouchers, the whole deal. They wanted this to be a gift for all of us ever since I mentioned it to them."

She hesitates for a beat, looking at Jax, then shakes her head with a small grin. "Okay… I'll admit, I wasn't sure about including *everyone*, but Addie's happiness comes first."

It's not harsh, just quiet protectiveness, the kind that makes it clear she's watching out for Addie. Even someone like me, who doesn't like favors, can't argue with that.

Counting with his fingers, Matthew calls out, "We only have a handful of weeks until we leave. We'll have played four games by then and there will be a game when we return." Turning to look at me and Liam, he adds, "We'll have to work hard before we leave and practice while we're in Barcelona."

Seeing the sense in that, I nod my head in agreement, alongside Liam. "Sounds good to me." I force a smile, but my nerves threaten to bubble to the surface. Barcelona isn't freedom. I tuck my hands into my pockets and stare at the floor, counting the days, already trying to figure out how to last.

***

As promised, Matthew works the team hard during practice the next few weeks, analyzing every play and doing his best to perfect any mistakes. The team calls us the Triple Threat, and we chest-bump every time the net shakes with our goals. By the end of the last game before break, we have won all our games of the season so far, putting us in an impeccable position to land in the playoffs should we continue our winning streak.

There's still a week left before the trip, and I've made a decision that has me completely on edge. We'll be flying to the hotel, which means no pills, no easy escape. The thought of going a week without them has me feeling sick, makes my hands itch and twitch even now. I can't risk extreme withdrawals while everyone else is celebrating and exploring, so I'm forcing myself to do the unimaginable this weekend.

Get sober.

Addie has agreed to help me, telling her mom she's spending the weekend at Zahra's house. Part of me wants to laugh at how small that sounds compared to the storm raging inside me. I'm tired of hiding it. Tired of the shaking hands I clutch beneath the table, the jittering leg I keep still while she's watching, the secret glances she shoots me when she thinks I'm not looking, as if trying to gauge how high I am that day.

Thinking about our group, I realize everyone has their own battles. Addie fights her reflection, her scars, the whispers she hides behind smiles. Liam wrestles with numbers that refuse to make sense, proving he's more than his dyscalculia. None of them reach for pills to cope, and yet here I am, addicted, craving, terrified. Maybe it's time I stop hiding and start fighting my own demons. If I can survive the weekend, maybe I can survive the trip.

Addie arrives at my place in the evening, an overnight bag hanging from her left shoulder. She sets her bag down and puts her coat and scarf in the closet. Cold rides in with her, clinging to her hoodie and the red tip of her nose.

"Ready?" she asks, even though none of us have a single clue what we're doing, all knowledge learned from the internet.

"No. But I'm as ready as a guy about to jump into ice water."

Her expression tightens as she takes in my trembling hands, worry flickering in her eyes. I can barely meet her gaze, my shame twisting. Without a word, she motions for us to move quickly, and we head upstairs. I grab the plastic bag of pills from my room, untouched for the last tempting twenty four hours, and hand it to her. Back in the kitchen, she fills a glass with water and dumps the pills in, letting them dissolve.

I gulp nervously, the familiar panic crawling up my spine. She nods toward the phone, instructing me to pull up Jay's number. My fingers hesitate, then she takes the phone and deletes his contact, erasing every trace of our messages. My irrational fear sharpens as I realize there's no going back, no other way to reach him. We stand side by side, waiting, the tension between us thick, the silence stretching, each second amplifying the dread and anticipation.

My hands have been shaking for half an hour, my forehead is clammy, and a cold sweat is creeping down my neck. She notices and sets a fresh glass of water on the table, her presence calm but alert.

We sink into the couch, her fingers flipping through channels until a baking show fills the silence. Three episodes in, food arrives, but nausea hits me before I can touch it. She orders chicken broth, hoping it'll be gentler, but the smell hits like a punch. My stomach revolts. I slam the bowl down and stumble to the bathroom, kneeling in front of the toilet.

I heave, retching up breakfast and lunch, my hands trembling against the porcelain. Addie stays at the door, worry etched across her face, pressing a glass of water into my hand. I wave it away, closing my eyes, letting the room spin as the withdrawal tightens its grip.

"This fucking sucks."

"Yeah," Addie agrees, "but you'll get through it."

Acid burns my throat and nose. I flush the toilet and stay there, afraid to move. I can feel Addie's hand come down and rub my back. Her hand is kind, but my nerves are raw wire. I flinch and she steps back.

I slump against the wall, finally taking the water in slow sips. Exhaustion crashes over me. Addie helps me to the couch, where my damp, sweat-soaked clothes cling to me. She drapes a blanket over my shivering body, sets a bucket nearby, and brings fresh water, sitting at the far end.

Time blurs. I lean over the bucket, heaving until nothing comes up, then curl under the blanket, shivering. Addie wipes my forehead, but even her touch makes me flinch and growl. I drift in and out of a restless, broken sleep, not opening my eyes until sunlight cuts through the windows.

"Addie, close the shades," I croak.

Not getting a response, I lift my head slightly and see that she's curled up, asleep at the edge of the couch. Feeling bad about the way I've treated her, I try to get up to close the shades myself. The room tips, the floor slides left, and the couch catches me. The aches in my body are screaming. Addie's eyes shoot open and she looks my way, her gaze bleary.

"What's wrong?" she asks sleepily.

"Just trying to close the shades," I respond. My voice cracks as I speak.

Addie slowly brings herself to stand. She dims the room one blind at a time. "Better?" I nod. We both exhale.

"Hungry?" she asks.

"No," I breathe out. "I fucking wish though."

"You're keeping the water down now. That matters. I think this may be the worst of it."

Without warning, a sudden pain radiates through me, tears spilling before I can stop them.

Addie rushes over, alarm in her voice, but I can't speak. I let the sobs shake me, disgust, fear, anger, guilt, shame, grief, all crashing at once. I let it out, raw and uncontrolled.

"I have to tell you something," I manage, voice shaking.

She sits close, patient, giving me space. I begin with the first heartbreaks that shaped me. When I was twelve, my mother became pregnant after so many miscarriages. I was thrilled at the thought of being a big brother. My dad spent hours building the crib by hand, teaching me carpentry in the garage so I could help.

My baby brother Alexander was born on the first day of summer. He was beautiful, and I vowed to make him proud. But weeks after his birth, my mother changed. She withdrew, refusing to care for him, crying in the bathroom, snapping at the smallest things. I tried to help, feeding and changing Alexander whenever I could.

One day, after he cried for hours nonstop, my dad rushed him to the emergency room. My mother refused to go, claiming she was too tired. Alexander never came home. He suffered a severe seizure, was placed on life support, and then declared brain dead. My dad and I grieved; my mother seemed almost at peace, untouched by the tragedy.

Her detachment persisted. I'd catch her talking to herself, pacing the house in the dark. She eventually refused to work, spending years in bed, leaving my dad and me to care for her the best we could. I didn't understand it then, but even as a teenager, I realized something was deeply wrong.

Then, on what would have been Alexander's birthday, I came home from practice. The house was empty and dark. And there she was. My mother, hanging, dead. I panicked, cut her down, held her for what felt like hours before calling the police. My dad arrived shortly after, collapsed on the front steps, head between his knees, crying. He shut me out in his grief, and I shut myself away, burying everything instead of facing it.

The nightmares started soon after. I'd see her body hanging, her face swollen and purple, or decomposed in a coffin. I couldn't bear it, couldn't face it sober, so I turned to pills. That's how it all began.

Addie doesn't speak; she just sits, hand resting on my knee, silent and steady. No judgment, just care. When I finish, I exhale long and shaky, a little of the weight lifted. She wipes her own tears, and I nod, grateful for her presence. I rise to wash my face, body sore, emotions raw, but at least I've finally let it out.

"I... I can't imagine how hard that was," she whispers, her voice soft. After a pause, she adds, "I know that the pills have helped you not feel all of that, but... the next step matters too. You'll probably need some help to actually stay clean."

I glance at her, hesitant.

"A therapist, Jax," she says gently, meeting my eyes. "Not to erase it, but to help you feel. To live without the pills."

"I don't know," I hesitate. "I'm not really into therapy or talking about my emotions."

"And that's the problem. You have to talk about it, Jax. Pushing it away? Look what good that's done. I know it's hard, but if you want to get through this, you're going to have to be prepared to get comfortable with the uncomfortable."

Reaching over to hold my hand, she continues, "Look, this isn't gonna be easy. You can't just rely on me cheering you on. Staying clean has to come from you, from your own choice. You're strong, Jax, and getting help doesn't make you weak. It actually makes you stronger."

Get more pills when you come back, that familiar voice hisses.

Then, a new voice creeps in. A stronger voice.

Let the light in.

Blinking a few times, I clear my thoughts. I give Addie's hand a squeeze.

"You're right." I let her words sink deep. "I won't lie and say that staying clean will be a success, but I'll try."

Getting help won't be easy, and the road feels long, but for the first time in a while, I don't feel entirely alone.

CHAPTER TWENTY-ONE
Adelina

Getting Jax through the weekend proves to be more emotionally draining, but after hearing his story, I'm beginning to feel as though I finally understand him better. I see how tightly he holds his jaw when silence falls, how his hands curl as if gripping something invisible. His wounds aren't gone. Just waiting.

Sitting on the couch, reading a new book, I'm waiting for Mami to finish a phone conference she's been in since this morning. When she comes into the living room, she takes a seat next to me, removing her glasses. Mami's hand comes down on my lap and she gives me a few light taps before settling her hand there.

"Everything okay?" I ask her.

"*Sí*, just took a bit longer than expected." She sighs.

"Mami, I need help with something."

"What is it?"

I take a deep breath before beginning. "I have a friend who could use some therapy. He's never tried therapy and he's nervous about opening up. Is there anyone in the office who can take him?" Pausing, I add, "Maybe a guy?"

Mami thinks for a second, her eyebrows bunching up the way they do when she's in problem solving mode. "I can check in a bit. Do you know what your friend is struggling with?" Mami asks.

Not wanting to give too much away, I keep the story simple and say, "He's been through a lot… lost some people close to him, and it messed him up. He's been trying to get better, though. It's just, no one ever really helped him deal with it."

"Let me speak to Samuel. He'll have more experience with that. I'll let you know if he's open."

The words barely leave her mouth before Mami squints at me. "Who is this friend, Adelina?"

"Um," I hesitate, "a friend from school. We have a few classes together."

Her eyes narrow even more. "You're not getting yourself into trouble, are you?"

"Mami," I sigh, turning to face her fully. "No. I'm just trying to help him. That's all." Then, I reach for her hands, but still maintain eye contact. "*Te lo prometo.*" The words steady me as much as they steady her.

A few seconds pass before Mami gives a small nod, trusting my word like she always does. She might be busy and gone more often these days, but she's always there when it counts. I hear her head upstairs to call Samuel, and about an hour later she comes back down, a post-it note in hand. "He'll take someone new," she says simply. I thank her, tucking the note between the pages of my book, quietly grateful that even when she's wrapped up in work, she never lets me down when I need her.

***

The day before Christmas Eve, I pull into Jax's driveway and spot him outside with a man who can only bc his father. They share the same sharp jaw and stormy eyes, though Jax's hold less life. They stand stiff, words low but heavy, tension hanging between them like fog. Jax's shoulders are rigid, his father's arms crossed tight.

I honk once, unsure, and both their heads snap toward me. Jax's expression flattens before his father mutters something and turns away. I wave awkwardly, pretending to dig through my bag until Jax finally starts walking over, the weight of whatever just happened still clinging to him.

"Hey," I greet Jax, stepping out of my car and giving him a hug.

He hugs me back before we both rush inside, trying to escape the cold. We shake the snow from our boots and leave them on a mat by the front door to dry.

"Was that your Dad?" I ask, taking off my sweater.

"Yeah, I ran into him on my way back from the store. He just dropped it out of nowhere... dinner on Christmas. Like last year never happened."

"That's a bad thing?" I ask, watching him from the edge of his bed as he folds a stack of clean clothes. His hands move slower than usual, but steadier, no more tremors like before. The dark circles under his eyes are still there, shadows of the last few days, and he doesn't stand as tall, shoulders slumped with exhaustion.

Still, there's something quieter about him now, something more real. Maybe this is who hc actually is beneath the haze. I don't know yet, but I want to. I want to see him keep healing.

"Not bad, just weird. He didn't care about spending Christmas with me last year, the first Christmas without my mom, so I wonder why he wants to spend it with me this year."

Thinking about it, I say, "Maybe he misses you? If neither of you speak to one another, you're just left assuming things. You assume he's ignoring you and maybe he assumes you don't want to speak to him." Working with the bits and pieces of information I have about Jax and his family so far, this is the best guess I can make.

Jax stops folding and sucks his teeth. "Why?" he whines.

So, I'm correct. "Why what?" I dare shoot back.

"Why do you do that?" he accuses. "Always with an answer." I blink, stung, then try to smile it off.

"That's not true," I defend myself. "I'm just looking at it as an outsider. Just because I like you doesn't mean I'm going to ignore reason. You never know what might come out of that dinner," I shrug.

Jax gives me a look before folding another piece of clothing and mumbles, "Yeah, yeah, yeah. You don't know him like I do."

Abruptly remembering, I bolt up and run out of the room. Returning out of breath a minute later, I ignore the look of surprise written on his face and hand over the post-it note. He reads it.

"You just have to call and set up an appointment. Samuel will probably have an opening when we get back from break. What do you think?"

Jax is looking down at the post-it note in silence.

"You don't have to if you don't want to," I add quickly. "The choice is yours."

He nods and puts the small paper down on his bedside table. "I'll call later today. You think they'll be open?"

"As long as you call before five."

"Sounds good then." Changing the subject, he asks, "What are your plans for Christmas?"

"Well, my family usually celebrates it on the 24th and we open presents after midnight. There's always a lot of music and dancing, so we sleep in and rest on Christmas Day. This year, Mami and I will be going to my uncle's house on the other side of town. Most of my cousins will be driving up from the city."

"Sounds like a good time," Jax comments.

"Actually," I begin, a crazy idea occurring to me, "would you like to spend it with us?"

"Christmas Eve?"

"Yes, then you can spend Christmas Day with your Dad."

"I'll be meeting your family then," Jax points out.

A rush of panic hits me, and suddenly my palms feel slick. "Yeah... would that be bad?" The words tumble out before I can stop them. Oh my God. Did I really just say that? My brain is screaming at me to shut up, to rewind, to take it back. This is way too fast. If he rejects me, I'm pretty sure I'll just melt straight into the floor and disappear. What is *wrong* with me?

Smiling, he shakes his head. "No, just a bit unexpected is all." He says it like it's nothing, but my panic still lingers. This is Jax stepping into my world. "Should I dress in anything special?"

Relief washes over me in waves. Doing my best to hide my mortification, I say "You should look nice, yeah." Then I suggest "Maybe nice pants and a button down?"

He walks over to his closet and takes out a long sleeve shirt and tries it on. Perfectly fitted, the shirt makes Jax look sculpted and the dark color brings out the green of his eyes. I nod my approval and he switches back to his other shirt, placing it back on a hanger in the closet.

"I think I have a shirt that's similar," I point out.

"Are you trying to match my outfit?" he jokes.

"Would that be weird? Because if it's weird, then we don't have to. Actually, we—"

Jax cuts me off. "It's a cute idea."

Cheeks turning red, I hide behind my hands and say, "I'll let you know what time to come over."

***

The kitchen aromas drift through the house, filling me with Christmas spirit. Sofrito and adobo thick in the air as Mami massages the *pernil* with her special mix. The sound of the mortar and pestle later fills the room, each *clack* of the *pilón* rhythmic and familiar.

I'm standing beside her at the counter, dicing onions and peeling carrots for the marinade, my fingers sticky from the work. Mami sings a soft tune under her breath, then glances at me.

"So, this is the boy you asked about last night? Jax, right?" she says casually, though there's a knowing gleam in her eye.

I nod, trying not to smile too much. She already said yes to him spending the holiday with us, but I can tell she wants to hear more about him.

"Is he a boyfriend?" she probes, scooping the paste out of the *pilón*.

I avoid her eyes and grab the next carrot. "Not exactly."

"Not exactly? *¿Entonces qué?* Oh, pass me the tomato paste."

"He's not my boyfriend, Mami. Just a friend." I lean over and pass her the can.

Mami makes a noise and then turns to look at me. "*Oye*," she wags the knife she's using in the air, "all I ask is that you're careful. You're already a young lady about to turn eighteen. I can't stop what you decide to do *pero sí te puedo avisar.*" Her knife thuds against the board as she lectures. I want to shrink into the tiles. "If you plan on having sex, I urge you to be careful and use protection. Babies are blessings, but transmitting an illness? *Eso no.*"

"Mami, please, no. This is so awkward! I don't want to talk about this. I'm done. Nope. Not doing this," I moan.

Picking up a red bell pepper, Mami resumes cutting.

"I want you to be careful. You're a smart girl, Adelina, but mistakes happen. Just know you can come to me if you need me. There's nothing to be embarrassed about. What do you want me to expect from you at your age? You're going to go off and live your own life soon enough anyways, but I will make sure, to the best of my abilities, that you're prepared before you leave this house."

"Thanks," I say sheepishly, suddenly red-faced and shy. I help peel the last of the vegetables before she waves me off. My heart kicks up. Time to get ready.

Several hours later, steam fogs the mirror as I shower and scrub until my skin tingles. Back in my room, I wrap myself in my robe and sit at my desk, trying to do my makeup the way Zahra would. After a few failed attempts, I cave and call her. She talks me through each step until the reflection staring back looks almost confident. Soft shimmer on my eyelids, a sharp wing, bronzed cheeks, and lips shaded a warm brown nude. My scar is still there, but the lipstick makes me feel...pretty. Real. Chosen.

I curl and temporarily pin up my hair, slipping on the outfit I picked last night. White jeans, red off-the-shoulder top, and heels that make me stand taller than I feel. Still, when I catch my reflection, a tiny voice in my head wonders what Jax will think. Does this look like too much? Too little?

My phone buzzes: On my way.

I knock on Mami's door and find her mid–wardrobe meltdown, clothes everywhere. She barely looks up when I tell her Jax is coming. "*Bueno*, let me fix this hair before your friend gets here," she mutters.

The doorbell rings before she even decides on earrings. I pull the pins from my hair, shaking out the long curls. My emotions twist with nerves and excitement, all tangled up, and then I head for the door.

"Coming!" I yell. I put the pins in my pocket, doing a quick hair check before opening the front door.

"Hello beautiful." Jax's solid arms wrap securely around me.

"Hi," I breathe out, happy to see him. Closing the door behind him, we walk over to the living room and sit down. "Would you like some water?" I ask.

"I would like whatever it is that's cooking. It smells delicious." Jax sniffs the air.

"Not yet. You'll have to wait until dinner." He gives me a sad look and I almost feel sorry for him. "Oh, by the way," I whisper, "pretend like you've never been here before when Mami comes in."

Jax nods. "Sounds good."

I sit down and he leans in close to me. "You smell really nice," he whispers in my ear. The hairs on my arms stand and I finish closing the distance between us.

"You smell good yourself," I whisper to him. "I always like how you smell."

He leans in closer, faces barely inches apart. Heat rises in me, but so does panic. "Not here," I hiss, the stairs creaking above.

"Sometimes I can't help it." His hand tilts my chin, pulling me into a kiss. Soft at first, it quickly turns urgent when I lower his grip, letting him close the distance. Desire courses between us, heat spreading from his hands to mine.

A sharp *click* of heels on the stairs jolts me upright. Jax freezes, sliding back onto the couch like nothing happened. My heart pounds as I scramble to pull myself together.

Mami appears in the doorway, radiant in a white dress and red heels, hair pulled into a tight bun. Gold earrings catch the light. I force a calm breath, trying not to show how close we were to being caught, my pulse thrashing wildly within.

"Mami, you look so pretty!"

"*Gracias*, Adelina," Mami says, smiling at me with that gentle, knowing look, like she sees everything. She turns to Jax. "And you must be Jax. Adelina told me a little about you earlier. *Un placer.*"

Jax glances my way, then stands and gives Mami a quick hug. "You look great. I see where Addie gets it from." Mami laughs, winking at me like she knows exactly what's going on. "Thanks for having me over," he adds, sliding back onto the couch. That easy, charming smile of his hits me again. I can't help but notice his lips, the same ones I was just pressed against.

Mami's voice pulls me out of my reverie.

"You're always welcome here. Now, *vámonos*. Let's get the food packed up. We're running a bit late!" Clapping her hands together, she begins to turn towards the kitchen.

"Mami," I point to her dress with concern, "you're wearing a white dress. Jax and I will do it. You go get the car ready."

She nods and walks over to the closet where she grabs her coat and car keys. Jax and I hurry through the kitchen, wrapping the food and securing it for the trip. He carries the bundles to Mami's car while I follow, watching her organize the backseat.

"Adelina, you know the way to Tito's?" she asks. I nod, and she directs me to ride with Jax so she can place the drinks up front. Once everything is set, I hug her goodbye and slide into Jax's car.

The drive will take over an hour, but he doesn't seem to mind. "An hour alone with you," he says with a grin as he pulls onto the street. My body warms as we talk, the conversation flowing easily while he keeps his eyes on the road, and I sneak glances at him, thinking about Tito's house and the feast waiting for us.

"Have you been feeling any better?" I probe when we're on the highway.

"Friday marks a week. My body's still dragging sometimes, but at least I don't crave it," he says, his eyes on the road. The way his hands rest easily on the wheel makes me wonder how often he hid his nerves. "My head, though... all over the place. Everything sets me off, I can't focus on shit, and some days I just feel dead inside. You'd think being clean would feel easy, but nope. This shit's brutal. I don't know how I would've done it without all of these days off from school."

The realization hits me mid-conversation. There's going to be alcohol at the party. I groan and smack my forehead, unable to hide the panic creeping up. Jax catches the shift in my expression, his eyes flicking toward me with a faint frown. He doesn't hesitate when I tell him what's wrong, patting my thigh lightly. He is calm and steady, even as he glances between me and the road. His presence alone is enough to slow my spiraling worry.

"Don't sweat it," he says. "I've got this. Someone's gotta be the designated driver anyway." I exhale, letting a small bit of relief wash over me, trusting him, but the flutter of guilt still lingers. "Now relax your forehead," he chuckles, "before you give yourself premature wrinkles."

Punching his arm softly, I ask "Were you able to call the office and speak to Samuel?"

"Yeah, he's got me booked for an intake the Monday we get back from break. Depending on that, he said he'd let me know how often he wants to see me. I'll let you know how it goes." His right hand comes back down on my thigh and he taps his fingers absently.

"I hope it helps, Jax." And I mean it from the bottom of my heart.

He squeezes my thigh then resumes tapping his fingers. "Yeah, same here. Just have to wait and see."

In the spur of the moment, I lean over and give him a kiss on the cheek. "I'm proud of you."

"Thanks," he tells me. "But how about you don't distract me with your kisses." He points to the road. "I'm still trying to follow your mom."

I laugh. "Yeah, sorry."

"You can kiss me later though. I won't say no to that." He glances slyly at me.

My face reddens. "Hm, I'll see what I can do."

His laugh spills into the car and he returns his eyes to the road.

***

We arrive at my uncle's house to find the driveway fully packed with cars. Mami drives down the block and Jax follows behind her until we're able to find parking spots.

Jax and I get out of the car and rush over to Mami's car, each of us helping to carry the food and drinks. Mami walks ahead to ring the doorbell and I see her sister open the door and embrace her in a hug.

"That's my aunt," I point out. "Just another fair warning. My family is a bit loud."

When we get to the front door, my aunt grabs a few trays from my hands and disappears inside. My cousin Patrick pops out a second later, taking the rest of what I'm holding, Jax's trays too. He balances them like a pro, and Jax steps up, introducing himself with an easy smile. I follow Patrick inside, trading quick hellos with my family elders before asking for their blessing and introducing Jax. My thoughts begin to race. I hope he doesn't mind all the attention.

"*Mamá, Papá, este es mi amigo, Jax,*" I say in Spanish. "I'm introducing you to my grandparents," I whisper to Jax who nods his head and waves to them.

Patrick saunters over and jokes, "*Amigo, no. ¡Más cómo novio!*" Heat slams my face. The room roars with laughter and I want the floor to open up.

"What's happening?" Jax whispers, but Patrick beats me to the response.

"Nothing, I just told them you're her boyfriend. We've all been waiting to see when Addie would bring someone!"

I give him a death stare.

"What? It's true!"

Jax laughs under his breath, and I sneak a pinch to his side. We move past Patrick, and I keep introducing him to my family, everyone playfully gossiping about my "*boyfriend*." At the back of the house, my cousins wave us over, and we join their huddle.

Spanish holiday music fills the air, and I dance a few songs with them, catching Jax grinning every time I glance his way. When the music pauses, my aunt calls everyone to the living room. She gives a quick thank-you in Spanish before my grandfather offers a blessing and prayer. Hands held, heads bowed, cheers erupt when it's over.

Hungry, I drag Jax to the kitchen line, groaning when I see a few relatives beat us there. We pile our plates with a bit of everything and return to sit with my cousins, the chatter softening as we dig in.

"Mph, this is really good!" Jax says with a mouthful of food. "What is *this*?" He points to his plate.

"That's called *Pastelón*. It's made with mashed sweet plantains, cheese and chicken."

"And this?" He points to his drink.

"This is *Morir Soñando* which translates to Die Dreaming. It sounds better in Spanish, trust me, but it's so good."

I glance around, making sure no one's watching, and Patrick leans over with a sly grin. "Here," he whispers, sliding me a small cup of something darker than I expected. I barely have time to thank him before I lift it to my lips.

The alcohol hits my throat like fire. "Oh, that's strong," I mutter, coughing as the burn slides down. When it finally fades, I offer to swap it for something weaker, hoping no one notices how red my face is from both the drink and my nerves.

Jax lifts his hand to stop me, laughing as he does. "Don't stress about me." He leans over, sniffs my cup, and winces just like I did. "I'll definitely stick to water tonight."

I grin, feeling at ease with him and my family around. I lift the cup again. "Well, can't let this go to waste," I laugh, taking another careful sip.

"You're enjoying that, huh?" he teases softly.

"Of course," I shrug, smiling at him. "When else am I going to get to drink something like this with my family?"

He shakes his head, a small laugh escaping. "Alright, don't let me ruin your fun."

CHAPTER TWENTY-TWO
Jackson

Addie's cousins have been cracking up for hours. We've finished eating and are sprawled in a circle, holiday drinks in hand. I stick to small sips of water, trying not to look lame while Addie's already on her third, her cheeks flushed and laugh louder than ever. She reaches for another cup, and I catch her hand. "Water now. Trust me," I warn, thinking about the ride later. Even half-drunk, she listens, smiling sheepishly as she obliges.

Patrick, the family's resident comedian, has everyone doubled over. Tears stream down their faces as he retells the time Marianna tried to run away after breaking Mom's favorite vase. I don't catch all the Spanish, but the English bits are pure gold. William, Marianna's older brother, jumps up clapping, unable to contain himself.

"Yo, I can't believe that really happened. She packed a bag and everything! When I asked her where she was going, she just kept saying, 'I'm leaving!'"

Marianna is hiding her face in shame. "I only did it because I didn't want to get in trouble!" she yells. "You all know how Mami gets. Next thing I know a *chancleta* is flying to my head."

This sends everyone into another fit and Patrick runs to the closet to get a sandal, lightly hitting Marianna with it.

"*Chancleta* means sandal?" I ask, half-laughing, half-scared.

"He doesn't know what a *chancleta* is?!" William shrieks. Shaking my head, Patrick waves the sandal in the air.

"Okay," starts William, "a *chancleta* is not only a sandal, but it is the holy grail of Caribbean weapons, a serious weapon used by our mothers. Whenever we do something we're not supposed to do, expect one of those to be thrown at you."

"And their aim is crazy good!" Patrick adds. "One time I dodged one and I don't know why I did. Mami just ran over and grabbed me by the ear instead."

"Oh my goodness," Addie snorts. "I remember that! I laughed and *Tía* got mad and hit *me* just for laughing."

"Our parents are crazy," Marianna tells me.

I laugh with the group, soaking in their stories and the easy chaos of their childhood. William grins, clearly proud of the messes and memories. Then, a sudden yell cuts through the room, and everyone's heads snap toward the living room. Patrick bursts past us, full of energy, sprinting off like the night's just begun. The clock hits midnight.

I'm beside Addie in the living room as we watch her family members open their gifts. Addie is given hers and she opens it. Her hands fly to her mouth when she sees the new laptop, eyes wide with disbelief. The perfect gift for a soon-to-be college student. She also receives small knick knacks from her cousins and several more gift boxes. A few contain clothes and one contains new books. Thanking everyone, she carefully places her gifts on the floor next to her.

Telling me that she'll be right back, Addie takes her mother's car keys and leaves the house. She returns with a present which she gives to me.

She holds out the box like it's a fragile secret. "Merry Christmas," she whispers.

I fumble with the little box in my hands, heart racing. Inside rests a simple silver chain with a small tag. I lift it out and notice the tiny engraving: the date she knows is my sobriety milestone. My throat tightens.

"It's... really nice," I finally manage, my voice thick. Warmth spreads through me. Not just for the gift, but for her. For Addie. It's always been her.

She bites her lip, a little nervous, her fingers brushing mine as she smiles. "I wanted it to mean something... for you."

I glance down at the tag again, then back at her. My heart lurches slightly, and I realize I don't need words. This is real. She's real.

We share a quick, quiet hug before sitting back down, the noise of the room fading around us. Somewhere deep inside me, something settles. I feel lucky, and maybe, just maybe, a little lighter than I have in a long time.

An hour after everyone finishes opening gifts, the room alive with laughter and chatter, I realize I haven't given Addie anything. My disappointment takes root. With everything I've been juggling, like staying sober, keeping my emotions in check, and just trying not to mess up, gift-giving has completely slipped my mind.

Addie, oblivious to my guilt, takes my hand and leads me over to her mother. "Mami, Jax has plans tomorrow and it's a long drive back. I'm also tired, so he's going to drop me off. Is that okay?"

Her mom smiles warmly. "*Sí, amor.* Just text me when you get there. Leave your gifts in my car before you leave." She stands and wraps me in a brief hug. "Be careful on the road. Thank you for coming. I hope we don't scare you off."

I chuckle, "No, anything but." I give her a genuine smile, keeping my voice steady. "Thank you for having me. Merry Christmas."

"*Feliz Navidad,*" she repeats warmly followed by "and behave!"

It doesn't take us long to put the presents in her mother's car and soon we're waving our goodbyes to the rest of the family. Addie stumbles into the passenger seat and closes the door. She cracks the window open.

"Don't you feel a bit hot?" she asks me. Her cheeks are rosy and she seems a bit flustered.

I laugh. "No. You're wearing a thick coat and you've been drinking. Try taking the coat off."

She does, throwing it in the backseat. "Okay, that feels better!"

I set the GPS to Addie's house and start driving towards the highway. "Tonight was fun," I hear her say.

"Yeah, your cousins are cool."

"I'm glad you think so. I wish I had more time with them, but we all live a bit too far. We used to spend our summers together when we were little. Now? Not so much."

"That happens. All part of growing up. People drift." I turn the wheel and get on the highway, carefully driving at the speed limit even though it's empty of cars.

"Do you think *we'll* drift?" she suddenly asks.

I'm not sure what I'm supposed to say. The question is so sudden that I suffer a momentary bout of word vomit. "What? You and me? I don't know. Why?"

"I just don't know what you see in me. Sometimes I feel like I'm waiting for a ticking time bomb to explode and bring me back to reality."

Taking a moment to glance her way, I think through what I should say next. "I see many beautiful things in you, otherwise I wouldn't be here."

"Yeah, but sooner or later you'll find someone prettier than me," she blurts out.

"Are you still drunk, Addie?"

"I don't know! No. Maybe. Okay, yes. I think so."

I sigh and grab hold of one of her hands. "Addie, relax. Why the hell would I do that to you?"

"Because I'm not pretty like other girls," she whispers.

"You are far more beautiful than any girl I've ever met. Your scars don't scare me. They just prove you survived."

"I just wish things could be different."

"I don't," I say, kissing her hand. "Why would I? You're beautiful, smart, funny, strong... all of it. And your scars? They've never changed how I see you."

It hits me as I say it. I really mean it.

Her scars were never what stood out. It's her heart, the way she gives without asking for anything back. She's done so much for me when she didn't have to. She could've walked away a hundred times, but instead she's been the current pushing me toward something better.

"You are beautiful," I repeat, needing her to believe it.

Addie goes quiet, leaning against the window, drifting in and out of sleep. By the time we reach her driveway, she's fully out, chest rising and falling slowly. I squeeze her thigh gently, once, twice, but she doesn't stir.

I grab her keys from her purse and fumble with the front door until it finally clicks open. Leaving it ajar, I return to the car, carry her inside up to her room, and set her on the bed. Her heels go beside it, and I leave her in her clothes, careful not to overstep. I start charging her phone when her soft, slurred voice calls my name.

"Yeah?" I say walking over to her.

She tugs me close, but I freeze, pulling back. "Not like this, not when you've been drinking." My heart pounds, and part of me wants to throw caution to the wind, but I can't. I've got to hold back, respect her, even when it's ridiculously hard. I bite the inside of my cheek, mentally groaning.

"Try and get some sleep. I'll check up on you in the morning."

Standing up, I bend over and kiss her forehead. Addie mumbles something as she turns the other way, eyes closing. Her breathing evens out and she falls into a deep sleep. I leave her house, closing the door behind me.

***

Waking up early, I feel the weight of not getting Addie a Christmas present. Sleep didn't stick, but wandering the mall is worth it when I find the perfect gift for her. For my dad, I pick something simple. A gold pocket watch. Maybe it can restart old time, or at least signal some kind of reset.

I drop Addie's gift into my already-packed suitcase. Her text messages tell me she's been poring over the school's travel itinerary for the senior trip, thinking about what to pack, joking that it's still going to be freezing over there. She has no memory of last night, which is fine. She seems happy, though a little headache slows her down. Her excitement about the trip makes me smile even if she can't see it.

A run at noon doesn't clear my mind as much as I hope. Dinner with my dad? My brows furrow. He's left me alone for years, even though we live under the same roof. Now he suddenly wants bonding, and I don't know if I trust it, let alone him. The easy option is to bail, like I've thought about a dozen times. But Addie's voice in my head stops me. Avoiding it won't help anyone.

Showered and dressed, I grab the watch and jog up to the door, trying to avoid the steady current of snow painting the town white. My dad opens it, looking put-together and sharper than I feel. He gives me a light hug, and I freeze for a second, unsure what this sudden warmth means, or if I even want it.

"Merry Christmas," I say awkwardly, tensely.

"Merry Christmas, son," he responds.

We head into the living room. The TV's on, a game just started, but it feels like everything else has paused. It's like a memory of a life where more of us used to be here, when things felt simpler, when Mom was still around.

"Sit, sit," he gestures, and I sink onto the love seat while he settles on the sectional. He passes me a small plate of chips and salsa with a soda, then cracks open a beer for himself.

I fidget with the gift in my hands, my silent anxiety twisting in the same fashion. "Pops," I say, holding it out. He turns, surprise flickering across his face. "Here."

He takes it gently, like it could break, and opens the small box. His green eyes soften behind his glasses. "I wasn't expecting this," he murmurs. "It's... really nice."

I look down at my hands, trying not to meet his gaze. "Yeah, I figured you'd like it."

He carefully cradles the watch and heads upstairs to put it in his room. I hear him mutter, "It may not be much..." and then return with a small velvet box. Sliding it open, I find a leather-bound notebook and a sleek black ink pen.

"Thank you," I say, more than just words.

"I remember how much you loved writing. Do you still?" he asks, cautiously, his shoulders tense, like he's measuring every word.

"Every now and then. Not like I used to," I admit, noticing the way he keeps his posture stiff, trying not to let the moment slip into awkwardness.

"Maybe this will help you get started," he says, hope threading his voice.

I nod, gently putting it on the table. "Don't let me forget it," I warn, trying to mask how tense I feel.

The game continues on the TV, but the room feels heavy, like we're both walking on eggshells. I notice the tight set of his jaw, the way his hands curl around the beer can. He's holding back, just like me, and in that shared hesitation, something flickers, fragile, but real.

When the game ends, I slip outside, thanking him for dinner and the gift. He reminds me to take it, and we exchange a hug, slightly warmer this time.

Before I can pull away, his hands rest on my shoulders. "I know this hasn't been easy," he says, eyes steady. "But we have to start somewhere, Jax."

I exhale, trying to mask the tension. "Easy's an understatement. What do you want me to say?" My tone is steel.

He steps back, palms up, surrendering. "Nothing I say will change the past. But I want a future... with you in it."

"I am in it," I reply, but my mind races. Only in theory. Only if I let him in. The anger surges, the years of neglect, the things he didn't do for me, for Mom. But what good is holding it all hostage now?

Finally, I ask, "What would that look like?"

He purses his lips, but there's a glint in his eye. "Dinner on game nights?"

I think it through. "Not all of them. Let's try Sundays."

He starts to respond, but I cut him off, not rudely, but enough to end the conversation, heading to the garage with my gift. Inside, I shift my focus to the senior trip, checking Addie's gift in my suitcase, reviewing outfits for the cold weather, including the senior hoodie Liam and Matthew pressured me to order, and making sure my passport is secure.

If you'd told me five months ago that I'd be here, attempting sobriety, with friends, actually keeping up with school, I would've laughed. But I'm here and it feels like maybe that's enough.

CHAPTER TWENTY-THREE

Adelina

"Adelina, let's go!" Mami calls from downstairs.

"Coming!" I shout back.

I grab my carry-on, roll it down the stairs, and toss it in the trunk. Backpack on my lap, I hop in. Mami pulls out of the driveway, navigating the crisp winter afternoon.

When we pull up to Jax's house, he's already outside with his bags, talking quietly to his dad. They exchange a quick nod as Mami and I wave. "They could be twins!" Mami whispers.

"I know, right?" I giggle.

Jax gives his dad a brief hug, loads his luggage, and slides into the back seat. Small talk passes between us while Mami drives. The rest of the holiday break came and went in the blink of an eye, New Year's turning out to be quiet and intimate with Mami, Jax having spent it with his own father. Today, sunlight slices through the clouds, warming the car against the cold air.

"Are all your friends meeting at the school?" Mami asks.

"Yeah," I say. "They're probably already there."

As we pull up to the school curb, chaos hits. Parents linger on the sidewalks, snapping last-minute photos and hugging kids tight. A few students proudly sport their senior hoodies, marking the milestone in bright school colors.

"I'll be calling Zahra's mom later to thank her for covering everything," Mami reminds me as we climb out of the car. "Call me when you land, take a lot of pictures, and don't get lost!" She hugs me quickly, then Jax. Just before driving off, Mami lingers, watching us as we walk towards the school, a silent prayer forming on her lips.

I squeeze Jax's hand. "Wow. Look at this. Everyone's so hyped, it feels unreal."

He glances around, a mix of nerves and excitement on his face. "Yeah... Barcelona. Senior trip. Can't believe it's actually happening."

I grin towards him, brown eyes meeting green. "Finally."

We make our way to the center of the lawn to meet Liam and Matthew where there is a different kind of chaos. Instead of the scattered drop-off frenzy by the curb, everything here feels condensed and electric. Clusters of seniors huddle around their luggage, comparing seat assignments and checking the itinerary one more time. Teachers move through the groups with practiced efficiency, directing students to their buses as they shout last-minute reminders.

"Where's Zahra and Yoona?" I ask, scanning the crowd.

"They went to the bathroom," Liam says, smirking. "They told us to wait, but now that you're here, let's get moving."

We haul our luggage to our assigned bus and help each other shove bags into the compartments. It isn't long before Zahra and Yoona join us. Inside, everyone slides into their seats, claiming spots. The doors to the bus close, shutting out the last remnants of cold air, and the trip feels like it is finally moving forward.

Mr. Alvarez and Ms. Chen, clipboards in hand, do a roll call and go over the itinerary, pointing out airport rules, safety reminders, and expectations for behavior. The bus fills with low conversation, laughter, and the playful groans of seniors already rolling their eyes at the rules.

Zahra leans over, whispering, "Since my parents paid the senior dues and then some, they pulled some strings. We got our rooms close together."

Yoona grins, wiggling her eyebrows. "And yes, we'll be sneaking into each other's rooms... we just can't get caught."

I laugh, nudging Jax. "So this is all a secret mission, huh?"

"Exactly," Zahra says, eyes twinkling. "Addie, your birthday's gonna be epic."

"What exactly are we doing?" I whisper, already imagining the surprises.

Yoona shakes her head. "Not telling. Can't risk spoilers."

Liam and Matthew start joking around, bantering about who's going to get stuck with middle-of-the-night wake-up calls. Jax smirks but keeps an eye on me, and I notice my nerves fluttering in that familiar mix of excitement and mild panic.

At Yoona's request, the six of us pose for last-minute selfies as the airport comes into view. The bus seems to hold one shared breath before the doors open and we begin clambering out.

***

One red-eye flight and another round of coach buses later, we pull up in front of a sprawling hotel touched by soft morning light. Everyone is bleary-eyed and jet-lagged as they drag luggage through the lobby, shoulders bumping, backpacks sliding, friends teasing each other about who slept the least.

Check-in moves quickly. Mr. Alvarez and Ms. Chen call out names and room numbers while we shuffle keycards and luggage. Jax and I share a quick grin when we realize our rooms are only a few doors apart from Zahra, Yoona, and the boys, exactly like they promised. The moment the teachers finish, everyone rushes off to their rooms, eager to unpack and wash the plane off their skin.

Once I am settled, I get a notification. Zahra.

Room 312. Come over. We need to go over our plans!

I grab my bag and head down the hall, slipping quietly into Zahra's room. The girls sit cross-legged on the floor, maps, itineraries, and a few travel brochures scattered around them like a miniature tourist office.

"Okay, so here is the plan. Well, part of it," Zahra says, her eyes bright with excitement. "For your birthday, we thought we would do something a little extra. The teachers approved it since it is technically an academic activity even though it's not on the itinerary."

I lean in, curious. "What is it?"

Before she can explain, her phone vibrates. She groans at the school app notification.

"Great timing," Zahra mutters. "We will finish this later. But you are going to love it."

We rush down to the lobby with everyone else. The group spills into the space in a wave of chatter, phones already out as people crowd together for selfies under the chandelier. Mr. Alvarez and Ms. Chen give a quick welcome speech, reminding everyone to stick together, stay hydrated, and get ready for a full city tour.

Our circle groups up as the grade splits into chaperoned clusters. We pile onto new double-decker buses, the chatter of voices blending with the steady movement of the wheels on cobblestone streets. Jax slides in beside me on the upper deck, our legs brushing from time to time, while Liam, Matthew, Zahra, and Yoona argue over which food spot they want to try first.

I lean over slightly and take in the city. Sunlight glints off terracotta roofs, narrow streets twist between old stone buildings, and plazas are already dotted with street performers even though the air is not the warmest. The smell of fresh pastries drifts in from an open bakery door when we stop at a light, and I cannot stop grinning. My birthday is almost here, and the whole city feels awake because of it.

CHAPTER TWENTY-FOUR

Jackson

Barcelona settles into a rhythm of tours, late-night laughs, and quick moments that feel like they pass before I can catch them. Then the morning of Addie's birthday finally arrives. Everything about the last few days felt fast, but this morning feels different. Trying to keep my nerves at bay, I stand outside her door with my backpack on one shoulder and the little box pressing against my ribs.

I take a deep breath and knock softly. Inside, I hear her moving around. She opens the door with a sleepy smile, her hair barely tamed and the last traces of morning still on her face. My nerves jump, and I have to focus on not tripping over my own feet.

"Hey," I say, keeping my voice steady. "Happy birthday, Addie."

"Thank you," she says, stretching a little, her eyes soft and tired. She looks incredible even half-awake.

I step in and sit beside her on the edge of the bed. Every moment feels stretched thin, like the minutes want to hold onto us. She talks about breakfast plans and the itinerary, and I pretend to be calm even though my hands keep shifting in my lap. Sunlight brightens the room and the sounds of the city drift up from below. Her laugh is light and makes the tension in my shoulders loosen, but not completely.

When our phones ping with the reminder from the school app, I hesitate. Part of me wants to stay here with her and let the morning stay slow, but we have to go. Zahra was able to organize a private scavenger hunt, just for us, in Barcelona's Gothic Quarter, claiming that Addie would love it given she wouldn't stop talking about it ever since it was revealed we'd be coming here. The Gothic Quarter wasn't one of the locations on our itinerary, but as always, Zahra pulled it off.

We head down, check in with the chaperones, and share our locations. The six of us come together. Me, Addie, Zahra, Yoona, Liam, and Matthew. The teachers give us the signal and we leave the hotel, all without revealing a single clue to Addie.

***

As we get closer, the buildings begin to change around us. Shadows stretch longer between the walls and the streets narrow, the stones under our feet looking notably older. Addie slows down a little, eyes scanning the tall, textured facades above us.

"Wait," she whispers, almost to herself. "This looks like..."

The Gothic Quarter opens up in front of us, all narrow stone alleys and lanterns strung overhead like a path leading into another century. Addie isn't expecting anything like this. The streets feel alive in a way none of us

240

can quite explain. Zahra reveals the surprise to her then: a historical scavenger hunt in the Gothic Quarter. Addie's excitement becomes instantly contagious, infecting all of us at once.

Despite this being Addie's birthday surprise, we all stare in awe at the magnificent architecture around us, full of history and untold stories. Our eyes roam excitedly as Zahra shoves envelopes into everyone's hands. The scavenger hunt starts immediately.

We split into pairs, racing through shadowed corridors, hunting for carved gargoyles, mosaic tiles, and little details Addie is able to finally appreciate in the flesh. With every clue she solves, she smiles brighter, a little more caught up in the magic of the place.

By the time we regroup, Addie is flushed and laughing, mouth still open at the wonders around her. Then the moment arrives. I share a quick look with the rest of them and Zahra shoots me a quick, subtle nod. Addie is still grinning, face tilted upward at a sprawling cathedral in front of us when she feels my hand touch her elbow, softly guiding her away from the others.

"Where are we go..." she starts, but trails off as we slip into a narrow stone alcove just off the plaza. It feels quieter here, like the Gothic Quarter holds its breath.

"Addie," I say, my voice tighter than I want. She looks at me with that open, curious expression that makes me forget what I am supposed to say. I swallow and try again. "I need to tell you something."

She tilts her head slightly, waiting.

"I have never had a girlfriend," I say. The words feel strange, almost too honest. "But I want you. I don't want to let you go."

My hand moves to my pocket, fingers brushing the small box. I take it out and offer it to her. "I got you something."

She lets out a soft, surprised breath and opens the lid. The little gold necklace catches the light, the garnet shimmering like it is alive. Her smile grows, warm and bright.

"Jax. This is perfect," she says.

I step closer, nerves rising again. "So... will you be my girlfriend?" My voice drops. "I know I will mess up sometimes, but I don't want anyone else."

Her smile widens. "Yes, Jax. I want you too."

Relief floods through me and I feel my whole body relax. I lace my fingers with hers and we stay there for a moment, sharing a piece of our own history with the Gothic Quarter.

***

We slip back onto the main street, the noise of the Gothic Quarter rising around us again, and I can feel Addie's hand brush against mine, just barely, but enough to make me smile. Her neck shines garnet, twinkling every time it catches light. Our friends wait a few spaces ahead, a mix of curiosity and barely contained excitement on their faces.

Zahra peers at us like a hawk. "So... spill!" she says, one eyebrow arched. "What'd we miss back there?"

Addie grins, cheeks pink, hand flying to the delicate stone resting at the base of her neck, and I can't help the little smirk tugging at my lips. Liam nudges Matthew and mutters something, probably about how obvious we were being. The air feels electric, like everyone knows something big just happened.

We tell them.

Cheers explode into the air, locals turning their heads our way. Liam and Matthew crush against me, as if this decision is the key to the final lock, solidifying our group, our friendship.

Yoona suddenly snaps a picture of Addie and me, grinning like she's been waiting for this moment. Then she spins around to capture a group shot, the medieval cobblestone streets extending behind us perfectly. I glance at Addie as the camera clicks. She's beaming, all warmth and light, her excitement for her birthday written all over her face.

We return to the scavenger hunt. Everything feels lighter now. Addie laughs as I struggle to read a clue in Spanish and I tease her right back. When the final clue leads us to a small café terrace, Matthew throws his hands up and says, "Lunch." The sun is warm and the streets glow a little brighter as we navigate the directions back to the hotel, teasing each other and planning what we want to explore next.

Addie looks over at me with a small grin. I know she feels the same flutter I have been trying to hide all morning.

***

That night, I glance down the hall, making sure it's empty and free of chaperones, and quietly slip to Addie's door. I didn't even hesitate when her text popped up, telling me to head to her room. Knocking softly, she opens it almost immediately and pulls me inside, wrapping me in a tight hug as the door clicks closed behind us.

"Thank you... for everything today," she murmurs, her voice soft.

I rest my chin on her head. "Anything for you."

She takes my hand, but there's something different in her eyes now, a steady, quiet resolve. The room is dim except for clusters of candles she must have lit earlier, their soft glow flickering across the walls. She leads me toward the bathroom, the shower already on.

The flickering candlelight inside casts a warm glow across the black stone tiles. Shadows dance along the walls, softening everything in the room. I notice her lip caught between her teeth, a tiny, nervous habit, and my gaze lingers, sharp and focused.

She steps into the room and closes the door behind us, leaving the two of us in the warm candlelight. I pull her gently into me, holding her close.

"What are you doing?" I whisper.

"Trust me," she answers, her voice low and breathless. It hits me then that she planned this, not for me but for herself, because she wanted this moment to be hers to choose.

The steam rises around us, curling in the candlelight. Every movement she makes is careful, hesitant, but deliberate, like she's stepping into something entirely new. I keep my eyes on her, not wanting to look away, letting the quiet intimacy of the moment speak for itself. The first thing she slips off is her top, her hands trembling just a little. Then, the rest.

"Addie?" Her name comes out deep, unable to hide my desire.

She doesn't respond.

Instead, she moves away from me and steps into the shower, the door closing behind her. Moments later, I see the silhouette of her body through the quickly steaming glass. She calls for me, an invitation, and I don't waver, walking over to open the glass door. My eyes go dark at the sight of her. I want to run my hands over her body. I need to feel the curve of her hips, the dip of her waist.

Addie's lashes flutter as she reaches out and tugs at my clothes, urging me to take them off. I succumb until steam curls around us both. She pauses, taking in my body with her eyes, mouth opening slightly when she trails them down. When she's seen it all, Addie pulls me under the warm water.

I turn her away from me and use the soap to gingerly lather her body, allowing my hands to learn every part of her. I want to be the first to feel every inch of her. I want to explore her and learn her in ways that no one else has. Addie moans under my touch and rests her head back on my shoulder. She sighs, and I catch the sound with my mouth.

I feel my desire beginning to grow and she feels it too. A brutish sound comes out of me. Picking her up, I carry her out of the bathroom and gently lower her down onto the bed, unable to contain the fire burning within me. We're both dripping wet, but I don't care and neither does she. I'm hovering over her and her hands pull me down.

"Kiss me," she pleads. "Make me yours."

"Are you sure?" I groan between kisses.

"Yes," Addie moans.

She leans over and takes something out of the bedside table. Holding the small wrapper up to me, she says, "I also found this," and then kisses me again.

I kiss Addie with everything I've got, reckless and hungry, and finally, we're together in a way that's only ever felt right between us.

***

I wake and find Addie still fast asleep, an arm draped over me. I glance at the clock and realize we've completely lost track of time. A flicker of worry hits me. What if one of our teachers checks in?

But then I look at her, chest rising and falling against mine, hair spilling over my arm, and all that worry fades. She grounds me. Centers me. In this moment, nothing else exists. I stroke her hair softly, memorizing the angles of her face, until her eyes flutter open. And in that quiet, something inside me finally settles. This is a better high than anything I've ever known.

"Hi birthday girl," I whisper and kiss her forehead.

"Hey," she whispers back.

"How are you feeling?"

"Amazing," she smiles and arches her back in a small stretch.

"And your body? Are you okay?" I ask, my voice quieter than I intended, a flicker of worry forming.

"Yeah, I think so."

"Good," I kiss her forehead again. The tension inside me eases a little, and I relax, holding her a bit closer under the sheets, letting the quiet and warmth of her presence fill the space between us.

"Do you think we can try this again?" she whispers. I laugh. "You mean shower or...?" When her eyes meet mine, there's no mistaking the curious desire in them, her cheeks flushing. "Right now?"

"Yeah." She pulls the sheets over her face and hides.

I look into the bedside table drawer and smile.

"Come out," I laugh and she slowly peeks her head out from underneath. Pulling the sheet so that her face and neck are uncovered, I kiss her shoulder and work my way down to her chest. She sighs and soon we're falling into each other once more.

No dream, no high, nothing I've chased has ever come close to what she gives me. The way that she has shown up for me when no one else has. Addie believes in me and, because of her, I think I'm starting to believe in myself as well.

"Thank you," I tell her. "Thank you for everything. Thank you for choosing me, Addie." I'm not very good with my damn words, this is as much as I can get out.

CHAPTER TWENTY-FIVE

Adelina

Since returning from Barcelona, everything feels different. The last day there was amazing, but the flight back? Brutal. Jet-lagged and dragging ourselves through the hallways, the seniors still manage to rattle off stories and flash photos, passing memories around like treasures, while juniors stare wide eyed, already dreaming of their own senior year.

Somewhere in all the chaos, I realize I don't feel that constant, gnawing weight I'd carried for months— the imaginary ticking bomb I thought was going to ruin everything with Jax. I'd been terrified of trusting him fully, afraid he'd get bored or find someone "better." Denial had built walls around my heart, thick and jagged.

But seeing him sober, seeing him really fight for himself, and for us, cracked those walls. Christmas Eve, sitting together, laughing until our cheeks hurt, feeling the warmth of him near me. Little by little, the fear loosened its grip, and what took its place was unmistakable. I love him.

Now I look for him the way lungs look for air. Jax teaches me how to accept and I teach him how to release. Words can't explain the way our bodies connect when we allow desire to take over, welding us into one seamless source of energy.

I can hear Jax's heart beating steadily as my head lays on his bare chest, feeling it rising and falling slowly, his breathing even as he sleeps. Underneath the blankets of his bed, we are undressed and exhausted from our earlier efforts.

Jax has been nothing but patient and gentle since I gave him something I'd only ever saved for the right person. He has made an adamant point to always go at my pace and for that, I am grateful. I never feel pressure or scrutiny from him and he certainly never makes me feel insecure about my own body.

Because of that, I have been able to let go and try new things, experiment with newfound desires while Jax guides me in the right direction until my body explodes with pleasure, his own explosion quickly following.

Thinking about this makes me stir and I reach a hand out to stroke his face softly. Feeling my touch, Jax's eyes slowly open and look down to me. His hand hugs my waist from outside the sheets and my body presses deeper into him.

"Addie," he mutters with his lips pressed against mine. "It's getting late."

"I know," I respond and let the sheets slide lower.

His eyelids come down and I feel his eyes rest on my body. I shiver against him as his hands trace my curves.

"We should make it quick then," I dare.

Using his strength, he pushes himself up to a standing position and I wrap my legs around him. Foreheads pressed, we move as if we've known this rhythm forever.

"I'm wide awake now," he says after collapsing in his bed with me, letting the adrenaline leave our bodies.

"Are you excited for tomorrow?" I ask him, standing to get dressed.

"Excited? No. I'm just trying not to think about how short the future feels."

"But what if, by chance, he happens to look your way?"

"I doubt that will happen. If the recruiter does, then he does. Anyways, it's Matthew and Liam he should be looking at," Jax tells me.

I kiss him on the forehead like he's done to me so many times before. "Well," I add, "who knows what tomorrow will bring? All I know is that everyone won't shut up about the game."

"It's the championship game. All or nothing tomorrow."

"I'm not much of a competitive person, but kick some ass. Yoona, Zahra, and I will be in the bleachers, cheering for you!"

"Thank you," he kisses me.

"Of course." I return the kiss.

Wrapping the blanket around his body, Jax walks me downstairs to see me off.

"Text me when you get home!"

I walk out and I assure him I will. Looking out of my car window, I wave at him and drive off.

***

Everyone's hyped for the final soccer match of the season. The energy in the school is electrifying. In chemistry, Jax looks totally chill. When I ask how he's feeling, he just shrugs and says he's good. In my other classes, a few soccer players keep sneaking glances at the clock, barely able to sit still until the bell finally rings. Then, like a herd, they bolt.

By the time I get to study hall, the library is practically empty. Now waiting for my college acceptance letter to arrive, I dive into studying for the next exam. We've moved past the basics by this point in the semester and are now into the heavy stuff. I'm so into it that when the bell finally rings, I jump, surprised it's already time to go.

At lunch, Matthew, Liam, and Jax are all missing, preparing for the game, no doubt. I sit with Zahra and Yoona, who immediately mention how empty the table feels without the boys. Nonetheless, we use the time to catch up with one another.

"Can you believe it's almost February?" Yoona exclaims. "Where has the time gone? The school year is going by so fast!"

"I know!" Zahra agrees. "I'm dying to get my college acceptance letters."

"I'm sure Addie will get accepted by them all," Yoona adds.

"No," I disagree, "I could very well be rejected. To be honest, I think my personal statement was complete garbage. I was satisfied with it at the moment, but the more I think about it, the more I wish I could go back and make edits."

Zahra rolls her eyes at me. "Oh please, you'll get accepted and probably with a scholarship."

"I feel bad for Liam, though," Yoona comments, reminding us of his struggles. "He's still pretty bummed that he has to wait until March to apply."

"Jax isn't even applying." I sigh and they both ask me why. "Well, I don't think it's really his thing. It's a shame though because he's really good with English lit."

"Is he?" Zahra says, clearly surprised.

"Yeah," I respond. "Math and science aren't really his thing, but he's a damn good writer from what I've seen. We still study every weekend and he's able to crank out an essay faster than I've ever been able to."

"That says a lot," Yoona whistles out.

"I get math and science. They're structured. Numbers don't lie, every action has a reaction," I say, taking a sip of water. "But Jax... he reads something and just *gets* it. Like he's inside the writer's head."

"That's sort of like art. The only difference is, I see images and he sees words," Yoona says.

"He's talented," Zahra says, softer now. "I just hope he knows it."

Her comment hangs in the air, but it's no longer tense. Zahra's always been cautious about Jax, but now I can talk about him freely without worrying she'll overreact. I don't need to share every detail with her, but it feels good to have that space to just be honest.

"I'm sure Liam will get his done in due time," Yoona says, hope riding on her words.

"When does the game start?" I question, looking down at my phone.

"An hour after school, I think," Yoona answers.

"Want to meet up when the last bell rings?" I ask.

Zahra nods, but Yoona is the one who responds. "Sounds good! We can walk over together."

***

When we meet up again, we head toward the soccer field. A bus is parked by the curb, the other team unloading while ours is already out running drills. I spot Jax kicking a ball with Liam while Matthew practices shots with the goalie.

We find seats on the bleachers, huddling together for warmth. Our breath fogs in the cold air, and a concession stand nearby is selling hot drinks, snacks, and hand warmers. I tell Yoona and Zahra I'm grabbing cider and offer to get them some too.

After paying for three cups of cider and hand warmers, I step aside to wait, when suddenly, someone grabs me and spins me around. I yelp, feet barely touching the ground, before landing face-to-face with Jax grinning like an idiot. I swat his shoulder, trying not to smile.

"I'm sorry," he laughs. "Did I scare you?"

"Scare me? You almost made my heart explode!" I reprimand him.

Jax kisses me deeply. Whispers rise around us, but I don't flinch. For once, I don't care who was watching.

"Where are you girls sitting?" Jax holds my waist.

I point over to our spot and he turns to wave. The girls look at us, their mittened hands waving back in the air.

I grab the drinks from the stand, and Jax helps me carry them back to the bleachers. After I hand them off to Yoona and Zahra, he kisses my forehead and jogs back to the field.

The stands are packed. Students from every school team fill the bleachers, chanting and waving banners. Football, baseball, and track are all here, hyping up the boys on the field. The cheer squad's down front, pom-poms flashing in the cold.

I check my phone. Only minutes to kickoff. Across the field, the opposing team huddles up, their coach giving a pep talk before they break into a roar. Jax claps Liam on the back, steady and confident, before our team circles in. The coaches give their last words, then Matthew's voice rises, leading the chant that rips through the air and sends chills down my spine.

A man steps onto the field, cutting through the noise of the crowd. He's dressed in all black, a long tailored coat brushing his knees, the kind you wear when you're here on business, not for fun. He walks straight toward our coach, shaking his hand before the two start talking. Whatever he says makes the coach's expression sharpen just a bit. The players don't seem to notice, they're too focused, too hyped, but something about the man's presence feels important.

Sitting between Yoona and Zahra, I nudge them and point to the man. "I think that's the recruiter," I tell them.

They both nod and Zahra says "Yeah, I think you're right."

The man shakes hands with the head coach and sits next to the other two coaches. "Yup, that's definitely him," Yoona confirms.

All heads turn toward the center of the field when the whistle blows, cutting through the noise. The ref stands between the two teams. "Clean game, no dirty plays, no funny tricks. If I blow the whistle, you stop. Got it?"

Both teams nod. Matthew and the other captain step up for the coin toss. The ref flips it. Heads. We kick off. Players take their positions, coaches shout from the sidelines, and when the next whistle rings, the game begins.

Pandemonium ensues as people start frantically yelling for specific players and teams. Both teams are holding their own during the first half-hour of the game and no goals are made. A foul is called on a player from the opposing team, who tripped one of our players and our team took the chance to regroup. When the whistle blows again, I notice Liam, Matthew, and Jax spread horizontally across the field, an equal distance apart.

The other team takes control, but Matthew intercepts and passes to Liam. With Jax and Matthew flanking him, Liam fakes a pass, shifting his feet and sending the ball the other way. Jax sprints downfield. It was a setup. While the defenders chase Liam and Matthew, Jax gains control. The two pass back and forth, dodging players until the goalkeeper loses track of the switch. Jax kicks. And scores!

The bleachers erupt, cheers and groans mixing in the cold air. My eyes find the recruiter, now leaning forward, elbows on his knees, fully locked in. The whistle cuts through the noise. Halftime.

Each team huddles on their side of the field to regroup and hydrate themselves. Players are substituted out on both teams, but Matthew, Liam, and Jax remain on the field. The recruiter is now walking over to Matthew and shakes hands with him. From my seat I can see that Matthew is giving his best face to the recruiter, who has now turned to shake hands with Liam as well.

"Oh shit, look! He's talking to Liam now!" Yoona says with excitement. The two boys seem to be having a deep conversation with the recruiter when I see the recruiter point a finger down the field. Oblivious to what's happening, Jax is passing the ball with another team member, who is being substituted into the game for the second half.

"Jackson!" one of the coaches calls out and Jax whips his head, a slight frown on his face as he runs over. Stopping in front of the coach, she sends him over to the recruiter who shakes hands with him. My eyes are wide as this happens and I stare intently at Matthew, Liam, Jax, and the recruiter.

"What do you think they're talking about?" Zahra whispers.

"I don't know," I say in awe.

"I'm going to get us another round of drinks, ladies. Same as the first round?" Yoona asks.

Zahra and I nod, both, apparently, having a hard time finding our voices. When Yoona returns, the game has already started.

Determination burns on their faces as Matthew, Liam, and Jax land the first goal within ten minutes, but the other team quickly answers with two of their own. The air is thick with tension; the crowd's gone silent.

Five minutes left.

Every pass feels like a heartbeat. Coaches are shouting from the sidelines, and the recruiter's now pacing, scribbling notes without looking away.

Two minutes to go.

Both teams are relentless. Jax shouts something to Liam, who nods and signals Matthew. Whatever plan they've cooked up sparks into motion. Matthew charges after the ball, Liam closes in for backup, and together they intercept.

People are now howling in the bleachers, one boy pulling at his hair, another girl jumping up and down in excitement. I'm leaning at the edge of my seat, intently watching and holding my breath.

Liam pulls back and receives the ball from Matthew, who shoots it over to him. A player from the other team runs over and they struggle for control when the ball suddenly shoots up into the air. Liam uses his height to his advantage and leaps into the air, head butting the ball in Jax's direction.

Jax runs towards the ball and meets it with a powerful kick. The ball flies into the air and this time hot cider splashes my hand but I don't feel it, my eyes glued to him.

It's going to miss! I scream internally because that's exactly what it looks like.

The goalkeeper, who is running to defend the goal, prepares to block the attempt. The post rings like a bell and the ball drops into silence.

For a moment, the world freezes. Then, the goalkeeper turns.

There it is. The ball rests in the corner of the net.

The field explodes.

Students leap to their feet, screaming; teachers cheer; the bleachers shake under the chaos. On the field, Matthew drops to his knees while Liam sprints with his arms wide, and Jax hauls Matthew up into a fierce hug before the team swarms them, lifting him into the air and chanting his name.

It takes a minute to calm the storm. Both teams finally line up, exchanging handshakes and sportsmanlike smiles. Off to the side, the recruiter utters something softly to our coach, slips his notes into his coat pocket, and disappears into the crowd.

"Come on, let's go wait for the boys," Zahra calls out.

The three of us can't stop talking about the game as we head toward the parking lot, our voices dripping with excitement. We toss our empty cups and snack wrappers into the nearest trash can, still replaying the final goal in our heads. It's a bit of a walk, and by the time we reach the lot, the boys are nowhere to be seen.

"Probably still in the lockers," Yoona says, reading my mind.

We stay there until I hear a loud commotion coming from one of the exits. The door slams open and Liam comes running out, screaming a victory chant. Matthew and Jax are close behind him, both laughing as they chant.

"That was incredible!" Yoona calls out to them.

"I thought I stopped breathing at one point," I add. "I couldn't believe it when I saw the ball in the net!"

"Honestly, I thought it hadn't gone in," Matthew reveals.

"Same," Liam cries, "but then I remembered that Jax is a complete beast!"

Jax, who has been silent as usual, just smiles and shrugs.

"How did you do it?" Yoona asks.

"The space just seemed right. The angle felt right. I didn't think I would make it, but I just went with my gut."

"Some damn good gut you have!" Liam's giddy voice yells out.

"Come on, come on, let's go to my house already! I'm starving and there's pizza waiting!" Matthew says, practically bouncing with leftover adrenaline.

We burst into laughter, the energy from the game still thrumming through us as we head toward our cars. The night air is sharp and electric, the kind that makes everything feel a little more alive.

CHAPTER TWENTY-SIX

Jackson

Pizza's already spread across the table, steam fogging the lids. My stomach growls, but my hands still shake from the game. Too much adrenaline, not enough food.

"Your brother wanted to come down and say congrats in person," Matthew's dad calls out. Tall and broad-shouldered, with the same strong features as his sons—though his hair is gone where theirs isn't—he looks every bit the part of a proud father.

Matthew's mom, tall and slender, with rich, deep satin skin that seems to glow in the dining room light, comes over to hug her youngest. His older brother, only home for the weekend given the spring semester started, settles in, and everyone starts talking over the game. I mostly stay quiet, happy enough to just enjoy my pizza next to Addie.

"It was really all because of him," Matthew points at me.

I raise my hands and shake them. I lift my slice in a toast toward them instead of arguing. "You two set the lane. I just kicked."

"He's being modest," Liam chides, peering over at me.

The conversation drifts to college, and Matthew's brother lights up talking about dorm life, classes, parties, and the independence it brings. Everyone hangs on his every word, excited about what their own college experience may bring.

I watch Addie laugh and ask questions, and a tight knot forms in my throat. I have her now, but college is coming. Fast. My mistakes, my past. What if I can't keep up with her on this next step?

Eventually, the pizza's gone and we help clean up, thanking Matthew's parents before heading out. Addie and I slip into my car, and I start the drive home, the city lights blurring past as my thoughts secretly spin.

"Liam was right, you know," she says once we're on the road.

"About?"

"About you being modest. You're insanely good!" she exclaims. Then, her face turns serious and she adds, "It's almost scary."

I laugh and hold her hand, a habit I've acquired when we're in the car. "I can get serious when I need to. Speaking of seriousness, I'm going to see Samuel tomorrow."

"Oh yeah?" Addie asks. "I thought you were meeting with him when we got back from the senior trip."

I tell Addie I had to reschedule because Matthew's training ran long, and she nods, understanding. Her hand finds mine, grounding me, and I realize I'm not nervous so much as bracing for what's ahead. Knowing I'll have to face the hard stuff eventually.

She squeezes my hand again, a quiet reminder that she's here for me, that this is my space to get things off my chest and leave them there. I press a kiss to her finger and feel a warmth spread through me. Pulling up in front of her house, we share a long, slow kiss before finally letting go.

I make a mental note to swing by tomorrow after my session. I still need her help for the exam next week.

"Sounds good. Mami will be here this weekend though," she responds.

"Will she mind if I'm there?"

"Oh no!" Addie exclaims, "Mami loves you."

"Does she know about us?"

"Yeah, I told her last week."

My eyebrows go up and I ask, "You did?"

Addie laughs and shrugs, saying it's obvious she's happier. Her mom even helped her contact her doctor about birth control. I tell her I'll grab more condoms too, and she grins, calling it teamwork. Her mom doesn't pry, thankfully. According to Addie, she tried "the talk" weeks ago, and she nearly died of embarrassment.

A gust of cold wind hits as she opens the car door. She leans in for a quick kiss, then darts inside, calling, "See you tomorrow!" I wait until she's safely in before driving off.

***

The alarm needles my skull. Yesterday's sprint lives in my quads. Hot water scalds me awake; the mirror fogs, and I practice saying my mother's name without flinching. No luck.

I throw on a black long sleeve, tie my sneakers, and grab my coat and cap before heading out. The drive to Samuel's is quick, twenty minutes, leaving me a few minutes early. Perfect.

At the house, I ring the doorbell and a cheerful voice calls, "Down here!"

I look down to see a woman no taller than my waist, blue eyes sparkling as she peers up at me, her black hair piled into a neat bun. I almost give myself whiplash trying to spot her.

"Good morning," I say.

She laughs and leads me to a cozy room on the side of the house. "Come, sit wherever you like," she says, gesturing to the couches. "Well... go on," she adds, a playful laugh coming out of her.

Exhaling a shaky breath, I thank her and take a seat.

"Do you want some water? Tea? Coffee?" she asks.

"Water is okay for now. Thank you."

"Young man, stop thanking me so much! You're a guest here. I'm Helena, Samuel's wife. He'll be with you in just a moment."

"Nice to meet you, Helena. I'm Jax." I smile back at her.

She gives me another bright smile that makes the corner of her eyes crinkle up. "I know, I work as his receptionist. He does all of the hard work though. But really, what would he do without me?" This time, she winks. "I'll be right back with that water."

My eyes take in the room: simple but cozy, cream colored walls dotted with seasonal forest paintings, and a bay window overlooking a lush garden. Three couches face each other around a small table, leaving enough space for Helena to weave through as she hands me water.

"Thank you," I say and she gives me a warm, friendly pat on the shoulder.

A man enters the room and smiles, coming over to shake my hand. Samuel is slightly shorter than me, but has black hair that looks strikingly similar to that of his wife's and the same smile to go along with it. Instead of blue, I meet his brown eyes and return his handshake.

"Alright, I'll leave you two to it. Do you need anything before I go?" Helena asks. Samuel looks at me and I shake my head. "If you need me, I'll be up in the study."

"Okay, sweetheart. Thank you," Samuel calls out to her as she exits.

Taking a seat on the couch across from me, Samuel crosses his legs and places a clipboard onto his lap.

"Before we start, I want to thank you for coming. Therapy is never an easy thing to commit to and it takes a lot of mental strength and self-love to show up."

Not knowing how to respond, I nod and stay silent.

Explaining the process, Samuel continues speaking. "I'm going to ask you a few questions first that I want you to answer as truthfully as you can. Remember, this is a space without judgement and what you say stays here between us. Do you have any questions?"

I shake my head.

"Let's begin then, shall we?"

I nod and take a sip of water, suddenly thirsty.

"What's your name?"

"Jackson Hurst," I answer.

"How old are you?"

"Eighteen."

Samuel asks about school, my plans, and who I live with. I tell him I'm in senior year, just trying to get through it. When it comes to home, I pause. I live with my dad, but we keep separate spaces. Him in the house, me in a converted garage. My mom? She's gone. The words feel flat even as they hang heavy in the room, a truth I've carried alone for too long.

"I'm sorry to hear that," Samuel says, leaning forward, and I can tell it's genuine.

"Well, that's why I'm here. I don't think I'm exactly over her death."

"Can you explain that a bit more?"

I speak reluctantly at first, but then the words flow out of me. Alexander dying. Mom's suicide. How my dad basically shut down after and left me to figure it out alone. I talk about the night terrors, the dreams that won't stop, the first time I took pills. I make it clear the overdose wasn't some big plan to off myself. I just wanted the noise in my head to shut up for once, but I pushed it too far. And then Addie, how she's the reason I'm even sitting here now.

I tell it all like I'm reading off a script, no cracks in my voice, no tears. But inside, I'm still pissed at my dad for disappearing into himself while I drowned. Samuel doesn't say a word or even glance at his notes. He just listens, locked in, and somehow that makes it harder to keep my hands from sweating as I finish.

"That's a lot to have to go through," Samuel finally says.

"Yeah, I guess so."

"I want to go back to that night of the party. What was your first thought when you woke up in the hospital?"

"Confusion," I say, then shake my head. "No."

A pause.

"Disappointment that I survived."

Samuel nods and writes something down in his pad. I suspiciously lean forward to see what he's writing. When he notices, to my surprise, he flips through his notes as he explains.

"I'm jotting down moments you've shared that we can use to set goals. Therapy is yours. You guide it, I just help. I think starting by disconnecting these tough moments could work. We tackle them one by one, then string them back together to see the domino effect since your brother's passing.

"The mind's complicated. Trauma gets shoved away. Sometimes we do it consciously, sometimes not. Either way, ignored feelings show up later, often in ways we don't realize. Make sense?"

I shrug when he asks about the first domino. Honestly, I'm not sure, too many moments blur together. Samuel just nods and flips his pad to a fresh page. He explains the homework: two columns, left for the event, right for the feeling I shoved away, arrows if it shifted. Simple enough, but knowing me, it'll still be a lot to think through.

He wants to see me twice a week. I nod, figuring I can handle it. No promises I'll like it, but it's a start.

With the first session done, I shake Helena and Samuel's hands, step into the cold, and slide into my car, unsure what to make of it all, but curious if I can actually tackle the timeline. Later, while studying with Addie, I tell her about the session and the homework. She laughs and cheers me on, hope practically radiating from her.

***

I shove study notes aside Tuesday night and finally tackle Samuel's homework. The blank paper stares back at me until I write: **Alexander's birth** → happiness. One arrow sparks another, and soon I'm chasing the dominoes of my life, trying to pin down feelings I'd buried for years.

I finish the events column, struggling to name the emotions. Some come easy, some leave me staring at empty spaces. I copy the timeline into the journal my dad gave me, letting the ink dry before finally crashing into bed.

At the next session, Samuel glances at it, nods, and smiles. "More than I expected. Good start."

I shrug. "Most of the emotions are missing."

"Starting somewhere is what matters," he says, pointing to the first few bullets. Week by week, we unpack them: Alexander's birth, his death, my mother, my dad. I realize I've been holding anger for him, blaming him for everything. But he was hurting too, not that it excuses anything. Just a reminder that he's human too.

I'm learning to forgive. To stop blaming myself. To let go of the weight that isn't mine. And it's changing things. Sleep comes easier. My runs aren't fueled by rage anymore. I'm laughing more with friends. Even talking to Addie about what's in my head feels possible.

I never thought therapy could feel like this, like actually healing. Men aren't supposed to cry, to talk about emotions, I thought. Samuel was right. It takes self-love just to show up. And maybe I'm finally starting to believe I deserve it.

Adelina

My eyes had been fixed on the window, mind a thousand miles away, when Zahra's voice cuts through like static. "Earth to Adelina!"

Coming back from my thoughts, I turn to look at her. "What?"

"Yoona asked you a question," she tells me.

"You did? I'm sorry," I turn to look at her. "My brain's on something else." The three of us are seated at our favorite cafe, having drinks to warm us from the lingering winter cold.

"Are you coming to my art show this weekend?" Yoona repeats.

"Oh my goodness, Yoona, of course. I wouldn't ever miss it. I was just thinking about acceptance letters. They're supposed to be coming soon and then my brain jumped to

Liam and I began worrying about him and it was just," I point to my head, "a snowball effect."

Yoona gives me a nod and forgives me. "I'm worried about Liam too. He did mention that he's passing math now. There's just one exam left and assuming he passes, he should have the math credit he needs to apply."

"When did he tell you that?" Zahra asks her.

"A few nights ago. I was over at his place," she responds. Zahra and I both snap our heads at her and stare. "No, no! Not like that. I was just making a portrait and he offered to be my model."

"Yeah right!" Zahra laughs, tossing a straw wrapper at Yoona like she's calling her bluff.

"No, seriously!" Yoona insists.

"You two would actually make a cute couple," I grin, half-teasing but secretly rooting for them already.

"What? He's always treated me like a sister." Yoona's voice is abnormally shrill and high-pitched.

"Matthew has always treated me like a sister and that doesn't mean anything," Zahra comments.

I'm about to respond to Yoona, but something Zahra says makes me abruptly stop and turn my head to look at her, eyes squinted.

I freeze mid-sip, lowering my cup. "What does *that* mean exactly?"

"Nothing!" she yelps, her eyes wide as though she has been caught doing something she wasn't supposed to. "I'm just saying people change," Zahra mutters, eyes darting anywhere but ours.

"What are you hiding from us?" Yoona studies Zahra's face.

"You *are* hiding something!" I accuse.

"Alright, alright! Yes, I'm hiding something," she finally confesses.

"Start talking," I pressure her.

"That night after the soccer game, I... texted Matthew that night. Just to say congrats. But then we kept talking, and talking."

Yoona and I spend the next hour poring over every message, analyzing each word until we are completely convinced Matthew is flirting with Zahra.

"How are you able to sit with him during lunch? Isn't it awkward?" Yoona asks.

"No, it's the opposite. He shoots me small winks when no one is looking and sometimes he walks me to classes. I'm hoping he asks me to prom," Zahra reveals dreamily.

"I'm sure he'll ask you when he's ready. This is so exciting!" I smile.

Yoona blurts out that she's just glad it's finally happening. She's tired of the tension between them, always pretending not to like each other. I laugh, and she joins me once Zahra shoots me a glare.

Standing up, Zahra puts her oversize sweater on and grabs her bag. "Let's go. We've got senior photos coming up, and I'm done being your gossip column," she says, half-laughing through her annoyance.

Yoona and I haul our stuff behind Zahra across the street to the mall. Hours later, we're juggling massive shopping bags in the parking lot. Zahra's bought way more than the two of us combined, so we help load her car. Trunk closed, she smiles and thanks us.

While we're packing, we can't stop talking about senior photos. We trade posing ideas, goofy faces, and outfit plans. The fear I once carried about being in front of a camera finally starts to ebb away. We even toss around ideas for our senior quotes, laughing at the cheesy ones and debating which quotes are actually "us." After hugs and a short walk to my car, I get a text from Jax.

Tried to find you after school. I miss you.

I respond.

The girls and I had an open schedule after lunch today. We decided to go shopping. Senior Photos? :)

I toss my bags in the backseat, cue up the radio, and let the late sun glaze the road.

That's right. lol, sounds like something you girls would enjoy. I'm going to wrap up here.

I text him that I'll head home to drop off my bags, and he says he'll let me know when he's done. Pocketing my phone, I back out of the parking lot and crank up some music, letting it ride over the last bits of sunlight.

Thinking about this school year, I let out a quiet, grateful sigh, rolling the windows down a crack to feel the cool air hit my face. Parties, trips, college acceptance letters, senior photos, prom, a boyfriend. Here I am, windows down, music up, life finally steady. The kind of peace that makes you forget how fragile it really is.

The roads are mostly empty as I drive home, street lights just starting to flicker on and the sun hanging later in the sky as spring edges closer. I slow at a red light, waiting to turn left, and when it finally changes, I pull forward.

Without warning, a violent slam rocks the passenger side, glass exploding in a glittering spray. My insides lurch as the car jerks hard, metal groaning like it's alive. I claw at the steering wheel, panic surging, but the car spins and flips, tires screeching against concrete.

My arms fly up instinctively, seat belt biting into my chest as gravity yanks me down. The world tilts and rings with a high-pitched scream in my ears. Spots of light dance across my vision, mingling with a warm trickle sliding down my forehead. The coppery taste of blood fills my mouth.

Through the blur, someone's running toward me. I want to call out for help, but the words never make it past my lips.

CHAPTER TWENTY-EIGHT
Jackson

I'm heading to class after a study session with Liam. He's been grinding nonstop for our next exam, cursing under his breath one second and flipping through notes the next. It's hard not to respect that watching him push through even when it's obvious he's struggling. Makes me want to do better, too.

I'm a few steps from the door when someone calls my name. I turn and spot a woman waving me over. Before I can ask what's going on, she's already leading me into a small office that smells faintly of coffee and printer ink.

She sits behind her desk, perfectly organized down to the last paper clip, while I awkwardly take the seat in front. Her nameplate catches my eye: *Mrs. Singh – College Advisor.* My stomach dips. Those banners, Harvard, UCLA, NYU, feel like they're mocking me. I look away, pretending the sting isn't there. *What the hell am I doing here?*

Mrs. Singh clears her throat, pulling me from my phone. When she flips her computer screen around, my less-than-stellar transcript stares back at me.

"I was going over students who missed the first round of college applications," she says, tucking a strand of hair behind her ear. "Your name came up."

I shrug. "Yeah, I'm not applying."

"Any reason why?"

"You've seen my grades. School's not really my thing." I say, trying to sound casual, even though the words taste like shame.

Her voice softens but doesn't lose its edge. "Four years of solid grades in English says otherwise. And your grades this semester, they're improving. That's not nothing."

"So?" I mutter. I don't mean for it to sound defensive, but it does.

"You've shown growth, Jackson. Real growth. I want to know what changed."

"I just want to graduate and get out," I say through gritted teeth. "Why does that matter?"

Instead of answering, she opens a drawer and slides a sheet across her desk. My eyes skim the list until they land on a name at the bottom: *Jackson Hurst.*

I look up. "What is this?"

"State University's recruitment list," she says with a small smile. "They want you on their soccer team."

The words hit like a punch and a gift at once. For a second, I forget to breathe. "I didn't even apply."

"Which is why you're here. If you submit your application in the next few days, you could earn a full scholarship."

I stare at her. "Full scholarship?" The word full spins in my head, like a door swinging open to everything I thought I'd lost.

She nods. "You've worked too hard to throw that away. Let's at least get your application started. You've got a story worth telling."

I lean back, torn between disbelief and something that feels like fear. For months, I've been clawing my way out of the mess I made and suddenly someone thinks I'm worth saving. That thought alone hits harder than I expect.

I nod slowly. "Alright. I'll try."

Hours later, I'm back in her office with a loaner laptop on my knees. The blank screen feels heavier than it should. Mrs. Singh types quietly behind her desk, giving me space. I put on my earbuds, open a new doc, and just... stare. Every line I start sounds fake, forced. I delete, rewrite, delete again.

Then I stop overthinking.

I think of Addie. My dad. Liam. Samuel. The nights I almost lost myself and the days I decided not to. And before I know it, my fingers move faster than my brain. The words pour out, raw, honest, real. My pain turns into something that almost feels like strength.

When I hand Mrs. Singh the laptop an hour later, she reads silently, her expression softening with every line.

"This is beautiful," she says finally. The same words Samuel might've said. I finally let myself believe it. "Don't change a word. Just spell check it and print."

I follow her instructions, and when I hand over the pages, she tucks them into a folder labeled with my name. "Come back tomorrow during study hall," she says. "We'll finish the rest. You're closer than you think."

I nod, standing to leave. "Thanks."

"Remember," she adds with a knowing smile, "you can always decide not to go."

I grin faintly. "Yeah. I'll keep that in mind."

***

I check my phone while walking across the lot. Still nothing from Addie. Weird. I call, and it goes straight to voicemail. She's probably busy, I tell myself, trying not to read into it.

At home, I drop my stuff on the couch and start filling out the rest of the college app. It's going fine until I hit the finance section. Great. I grab the folder and jog next door, teeth chattering from the lingering cold.

Dad opens the door, surprise flickering across his face. We're still learning how to act around each other, but it's not as awkward anymore.

"Pops, I need your help."

He steps aside, eyeing my short sleeves. "You ran here? In this weather?"

"Just... come on," I say, already spreading the papers across the coffee table.

When he spots the college header, his brow lifts. "You're applying?"

"Apparently. State's looking to scout me for soccer."

That gets a real smile out of him. "That's incredible, Jax. I didn't know you were playing again."

I shrug, unsure what to say to that, and let the silence pass.

He dives into the forms while I raid the kitchen for food. It's strange how normal this feels. Like something we used to have before everything broke.

When I come back with a sandwich, he's already halfway done. "You got through that fast," I say.

"Pretty straightforward. Needed a few tax numbers, but you're set."

As I'm chewing, I glance at my phone again. Still no reply. A sliver of fear settles in my mind. I text Liam and Matthew.

You guys heard from Addie?

Liam: Nope.

Matthew: Me neither.

My fingers clench around my phone. This isn't like her. I picture her car, her quiet house, the way silence sometimes used to mean something worse. Don't go there. Not again. I take a breath, grounding myself like Samuel taught me. Addie's fine. She has to be.

Dad's voice pulls me back. "There's a game on tonight. Want to watch?"

I almost say no, but stop myself. "Yeah. Sure."

He tosses me a soda, and the hiss when I open it sounds... safe. Familiar. We yell at bad calls, argue over plays, and by halftime, the air between us feels lighter. It's not perfect, but it's something. The kind of something I didn't think we'd get back.

I glance over at him, laughing at the screen, and realize maybe this is what healing looks like. Not forgiveness, not forgetting, but just trying again.

***

Addie's seat is empty in chemistry the next day, and my worry spikes. She never misses class. Ever. I try to focus on the formulas on the board, but the letters blur together. That hollow, twisting feeling I know all too well spreads. "Where the hell is she?" I whisper under my breath. I slide my phone out under the desk and shoot her another text. Still nothing.

By lunch, I've checked my phone so many times it's pathetic. When I spot Liam and Matthew, I head straight for them.

"You guys hear from Addie?"

They exchange a look.

"Maybe she's sick," Matthew offers.

"Yeah, that's the only time she skips," Liam adds.

I rub the back of my neck, the silence between our words filling with static. "Something feels off."

"I'll check with the girls," Matthew says, trying to sound reassuring.

Liam grins at me, clueless. "Hey, congrats on getting scouted, man! You submitting the app?"

"Yeah," I say distantly. "Working on it." My voice sounds far away, even to me.

The cafeteria noise is too loud, too normal. I bail and head for Mrs. Singh's office instead. The hallways blur. She lets me in, smiling that polite counselor's smile, and I hand her my folder.

"It's all done. Except for that last section."

"Did you decide on schools?" she asks.

"Just put State at the top," I mumble.

She double checks, fills it in neatly, and scans everything over. "I didn't think we'd finish so soon."

"Guess I was motivated," I say, though it sounds hollow.

She wishes me luck and says something about hearing back in April or May. I nod, thank her, and walk out.

The day drags. Every second without a reply crawls under my skin. I keep telling myself Addie's fine. Her phone's dead, she's busy, something simple, but my brain keeps reaching for the worst case scenario. It's like every dark possibility plays itself on repeat. By the time the final bell rings, I'm already halfway to the parking lot, scrolling through our old texts just to feel close to her.

Then I hear my name being yelled. I look up and see Zahra sprinting toward me, face pale, curls flying everywhere. My phone goes off in my hand, it's her calling me, but she hangs up the second our eyes meet.

"Jax!" she gasps when she reaches me. "It's Addie! She's in the hospital."

The words don't hit right away. Then they slam into me all at once, like the ground's been ripped out from under my feet. "What?" My voice cracks.

Zahra's crying, breath hitching between words. "Her mom said she was in a car accident. A drunk driver hit her. Her car flipped. The other driver's dead."

My hands tighten around the steering wheel before I even realize I'm driving. "When?" My voice is rough, shaking.

"Yesterday," Zahra says through tears. "We parted ways after the mall, but she never made it home." Her hands shake as she tries to buckle her seatbelt.

"Fuck!" I slam my palm against the wheel. "I knew something was wrong! She wasn't answering—"

"Her mom didn't want to worry us," Zahra says, sobbing harder, "so she didn't say anything until now."

We reach the hospital in what feels like seconds and hours all at once. I barely remember parking before we're running through the sliding doors. The fluorescent lights hiss quietly overhead, too bright, too real. Zahra talks to the nurse; I just stand there, my veins threatening to explode.

They lead us to the ICU waiting room. Addie's mom, Lucía, stands when she sees us, eyes red and glassy. She pulls Zahra into her arms, sobbing.

"I'm so sorry," she manages. "Everything happened so fast."

"What's happening now?" Zahra asks.

"They've taken her into surgery. There's fluid around her brain. They're draining it."

The room tilts. I drop into a chair before I can collapse. Lucía sits beside me, her hand trembling as it rests on my knee. Zahra paces, crying into her sleeve.

When the doctor finally appears, we all stand like we've been waiting for a verdict.

"She made it through the surgery," the doctor says softly, "but... she's fallen into a coma."

The world folds in on itself. No sound, no air. Just my heartbeat slamming against my ribs. Lucía gasps, Zahra cries out, but it all sounds muffled, like I'm underwater.

"This is my fault," I whisper. "She was supposed to come to my house after the mall, but I ran late. If I hadn't stayed at school... if I'd just finished sooner, she would've—" My voice breaks. I can't breathe.

Lucía grabs my hand, firm despite her shaking. "*No es tu culpa*, Jax. She's strong. Like her father."

Zahra wipes her face. "I'll tell the others," she says quietly.

My phone blows up a minute later, our group chat flooding with messages. Shock. Fear. Disbelief. Zahra tells them not to come, not yet.

I stare at the screen, unable to type, unable to move. The shoe finally drops. Everything good—college, soccer, my dad, Addie—it all feels like it's about to crumble.

Because I knew. Deep down, I fucking knew. Things were too good to last.

***

The three of us sit in silence until a nurse appears at the doorway. "She's been given a room," she says gently. "You can see her now."

We all stand at once, the scrape of our chairs echoing too loud in the sterile quiet. The nurse leads us to another floor, the hall so white it almost blinds. Every step sounds heavier than the last. My ears ring with silence, tuned only to my own breath.

She stops in front of a closed door. "Before you go in," she warns, "there are a lot of machines. And she has a few IVs running through her arms."

Lucía nods. Zahra wipes her face. My hands won't stop shaking.

Then the nurse opens the door.

We file in slowly, like we might wake her if we move too fast. The air smells like antiseptic and metal, sharp and cold. Addie lies there, still and small, almost unrecognizable beneath white sheets and a forest of wires.

It's not the bruises. It's not the wires. What kills me is how still she is. Like her body's forgotten how to be alive.

Her head's wrapped in bandages, a few strands of hair poking through. One eye's swollen shut. Scrapes cross her cheeks like someone tried to erase her. The brace at her neck meets the seatbelt burn that slashes down her collarbone. Her breaths come slow and uneven through the mask covering half her face. The hiss of the oxygen line syncs with the steady beeping from the monitor.

I freeze.

For a moment, it's not Addie lying there. It's my mom.

I'm sixteen again, standing in another room, watching my dad crumble against the wall while I stare at her body, so peaceful I almost believed she was asleep. They'd fixed her hair, painted her face. Said I could touch her hand if I wanted to. I did. It was cold. Too cold.

The same chill crawls up my arms now.

I blink hard, forcing myself to see Addie, not her. But the two memories keep bleeding together. The same stillness, the same silence, the same terrifying thought whispering at the back of my skull: *What if she doesn't wake up either?*

"How long will she be like this?" I hear myself ask, but my voice sounds distant, like it's coming from somewhere else.

The nurse lingers by the door. "We don't know," she says softly. "Her body will heal, even if it takes time. We'll take care of her."

Lucía sobs out a thank you. Zahra nods, biting her lip.

I can't move. My feet feel nailed to the floor. The nurse leaves, and it's just the three of us, standing there, breathing the same sterile air as the machines keeping Addie alive.

The beeping fills the silence, steady, fragile, human.

I shove my hands into my hoodie pocket, trying to keep them still. My fingernails dig into my palms until it hurts. I tell myself pain means I'm still here, still breathing.

I should say something. I should tell her I'm here. But the words stick in my throat. Because what if she can hear me? What if she can't?

My chest caves. Everything inside me feels like it's collapsing inward, folding under the weight of that single thought: *I can't lose her too.*

CHAPTER TWENTY-NINE
Jackson

When visiting hours are over, I leave Zahra and Addie's mom in the hallway, promising to come back tomorrow. Lucía hugs me tight, her face still wet with tears. Zahra gives me a wave and a tight smile that doesn't reach her eyes. I return one just the same. My heart isn't in it. My heart isn't in anything. It feels like someone hit mute inside my head. The world plays on, but all the sound has drained away.

I drive home on autopilot. The tires rolling steadily, the stoplights, the streetlamps streaking by. All of it happens around me, not to me. When I park, I don't move. I just stare at the black stretch of road ahead, my hands gripping the steering wheel until my knuckles blanch. Then something inside me clicks, soft, poisonous, and I reach for my phone.

That voice, the one I thought I'd buried, slithers up my spine. *It was only a matter of time, Jax. Look what you've done to her. Look what you've become.* My blood races. I scroll through my socials with trembling fingers, not even sure what I'm searching for until I find it. Jay.

`Hey, it's Jax. Lost your number. Can I swing by?`

The reply comes before my shame can catch up.

`You coming to score?`

My thumbs pause for a split second.

`Yeah. Regular.`

Jay's dorm smells like smoke and dust and bad choices. The deal is quick, practiced. His hand, my money, the small plastic bag. A mutual silence we both understand too well. He starts to say something, maybe even a warning, but I'm already walking away.

The drive home feels endless. I can hear my heartbeat over the engine, feel it pounding in my temples. When I finally step into the kitchen, I toss the bag onto the table. It skids across the wood, the sound sharp and small. The pills inside click like teeth.

You know what to do, the voice purrs.

My hands sweat. I fill a glass of water and sit down, staring. The pills are so ordinary-looking. Round, pale, harmless. Like they couldn't possibly be the reason I once almost died. My hands hover over the bag. I open it, dump them out in front of me, and they scatter like spilled bones. My breath stutters.

Then, my mother's face flashes before me. Not how she was before. How she was *after.* The way her lips had looked painted but wrong… too blue. How she'd looked like she was sleeping, except no one sleeps that still. The scent of the lilies from the funeral hit me so hard I almost gagged.

"What the fuck!" I slam my fist against the table, the sound cracking through the kitchen. The glass goes flying against the wall, shattering. I fill another, ignoring the shards glinting around my feet.

Pull yourself together, the voice growls, now deeper, darker. *You're weak.*

I scoop the pills into my palm. They feel cold and light, like they're already inside me. My heart is hammering so hard I can taste blood. The pills hit my tongue. The bitterness blooms. Silence rushes in.

A chime slices through it, Samuel's generic ring, not Addie's.

The sound cuts the world open. I spit the pills onto the table and choke out a breath I didn't know I'd been holding. My body folds in on itself. I slide down to the floor, knees to my chest, trembling. The phone rings again, twice. I crawl for it, hit the callback.

"Jax?" Samuel's voice is calm, low, the kind that fills a room even through static. "Hey, I just heard about Addie. I wanted to check up on you."

"Hey," I croak.

"Is everything alright?"

"No," I whisper. "I'm not alright."

"What happened?"

"I almost…" I don't finish. He doesn't make me.

"Alright," he says. "Stay on the phone with me, but text me your address. Can you do that?"

I send it. He doesn't hang up.

Samuel runs a local outreach program on the side, sponsors recovering addicts, leads late-night meetings for kids like me. He's the only adult in this town who doesn't treat me like a lost cause. So when he says, "I'm on my way," I believe him.

He talks me through grounding: feel the floor, name five things I see, four things I can touch, three things I hear. I try to listen. I don't realize how long it's been until I hear his knock. The door's unlocked. He finds me in the kitchen, sitting on the floor surrounded by glass and spilled pills.

He kneels beside me, picks up my phone, switches it off. Doesn't say a word for a long time. Then, quietly, "It's brutal to face life sober," he says. "I used meth for years. Lost my scholarship, my fiancée at the time, my mind. My sister found me and didn't let go. That was my first domino." He glances toward the table. "Relapse starts as a whisper. Then it becomes a thought. Then a craving. We'll build the part of you that can outlast the thought."

I stare at him, silent.

"We'll strengthen your will until it's indestructible."

He stands, holds out his hand. I take it, and he pulls me up, then, unexpectedly, into a hug. The contact cracks something in me open.

"Now," he says softly, "let's go clean up this mess."

We sweep the glass, flush the pills, wipe the counters. I tell him everything. About the voice. The shaking. The rage that comes and goes like a storm. The feeling of the world closing in.

"I don't think I'm hearing actual voices," I tell him. "It's more like… there's a war in my head, and I can't always tell who's winning."

"I don't think you're hearing voices," he says. "You're human. We all have our shadows. Yours just talk louder than most."

He teaches me a few breathing techniques, grounding exercises, things to grab onto when the storm hits again. We sit on the couch. He listens as I pour out my fears about Addie. Her not waking up, the guilt that I might lose her, too.

When he stands to leave, he says, "Try journaling. You need a place to empty what your mind can't carry."

I give him a skeptical look. "That's not really my thing."

"Have you tried it?"

I stay quiet. He smiles faintly. "Try it three times. Then tell me it's not your thing." He heads for the door, then stops. His tone sharpens, almost fatherly. "You're choosing life, Jax."

After Samuel leaves, I delete Jay's number again, block his accounts, erase every thread connecting us. The dark voice hisses, *You're an idiot.*

But this time, I don't argue. I just notice it, acknowledge it, and let it drift away.

And it does.

***

Day 28. Same garage level. Same pump of sanitizer. Same two deep breaths before I push her door open.

Zahra and I have fallen into a routine. Arriving at the same time, staying until visiting hours are over, leaving together in silence. Today, though, my session with Samuel runs longer than expected, and by the time I reach Addie's room, the sky outside the window has already darkened.

Zahra's curled up in the chair by Addie's bed, laptop open, earbuds in, foot bouncing in rhythm. Her braids are pulled into a tight bun, pencil tucked behind her ear. When

293

she hears my stomach growl, she looks up and gives me a faint smile, more of a peace offering than anything else.

"I'm going to grab something to eat," I say. "You want anything?"

She hesitates, then nods and reaches for her wallet.

"Don't worry, I got it." I leave before she can argue.

When I come back, I hand her a sandwich and sit beside her. For a while, the only sounds are the crinkle of wrappers and the hum of hospital machinery. The smell of coffee lingers faintly in the air.

"The letters have started coming in," Zahra says after a moment, her voice soft.

"The acceptance letters?" She nods. "Did you open them?"

Shaking her head, she stares at Addie's still form. "No. I want to open them with her. Her mom said she's been getting letters too."

I follow her gaze. Addie's body looks more like her now. No more bandages around her head, no more oxygen mask, no more neck brace. The cuts on her face have faded into faint pink streaks, and the bruises are gone. Only the thin yellow mark of the seatbelt burn remains. Her hair's smooth and brushed, shining under the soft light. If I didn't know better, I'd think she was asleep, about to open her eyes and call us idiots for talking over her again.

"You'll open them together soon," I tell Zahra, but my voice cracks halfway through.

Zahra doesn't respond right away. "I watched you read to her yesterday," she says eventually. "You kept explaining the plot like she could answer you."

I let out a small laugh. "Yeah. Old habit, I guess."

She sets her sandwich down, studying me with quiet intensity, a look so similar to Addie's. "You know, I never really believed that whole *'we met in chemistry class'* story."

I raise an eyebrow. "Oh yeah?"

"You're not exactly the 'meet cute' type," she says flatly. "And Megan, well, she made sure everyone knew what kind of guy you were. Sleeping around. Partying. You weren't exactly the poster child for healthy relationships."

Her words sting, but I don't argue.

"I warned Addie about you," she continues. "Told her she deserved better. She didn't listen, of course. She never does." She exhales slowly. "But lately…" Her voice softens. "Lately, I think maybe I was wrong about you."

I glance at her, surprised. "What makes you say that?"

"You're not the same person," she says simply. "You don't hide behind that angry, untouchable *thing* anymore. You actually smile now. You talk to people. You show up. And Liam said you applied for college at the same time he did—" she shakes her head, half smiling. "I almost didn't believe him."

I take a sip of my soda to hide the small grin pulling at my mouth. "Guess I'm full of surprises."

"You're not making this easy, you know."

"What, being likable?"

She laughs, quiet and genuine. "Exactly. I want to dislike you, Jax. I really do. But…" She trails off, eyes flicking to Addie. "I can't. You love her. And she loves you. That means something. So, yeah, I guess I kind of have to love you too. In a *'don't screw this up or I'll kill you'* kind of way."

I smirk. "I'll take what I can get."

Silence falls between us again, but this time it's lighter. Easier.

"You're good for her," Zahra confesses quietly after a moment. "She laughs more when she's with you. She's bolder. Like she finally believes she deserves to be happy."

"She's finding her way," I say, watching Addie's chest rise and fall. "I'm just lucky to be a part of that."

Zahra nods, eyes glassy. "You're helping her."

"Cheering her on," I correct softly. "The same way she cheers me on."

Zahra smiles then, warm, real. "Yeah," she says quietly. "I guess you are."

I lean my head back against the wall. "Friends, then?"

She lets out a long breath, thinking. Then she extends her hand across the space between us. "Yeah. Friends."

I shake her hand and the air in Addie's room feels almost normal. Almost peaceful.

CHAPTER THIRTY

Jackson

A week into April, Yoona, Zahra, and Matthew get their college letters. They leave them unopened, the envelopes lined up like sealed promises. No one says it out loud, but we're all waiting for Addie. Waiting for her to wake up and open hers first, because it feels wrong to move forward without her. I think they're waiting for me and Liam too, but mostly it's her.

Zahra and I take turns collecting Addie's schoolwork from her teachers, who always ask how she's doing and tell us to send love. They tell us we don't need to bother with the assignments, but we do anyway. Addie would hate falling behind. She missed senior photo day, her yearbook quote, class pictures, the spring festival, the senior breakfast, the last-minute college fair.

Every milestone comes and goes, and it's like we're all holding our breath until she can catch up. When we

hand the stack of papers to her mom, Lucía, she thanks us like it matters. And maybe it does. Maybe it's a way of keeping Addie's life ready for her return.

Second week of April. Sixth week of hospital visits. The same walk down the same sterile corridor, same antiseptic sting in my throat. I've already collected her homework for the week, but Zahra texts me to go on ahead. So I drive over, the unopened envelope with my college letter sitting on the passenger seat.

Lucía greets me with a hug. "*Hola*, Jax."

"Hey, how is she today?"

She smooths the front of my hoodie, plucking off a piece of lint like it's second nature. "She's stable. I have to see a client for a bit, but I'll be back soon."

"Okay. Zahra will be here later," I tell her, and she nods, squeezing my shoulder before heading out.

Inside Addie's room, the sunlight spills through the window, warmer now, like summer's already knocking. A vase of fresh flowers sits by her bed, bright and hopeful. I pull a chair close and sit beside her.

"So," I start, my voice low, "this morning my Dad handed me an envelope. State University stamped in the corner. It's sitting unopened in my car. I'm afraid to touch it." I take her hand, rough between my palms, and press my lips to it.

"He wanted me to open it right there, but I told him we're waiting for you. All of us. Liam should be getting his soon, too." I pause. "You'd yell at us if we opened them without you."

Her hand is cool, her pulse steady beneath my thumb. I trace the lines of her palm like they might tell me when she'll wake up.

"I miss you," I whisper. "Every good thing lately feels borrowed from you. Samuel's been helping me a lot, and Zahra's... surprisingly not terrible. Bossy as hell, though." A quiet laugh leaves me. "She reminds me of you sometimes. When she talks with her hands, or when she looks at someone like she already knows the answer."

I stand, walking over to the window. The light hits me, warm, real. For a second, I imagine it spilling over Addie too, washing away the gray hospital light. I take my cap off, run a hand through my hair, and put it back on.

Then I hear it. A small sound. A scrape of breath.

My heart stops, then starts racing. I spin around and rush to her side, gripping her hand tight enough to turn my knuckles white.

Her lips move. I lean closer.

"Don't break my hand, you beast," she croaks.

The sound that comes out of me is somewhere between a laugh and a sob. I can't stop it. Weeks of holding everything in just break open all at once.

Addie's eyes blink open, amber, unfocused, but alive. She smiles faintly, and it's like the world exhales.

The door bursts open. Zahra walks in, bubble tea in hand.

"Look!" I shout, still half laughing, half crying.

Zahra freezes. Addie blinks up at her, smiling wider this time.

Zahra's jaw drops. "Of course she'd wake up when she's alone with you."

I want to tell her it's not a movie.

But for the first time in weeks, it feels like one.

Addie laughs weakly. I laugh louder. I can't help it. I lean down and kiss her face, her cheeks, her lips, every place I can reach.

"Gross," Zahra says, rolling her eyes but grinning. "I'll get the doctors."

"How do you feel?" I ask, brushing hair from Addie's forehead.

"Like I want to sit up. What happened?"

I adjust the bed so she can sit, but before I can explain, doctors rush in, nurses, too, a small army of movement and noise.

"They have to check her," Zahra says, tugging me back.

I nod, stepping away, palms open, heart full. For once, I don't try to hold on. We stand together against the wall, watching them hover around Addie.

"Right," I say quietly. "That's important."

"Mhm, lover boy. Very important."

"Shut up."

CHAPTER THIRTY-ONE
Adelina

Waking up feels nothing like waking from sleep. For weeks, maybe months, I drifted in a place without color or time. Not dreaming, not feeling. Just floating in dark silence. Sometimes I heard faint voices, sometimes I felt warmth, but it never lasted long before I sank again.

People like to say you wake up because someone loves you enough to pull you back. I wish that were true. I wish I could say it was Jax's voice or Mami's kisses or Zahra's perfume that brought me back. But in reality, I just... open my eyes.

The darkness snaps. My first thought is, *Where am I?*

Then I smell him. Cedar, sandalwood, coffee.

"Don't break my hand, you beast," I croak.

The crushing stops.

It takes effort to peel my eyelids apart. Jax's face swims into focus above me, blurred by tears. His mouth is moving fast, but I'm too busy trying to make sense of the room around me. Machines whir softly. Light presses through blinds. My brain feels fogged, like I've been underwater too long. Despite it all, I see Jax and I smile.

Zahra is here for a moment, a look of shock and relief on her face, before exiting the room quickly to call the doctors. I mumble about wanting to sit up, and Jax helps shift me to a more comfortable position. He's just about to answer my question when a swarm of doctors enter my room.

Then chaos. Voices, footsteps, flashes of white coats. Someone shines a light in my eyes. Someone else asks my name, where I live, what year it is. I answer everything correctly, and a few smiles flicker around the room.

Everything seems fine until I notice how still my body feels.

The doctors keep talking, but their voices turn distant, muffled under the weight of a new thought forming in my mind. I try to move my legs. Nothing. I try again, still nothing. My heart stops.

A doctor taps my knee. "Just a reflex check."

No bounce. No feeling.

"What's wrong?" I ask, my voice breaking.

They don't answer. Their faces tighten, their eyes meet in that quiet way people do when something's not right.

"Wiggle your toes," another says gently.

I do. Or at least, I think I do. But the sheets don't move.

"I *am,*" I whisper.

My throat goes dry. I ask for water, mostly to stall, but Jax's hand is already there, steady and warm. He kisses my forehead and strokes my hair. The doctors step back to talk in low voices. I can't hear a word.

Mami bursts in, eyes red, mouth trembling. "*Mi hija!*" she cries, wrapping her arms around me. Her body shakes against mine.

I stare at my legs, willing them to move, but they lie there like they belong to someone else. Panic claws up my throat. I slap my thigh. Hard. Then again. Nothing. Just the sound, dull and far away. Jax is already trying to stop me, grabbing my wrists, but I thrash harder, hitting myself through the sheets.

"Addie, stop!"

"Let go of me!"

"Addie," Zahra says, her voice steady, calm. "Breathe."

But I can't. I can't because my body isn't *listening.* The strength drains out of me, leaving only shaking and silence. Jax's arms catch me as I crumble.

"Addie, it's going to be okay," he whispers. His lips brush my forehead. I press my face into him and sob until the sound doesn't feel like mine anymore.

Eventually, the doctors lead Mami and Zahra outside, leaving the two of us alone. Jax lies beside me, one hand in my hair, the other tracing circles on my back until my tears fade into exhaustion. I fall asleep like that, held, but hollow.

When I wake again, Mami's at my side with a small cup of water.

"There's food if you're hungry," she murmurs.

I shake my head. "Why aren't my legs working?"

"They don't see spinal damage," she says softly. "The doctors think your body just... forgot how to move after being asleep for so long. Therapy can help remind it."

I stare at the blanket over my legs. They look perfectly fine. They look like mine.

"Mami," I whisper, my voice small. "What happened to me?"

She glances at Jax and Zahra. They exchange a look, one I don't understand, before she begins to tell me. The car. The crash. The other driver. The words land like stones in my stomach.

When she's done, I can barely breathe. "The other driver... died?"

Her silence is answer enough.

The air feels heavy. I take a deep breath, let it out slow, and try to swallow the grief rising in my throat. But it wins. The sobs come, raw and endless.

***

I stay in the hospital for another week after waking up. The doctors say recovery takes time, but I can't help feeling impatient. My legs are still numb, and physical therapy feels like a daily reminder of everything I've lost. Still, I try to hold onto the small victories. I can shower now, sitting, of course, and I washed my hair for the first time a few days ago.

Mami hovered the entire time, ready to catch me if I slipped, but I didn't. I did it. I can also use the toilet on my own, and I've learned how to maneuver from the bed to the wheelchair without someone guiding me. It's strange how something so ordinary can suddenly feel like winning gold.

There's this ache that's been creeping up on me, though. Not physical, but emotional. I never cared much for senior year before. The soccer games, the pep rallies, prom, none of it felt important. I just wanted to finish and move on.

But now, realizing how much I've missed, it hits harder than I expected. I wanted to push myself this year, to try, to say yes more. For once, I actually wanted to live instead of watching from the sidelines. Maybe that's what hurts the most. But I'm not giving up. Not when I've already made it this far.

On my last day in the hospital, Jax is with me for another round of physical therapy. The room smells like antiseptic and sweat, and there's a set of black handlebars on either side of me. My wheelchair is centered between them. Paul, my therapist, straps my legs into a support harness, then gives me a quick nod. "Ready when you are, Addie."

Jax steps closer, his warm hand steady against my back. "I've got you," he murmurs. His voice always finds a way to ground me.

I grip the bars and pull myself up. My arms shake under the effort, and Jax shifts to bear some of my weight until I'm upright. I don't feel like I'm standing. My legs are still foreign, disconnected, but I'm up. It's something.

"Alright," Paul says from behind me. "We'll start slow. Right leg first."

I glance down, trying to focus, and feel the tug of the harness as he pulls on the rope. My leg moves, barely, but it moves. My balance wobbles, and Jax's hand tightens around my arm to steady me.

"Keep it steady," Paul reminds. "Good. Now the left."

He pulls again. My body obeys like it's on autopilot, mechanical, unfeeling, but still responding. Each small motion feels like climbing a mountain, and by the time both legs have shifted forward, my arms ache and my breath is uneven.

"You're doing great," Jax says quietly, close enough that I can hear the smile in his voice.

"Sure," I grunt. "If great means sweating through my sweatpants."

Paul chuckles. "Let's try something new. I want you to take the next step yourself."

My head snaps toward him. "What? We've never—"

"Today's the day," he says simply. "Give it your best."

I glance at Jax. He nods, confidence radiating off him like sunlight. For a second, I forget how scared I am.

"Okay," I mutter under my breath. "Fuck it."

The word slips out before I can stop it, and Jax laughs softly. I focus everything I have on my right leg. My fingers tighten around the bars. My shoulders tremble. Nothing happens. I try again. My muscles burn. Still nothing.

Come on, Addie. Move. Do something.

I pull again, harder this time, and suddenly, something shifts. My right foot scrapes the ground. The tiniest movement, but it's *mine.* Paul shouts, "That's it!" and Jax lets out a breathy laugh, his eyes wide with pride.

"Did I... did that just happen?" I pant.

"It happened," Paul says, grinning.

The disbelief floods me all at once. I start laughing, this shaky, tearful sound I can't control. Jax joins in, his own laugh breaking the tension in the room. I lift my hands in victory, forgetting completely that I can't balance on my own, and of course, I topple.

"Whoa, easy!" Jax catches me before I hit the floor, still laughing.

Back in my wheelchair, I can't stop smiling. Paul keeps talking about progress, unstrapping my legs as he does, but I can hardly focus. I'm still replaying that single step in my head. That *moment.*

Then something strange happens. I stop laughing mid breath. Jax notices right away. "Addie? You okay?"

I lean forward, frowning. There's a new sensation, so faint I almost think I imagined it. My heart starts racing.

"Wait." My voice comes out in a whisper. "Hold on."

I stare at my foot. Concentrate.

And then, it happens. The tiniest twitch in my right big toe.

A sound leaves me before I can stop it. Half gasp, half cry. "I felt that."

Paul freezes. "You—what?"

"I *felt* that," I repeat, louder this time, breathless, stunned. Tears blur my vision.

Jax crouches in front of me, eyes wide, his hand finding mine. "Addie," he says softly, voice shaking now too. "You did it."

***

I'm discharged by the second week of May. I'm not walking completely on my own yet, but with my forearm crutches, I can get around just fine. Mami says school approved two extra weeks of leave, which gives me time to finish my makeup work. Every teacher told me not to worry about it, but of course, I did anyway. I've almost caught up on everything. Soon I'll be submitting assignments on time again, thanks to Zahra and Jax dropping them off after class.

They also take turns driving me to physical therapy. Mami's back at the office now, less hover-y but still calling every few hours to check in. My friends visit almost every other day—Liam, Yoona, Matthew—sometimes bringing snacks or making me show off how far I can walk now. They cheer like crazy every time I take a few extra steps, which makes me laugh even when I'm sore.

One afternoon, we're all at my place. I'm on the floor stretching while Jax helps me, and the others are spread across the couch with half-eaten takeout containers. Liam clears his throat, which immediately gets everyone's attention.

"So, um… I'm not sure if this is the right time," he says, fingers raking through his hair the way he does when he's nervous. Then he reaches into his backpack and pulls out an envelope.

"Is that from State?" Zahra whispers.

He nods.

"Have you opened it?" Matthew asks.

Liam shakes his head. "We said we'd all wait for Addie."

Yoona says, grinning, "You know the deadline's in two weeks, right? We all have to make it an event."

"Wait, *you* applied?" I ask Jax, turning to him.

Before he can answer, Zahra bursts out laughing. "You didn't know? Mrs. Singh basically hunted him down until he filled out the application."

Jax shrugs, looking sheepish. "I only sent it because of her. The same day as… well, the accident." The room goes quiet. "After that, I just… forgot."

I stare at him. "You *forgot* you applied to college?"

He grins a little, and I smack him with a pillow. "You should've told me! That's huge, Jax!"

He rubs the back of his neck. "I'm still not sure I even want to go. I mean, what would I study?"

"English," I say without missing a beat. "You edit Liam's essays even when you pretend you're not."

He squints at me. "And what do I even do with that?"

"Lots of things," Liam says. "Writer, editor, journalist. You could even go into PR."

Jax doesn't answer, but I can tell he's thinking about it.

"So," I say, trying to steer the mood back up, "where should we open the letters? It has to be somewhere special."

Matthew perks up. "My parents' cabin by the lake. They've been trying to get me to use it before graduation. It's got enough room for all of us."

"That's perfect," Yoona says, instantly on board.

"Wait, they'd actually let all of us go?" Zahra asks skeptically.

Matthew laughs. "They love you guys. As long as we don't burn it down, we're good."

Everyone starts talking at once, planning snacks and playlists and who's riding with who. For the first time in months, it feels like the world is finally spinning the right way again.

Later, when everyone leaves, Jax stays behind. Mami's still at work, and the house feels calm. I grab one crutch and hobble toward the couch. He offers me his arm, but I wave him off.

"I've got it," I say, lowering myself carefully.

"You're getting stronger," he says softly, brushing a kiss on my cheek.

"I'm trying," I grin. "Pretty sure I'll have superhero arms by summmer."

He laughs, pulling me closer. The quiet stretches between us, comfortable and warm.

"When was the last time it was just us?" I murmur.

"Feels like forever."

"I missed this," I whisper.

"Me too." His voice is low now, close.

When he kisses me, it feels like breathing again, slow and certain. For the first time in months, I'm not thinking about hospital beds or wheelchairs or scars. Just us. Just this.

"Are you sure?" he asks, searching my face.

I nod. "Yeah. I'm sure."

He lifts me carefully into his arms, and somehow, I don't feel fragile.

CHAPTER THIRTY-TWO
Jackson

Samuel's looking at me with that calm, poker-faced expression that means I've been quiet for too long. I already told him about the plan. The cabin trip, all of us opening our college acceptance results together. But when he asks, "Why don't you want to open yours, Jax?" I don't have an answer that doesn't sound weak.

"I'm not scared of a no," I finally say. "I'm scared of the look after. The one people give when they expected more."

Samuel tilts his head. "What were you planning to do after high school?"

"I don't know."

"How were you going to make a living?"

"No idea."

"Just... wing it?"

"Pretty much." I sigh, leaning back. "It's like everything's shifting now."

He raises an eyebrow. "Afraid of failure?"

I shrug, but the word lands heavier than I want it to. Failure isn't new to me. What's new is that people are watching again. Addie, Liam, Matthew, Zahra, even Samuel. I've got people in my corner now, rooting for me, waiting to see if I'll mess up or make it.

"Either way, I disappoint," I mutter.

"Or," he says, leaning forward, "you stop performing for the crowd. You've got the pitcher in your hand, Jax. Maybe it's time to fill your own glass."

He's got this way of saying things that sound like fortune cookie wisdom, but still hit deep. And he's right. I *am* building something different this time. Still, I can't shake the feeling that if I open that letter and it says *no*, it'll confirm every shitty thing I've ever believed about myself.

We wrap up and Samuel walks me out. "You've been creating a new reality for yourself," he says before I leave. "Don't stop now."

When I pull up to Addie's house, she and her mom are already outside. Addie's standing, no crutches. Just her, steady and solid, sunlight bouncing off her hair. Her mom's holding the crutches anyway, just in case, but Addie doesn't reach for them. She just smiles and waves before making her careful way toward me.

It hits me how far she's come.

The girl who used to hide behind diverted conversations and silence now has a spark in her eyes again.

She slides into the passenger seat and buckles up. "Hi," she says, like it's any other day. But it's not.

"Hey yourself," I say, grinning.

Halfway to the hospital, I notice a string around her neck. "What's that?"

"Oh, it's my swimsuit. Paul's starting me on pool therapy today!" she says, practically glowing. "He says it'll help my muscles relax and build strength faster."

"That's actually kinda badass," I tell her, bringing her hand to my lips and kissing her knuckles. "Look at you, mermaid rehab edition."

She laughs, that soft belly laugh I've missed. The sunlight hits her face and for a second, everything, the accident, the pain, the nightmares, feels like something we outran.

"I love you," I tell her quietly.

She squeezes my hand. "I love you too."

***

At the hydrotherapy pool, Paul meets us with his usual grin. Addie does a quick outfit swap and joins him by the shallow end. I sit on the bleachers, watching her wade in as the floor slowly lowers. It's weirdly emotional, like watching someone reclaim a piece of themselves.

Paul calls out gentle cues: "Water walking, slow knee lifts, shallow squats."

By the time she's doing thigh pulses, she's grinning and breathless. "I swear I'm not wet! This is *sweat!*" she yells, cracking herself up.

I shake my head, laughing. "You're ridiculous."

After she's dry and dressed, Paul gives her the update: she's cleared to ditch the crutches. "Just keep the cane nearby for support," he tells her.

Addie beams. "Do you think I'll still have it by prom?"

He snorts. "At the rate you're going? Doubt it."

Addie nearly jumps for joy, well, almost, and thanks him about fifty times. She also fills him in on how she's been catching up with everything:

She made up all her missed assignments, retook her senior photo just in time for the yearbook, and added her quote. She's even been doing virtual college tours with Mrs. Singh too, something she used to roll her eyes at.

It's like she's piecing her life back together, one line, one step at a time.

We walk out of the hospital, sunlight glinting off the cars in the parking lot. Addie's moving without the crutches now, holding steady, the cane tucked under her arm just in case.

"I'm trying to dance for at least a few songs at prom," she says, sliding into the passenger seat.

"I thought you were anti-prom?" I tease.

She looks at me, calm and sure. "Prom. With you."

I blink. "Are you asking me out?"

"Well, seeing as I almost died," she says, grinning, "I don't really care about tradition anymore. I want to go. And I want to go with you."

Something in me twists with pride, awe, and love, all tangled together. The Addie in front of me isn't the girl who flinched from being seen. She's standing in her scars, not hiding from them. And I've never seen her look more alive.

"Damn," I say, smiling. "What happened to my girlfriend?"

"She grew up," she says softly.

I reach over, brushing a thumb along her jaw. "Guess I better catch up then."

She smirks. "So... is that a yes?"

"Yeah," I say, laughing. "It's a yes."

She leans over, kisses my cheek, and whispers, "Too bad I beat you to it, sucker."

***

The six of us are in front of Matthew's house, loading the cars for the cabin trip. Liam's driving with Matthew and Yoona; I'm taking Addie and Zahra. The morning air is warm, sunlight just starting to sharpen, and our clothes stick lightly to our skin as we haul boxes of food and coolers into the trunks.

Addie sits on Matthew's porch, chatting with his parents, probably about her recovery, while we finish up. When Matthew whistles, she gets to her feet, careful but steady, and his parents follow her down the steps.

"Drive safe!" Mr. Wright calls.

"Call us when you get there!" Mrs. Wright adds, waving as we pull away.

The drive is easy and bright, open fields giving way to thick woods as we near the campground. Addie and Zahra nap most of the way, but wake up restless and giddy once we roll through the forested gates just after noon.

Matthew sprints into the lodge to check us in, and comes back tossing room keys at us like souvenirs. I follow Liam's car down winding roads lined with tennis courts, a bathhouse, and a spa.

"Addie, look! A spa!" Zahra gasps.

"I saw it!" Addie grins. "We're definitely going."

"Your legs will thank you," I tell her, catching her smile in the rearview mirror.

By the time we reach our cabin, the "cabin" turns out to be a three-story cottage. Polished wood, solar panels, wide arched windows, a wraparound porch.

"This is a *cabin?*" I mutter.

Zahra whistles. "Guess we're roughing it in luxury."

Addie offers to help unload, but Yoona gently tells her to sit and rest. She listens, mostly, and limps up to one of the porch chairs, cane resting by her leg.

Yoona moves quietly through the chaos of unpacking, checking that everything's in place. There's a nervous edge to her movements, like she's carrying an invisible weight, but when Matthew cracks a joke, she laughs too quickly, too brightly. It's the kind of laugh that says she's been waiting for this moment of freedom longer than she'll admit.

When everything's inside, Matthew gives us the grand tour, complete with commentary. We pick rooms without question, and Addie and I slip into one together.

"This is pretty cool," she says, brushing her fingers along the window frame.

"Cooler than I expected," I say. "Or maybe I just like seeing you unpack instead of rehabbing."

"The first thing I'm doing is the spa house," she says. "My legs deserve it."

"They sure do," I murmur, squeezing her thigh, making her giggle.

She offers shyly, "You could join me. Like... a couple's thing?"

"Yeah," I say easily. "After the pool."

Addie frowns. "It sucks, we'll have to drive down there every morning."

"Uh..." I point toward the window. "I don't think that'll be a problem."

She peers out and gasps. In the backyard sits a glass-roofed pool house, sunlight glinting off the water.

"Oh my god," she says, laughing. "That's *ours?*"

Before I can answer, we're both changing into swimsuits. In the hall, we bump into Liam, already shirtless, towel slung over his shoulder.

"Pool?" he asks, grinning.

"Pool," Addie confirms, and he bolts ahead like a kid.

The water's perfect. Cool, clean, and echoing with laughter. Addie moves through her rehab stretches while Zahra and Yoona cheer her on, talking prom dresses and playlists. Liam, Matthew, and I hang by the deeper end, throwing a football back and forth until conversation drifts to prom.

"You two going together?" Liam nods toward Addie.

"Yeah," I say. "She asked me."

Matthew nearly chokes. "*She* asked *you*?"

"Beat me to it," I grin. "Didn't stand a chance."

Liam whistles. "Power move. Respect."

Matthew shakes his head. "Guess I need to level up before I ask Zahra."

"Ask her," I tell him. "If she says no, she says no."

He hesitates, and Liam elbows him. "Or you prove her wrong."

They start play-fighting in the pool before Zahra yells at them to cut it out. Yoona shakes her head, smiling faintly, but her eyes flick toward the trees beyond the glass windows. For a fleeting moment, she looks far away, like she's thinking about someone who wouldn't approve of her being here. Then she's laughing again, joining the others, the moment gone.

Later, Addie calls me over. "Ready for the spa?" she asks, checking her phone.

"Only if we eat first," I say.

"Buffet at the lodge?" Yoona suggests, paddling by.

Addie raises an eyebrow at me. I shrug. "Good enough."

We dry off, head back to the cabin, and shower together. The warmth of the water, her laughter against my shoulder. It feels normal again. When she dresses, I zip her up and watch her put on the necklace I gave her.

"Ready?" she asks.

"Are we going to the spa or on a date?"

She grins. "Both."

We skip the buffet and find a quiet place in town instead. Sitting on the patio, we eat slowly, hands brushing, feet tangled under the table. Addie's hair catches the light, her skin golden and freckled.

"You look happy," I tell her.

"I *am* happy," she says simply.

By dessert, we're stealing bites from each other's plates and laughing over nothing. When the check comes, she snatches it first. "We're splitting," she says.

"Fine by me," I grin. "I'm done hiding behind the card anyway."

She squeezes my hand, eyes soft. The air smells like lemon and pine. "Spa time," she announces when we reach the car.

I glance at her as I start the engine. "Yeah," I say, smiling. "Spa time."

***

By the time Addie and I return to the cabin, the sun is dipping behind the trees. Zahra bursts through the door, shouting for Addie and Yoona, and disappears inside with them before I can ask what's going on. Yoona follows a moment later, her hair pulled up and cheeks flushed.

"Liam and Matthew are waiting for you outside," she tells me, a knowing glint in her eye. "You should go."

I find them in Liam's car, music low, windows down, the evening air warm and easy.

"I take it things went well," I say, sliding into the back.

Matthew grins, cheeks red. "Better than well. I asked Zahra to be my girlfriend."

"Not to prom?" Liam teases as he begins driving.

"Skipped right past it," Matthew laughs. "Guess I panicked."

We clap him on the shoulder and he looks like he's floating.

Then Liam clears his throat, hesitating. "Well... I guess I should come clean too."

Matthew and I share a look. "Oh?"

"I've been seeing Yoona," he says, voice low, like it might disappear if he says it too loud.

That gets our attention.

"What? Since when?" Matthew asks, eyes wide.

"A few months," he admits. "It started slow. We didn't want to make things weird with the group, or with her parents."

He rubs his palms over the steering wheel. "They're really traditional. Old school. She has to lie just to hang out with us on late nights, saying she's sleeping over at Addie's or Zahra's. She hides it well from the rest of us. Her parents think boys are trouble, and I guess they wouldn't be wrong if they knew she was sneaking out to see me."

He tries to laugh, but it comes out thin.

"My family's different. With my parent's bakery, we're not struggling, but we're not... them," he says, nodding toward some invisible idea of Yoona's world. One made of rules and money and pressure. "She's supposed to end up with someone who speaks Korean fluently, comes from the same kind of family, has the same expectations. That's not me. But she says she doesn't care."

There's a beat of silence before Matthew says, "She wouldn't go through all that lying if she didn't mean it."

Liam smiles faintly. "Yeah. Still feels like we're fighting gravity sometimes."

He turns onto a quiet road, and the world opens up around us, neat brick townhouses, trees framing a wide green field. "This is the State University," Liam says, parking by the curb. "That's where we'll play… if everything works out."

We stand at the railing, staring out over the soccer field. The grass is cut short, perfect, waiting.

Matthew folds his arms. "Man, imagine us here in the fall."

Liam nods, shoulders finally relaxing. "New place. New start."

I glance between them and smile. "New home."

The words settle in the air, soft but certain.

CHAPTER THIRTY-THREE
Adelina

While the boys are gone, Zahra tells us everything about her and Matthew. How it happened, what he said, how she almost didn't believe it was real. Yoona and I squeal so loudly that Zahra can barely finish her story, but she doesn't stop smiling the entire time.

When she's done, Yoona goes quiet for a beat before saying softly, "I need to tell you guys something too..."

Zahra and I both stare at her. "Tell us what?" I ask.

"I've been seeing Liam," she admits. "For a while now."

Our mouths drop open, and Zahra practically chokes on her drink. "Are you serious?!"

Yoona laughs nervously. "Yeah, since before winter break. We wanted to keep it quiet because of my parents. They're... very traditional. Getting permission for this trip took weeks of convincing. I told them it was an academic retreat." She shrugs, eyes down. "They wouldn't understand. Especially not about Liam."

Zahra's face softens. "Because he's not Korean?"

Yoona nods once. "Because he's not who they'd expect me to bring home. But he's... kind. He asks about my art, sends me ideas for sketches. He believes in me, even when I don't. I like who I am around him." Her voice goes quiet. "And I don't have to hide that part of myself when I'm with him."

We don't press her any further. Instead, Zahra reaches over and squeezes her hand. "Then he's worth it."

Before I can say anything, my phone pings. A photo lights up the screen. Liam, Matthew, and Jax grinning in front of the State University sign, arms thrown over each other's shoulders. I can't help smiling.

"Okay, new plan," I announce, slipping my phone away. "We're celebrating right. Come with me to the supply store. I need a few things for later."

By the time we get back, the air smells faintly of pine and campfire. Zahra and Yoona head straight to the backyard to get the fire going while I lay out the letters on the kitchen table. Six envelopes, six pens, and six glasses of chilled sparkling cider, each with a cherry dropped in.

The boys barrel through the door a few minutes later, sunburned and grinning like idiots. "Smells like smoke," Liam says, sniffing the air.

I gesture toward the table. "Perfect timing."

Once everyone settles, I explain the plan. "Each of us has a letter from the college of our choice. But first, we write something down. The fear, the thing we'd let go of if we could, and then we'll give it to the fire before we open the letters that could change everything."

Matthew blinks. "That's... deep, Addie." Zahra elbows him, and he quickly adds, "I mean, good deep."

Within minutes, we've all disappeared to different rooms to write. When the timer goes off, we return to the backyard one by one, written letters in hand. The fire crackles, sparks rising into the dark.

Yoona goes first, her face lit by the flames. "To new beginnings," she says, tossing her paper into the fire. One by one, everyone follows, until the last ember fades.

Then come the envelopes.

"Addie first," Zahra insists.

I open mine slowly, heart in my throat. The words blur for a second before I finally look up. "I got in," I whisper, and then louder, laughing, "Full scholarship, honors program!" Cheers erupt and Jax lifts me in a hug.

Yoona tears open hers next. "In!" she grins, eyes wide. Zahra follows and screams. "College, here I come!"

The energy around the fire builds until it's almost electric. Matthew opens his letter, staring for a long moment before shouting, "Both in the school *and* on the soccer team!" He runs a victory lap around the fire while Liam and Jax howl with laughter.

But when it's Liam's turn, he hesitates. "What if I didn't—"

"Don't," Jax says gently. "You've got this."

Liam looks away as Jax opens the letter for him. Jax's eyes hurriedly skim the page. When Jax finally hands it over, Liam stares down at the letter, shoulders trembling.

Liam folds into Jax, a rough laugh breaking into a cry. Jax steadies him with one arm, no words needed. Liam dries his tears with the back of his hands and turns back to us.

Jax steps away, giving him some space, and says, "Go ahead, tell them."

Liam sniffs. "I got in," he rasps. Then he laughs, a raw, shaky sound, and turns to us. "Full ride. Soccer team too."

Matthew runs over to him and embraces him in a hug, tousling his messy red locks of hair. "Bro, I knew you could do it. I fucking knew it."

Turning to Jax, Liam points at him. "Come on, man," he says with a sniffle. "You're the only one left. We need you to complete us."

Jax opens the envelope and takes the letter out. When he reads it, his eyebrows furrow together and he squints his eyes. Now sitting, the hand holding the letter drops between his lap.

"You said I could be an English major, right?" he says, finally lifting his head and grinning at me. I nod, heart thudding.

He looks back down at the letter and lifts it high. "Then I'm in!"

The group explodes, Zahra jumping up and down, Yoona half crying, half laughing.

"Three of you on the same team?" Zahra says, shaking her head. "That's insane."

"Practically impossible," Liam adds, still grinning.

Yoona grabs the s'mores and I remember the glasses waiting inside. Jax helps me carry them out, the firelight catching in the bubbles. Our fingers are sticky with chocolate, faces glowing with smoke and joy.

We raise our glasses together. "To new beginnings," we say, echoing Yonna's earlier words, and the stars above us burn just a little brighter.

***

Prom night feels like the final page of a story we all wrote together. After months of rehab, exams, and countdowns, it's here, our night to celebrate. The school halls that once felt endless suddenly feel too small to hold what's coming next.

We're at Zahra's house, the three of us crowded around her vanity, buried in curling irons, setting powder, and laughter. Zahra's playlist blasts old throwbacks, and we sing along between mascara coats. She's in a cream, one-shoulder jumpsuit that makes her look like she belongs on a red carpet. Yoona's wearing a traditional lace dress that hugs her perfectly, her hair swept up with a tiny jeweled brooch I helped pin in.

And me? I'm in a deep plum silk dress that glows under the light. My scars peek through my makcup faintly, but for once, I don't hide from them. My reflection looks back at me, steady, confident, and finally unafraid. "Can someone zip me up?" I ask, not even pretending to be shy. Zahra comes over, smoothing my hair.

"You look insane," she says.

"You both do," I tell them, and it's true. We're dazzling in our own ways, three different stories written in glitter and silk.

When the doorbell rings, we glance at each other through the mirror. "Ready?" Yoona asks.

"Ready," Zahra and I answer in unison.

Downstairs is chaos, the good kind. Parents snapping pictures, someone shouting about lighting, camera flashes going off like fireworks. Liam and Matthew posing together, handsome in their crisp suits. And then I see him. Jax. His garnet bow tie matches my dress, his black suit fitted just right. For a second, everything else fades out.

He walks straight to me. "You will never cease to take my breath away," he whispers before pulling me in. I beam against him, no longer feeling like I need to shrink.

The six of us group together to do the whole photo thing. I'm the one dragging everyone together this time, adjusting Zahra's curls, fixing Liam's tie. For once, I'm not the one trying to disappear behind someone taller. I'm front and center, smiling wide.

When we finally head outside, the real surprise waits. A black limousine gleaming under the porch lights. Zahra's dad explains that all the parents chipped in for it. We scream like little kids, pile in, and wave goodbye, music already spilling out before the door even shuts.

The ride feels like a dream. City lights flashing by, our laughter louder than the bass in the limo. Liam and Yoona are sitting close, their fingers brushing, finally dropping their act now that our parents are not around. Zahra's head rests on Matthew's shoulder. Jax's hand fits over mine, his thumb tracing lazy circles on my palm.

The venue itself looks like something out of a movie. String lights, balloons, a giant "SENIOR PROM" banner drooping slightly to one side. Teachers stand at the entrance, handing out glow sticks and smiling like proud parents.

Inside, everything is gold and glitter and heat. We dance, we laugh, we take more photos in the booth making ridiculous faces. Someone spills punch on their tux. The DJ plays everything from slow classics to songs that make the floor shake.

When "our" song starts, a slow one with a familiar piano melody, Jax stands and holds out his hand. "Dance with me," he says, and it's not a question.

He leads me out onto the floor. His hand slides to the small of my back, steady and warm. I rest my head on his shoulder, feeling the rhythm of him thud against my cheek. "You dance well," I breathe.

"You follow well," he teases. He twirls me, pulls me back in, and I'm laughing as my heels scrape the floor.

The lights spin above us, soft and gold. "You've turned my world upside down, Adelina," he says against my ear. "How do I ever repay you?"

"You already have," I whisper. "You showed up."

He smiles, the kind that reaches his eyes, and for a moment, the world feels small enough to fit just us.

Later, when the prom king and queen are crowned (neither of us, but we cheer anyway), we scream-sing the final song until our throats burn. By the time we stumble out, the night air is cool and sweet, carrying the sound of laughter and camera flashes behind us.

Zahra's barefoot, holding her heels in one hand and Matthew's arm in the other. Liam and Yoona are sticky with sweat, her hair coming undone, their smiles bright and real.

Back in the limo, we collapse in a heap, our clothes wrinkled, our hearts full. "Next stop, graduation!" Yoona yells, and we all shout it back, the words echoing louder each time until the driver's laughing in the mirror.

We're not the same people who walked into senior year. We're better. We're freer. We're ready.

The night rolls past in flashes of light and laughter, and I finally don't feel like I'm catching up to everyone else.

I'm right there with them.

CHAPTER THIRTY-FOUR
Jackson

It's a furnace outside, and my black gown feels like a portable oven. I'm fanning myself with my cap, trying not to melt before we even get inside. Finally, the auditorium doors open, and a wave of air conditioning saves us.

The graduates are herded into a side room, parents heading in to find seats. Addie and I stand against the wall, sipping the free lemonade Matthew brought over. Zahra, Yoona, and Liam drift toward us, all nerves and smiles, and for a few minutes, it feels like time's paused. Just us, laughing about nothing before everything changes.

Then, an announcement cuts through the chatter: "Seniors, please line up."

I stretch my neck, scanning the crowd until I spot Addie near the front, valedictorian sash gleaming, posture straight as ever. The band starts playing, brass and drums beating like a single, synchronized beat. My palms go slick. I wipe them on the folds of my gown, my legs slightly trembling as the line begins to move.

We march down the hallway, the heavy auditorium doors swinging open to a burst of light, sound, and cheering. I blink hard, half-convinced I've stumbled into someone else's story.

Halfway down the aisle, I hear it, "Jax!", and turn my head. My dad's standing there, grinning wide, phone in hand. He's got that same look he used to have at my soccer games, loud and proud. Next to him, Addie's mom lifts her phone, both of them snapping pictures. Two different worlds standing side by side, and somehow, it works. My throat tightens.

Family doesn't have to be perfect. It just has to show up.

I take my seat, hands still shaking. Speeches blur by, teachers, the principal, a guest alum who probably rehearsed his talk in the mirror. But when Addie walks up to the mic, the room quiets in a way that feels sacred. She talks about perseverance, about how every scar, visible or not, tells a story of survival. Her voice doesn't waver once. I clap until my palms sting.

Lastly, the seniors are welcome to the stage, by row, to accept our diplomas. Then my name echoes through the speakers. "Jackson Hurst."

The crowd erupts. My dad's cheer is the loudest, louder than the brass, louder than everything. I walk across the stage, shaking hands with the principal, my grin stretching so wide it hurts. The diploma feels light in my hand, but the weight behind it, everything it took to get here, feels huge.

At the edge of the stage, I pause for the camera. The flash blinds me for half a second, but I stand tall, facing the light.

As I return to my seat, something shifts. I close my eyes for a moment and whisper, "Mom, if you can see me... I made it."

For a long time, I blamed her for leaving. For breaking the world in half and expecting me to live in it. But sitting here, diploma in hand, I realize she didn't leave to hurt me. She just couldn't stay. And I think, no, I *hope*, she's watching now, proud of the boy who finally learned to keep living.

When the principal gives the final words, "Graduates, you may now turn your tassels!", the room explodes. Hats fly. People scream, laugh, cry. I throw my cap as high as I can, yelling until my voice cracks.

And somewhere between the confetti of tassels and the noise of it all, I laugh and cry at once.

***

"Your speech was amazing," I tell Addie, wrapping my arm around her waist. I kiss her cheek. "Seriously, you killed it."

She laughs. "I was so nervous!"

"No one could tell," I assure her. "You made half the class cry."

She bumps her shoulder into mine. "Including you?"

"Maybe."

Hours later, the caps and gowns are gone, replaced by summer clothes, music, and the smell of barbecue drifting from Addie's backyard. Her mom's gone all out. String lights, tables stacked with food, balloons in school colors swaying in the warm evening breeze. A handmade banner hangs by the porch: *Congratulations, Seniors!*

Everyone's here. Parents chatting, cousins and siblings mingling, laughter spilling from every corner.

Samuel's manning the grill with Matthew's brother, arguing about the "proper" way to flip a burger. Zahra's brother Nathaniel is surrounded by Addie's cousins, all of them trying to one-up each other with stories that keep getting louder and more dramatic.

At one of the tables, I spot Yoona and Liam sitting across from Yoona's parents, who he's talking to *way* too politely. Liam keeps running his fingers through his hair every five seconds, and Yoona's pretending to text while her face turns bright red.

Addie nudges me and whispers, "Think they've been caught?"

I snort into my drink. "Not sure, but the poor guy's about to combust."

"Better him than us," Addie teases.

As the sun sets, the crowd starts to thin, conversations fading into soft music and the faint stir of summer bugs. Addie and I sneak away from the noise, slipping out to the porch steps with two slices of cake and the kind of silence that only feels comfortable when you've been through hell together.

She leans her head against my shoulder. "Feels weird, doesn't it?"

"What does?"

"Knowing it's over. High school."

"Yeah." I glance at her. "We actually made it."

She smiles. "We did."

I think back to where we started. The fights, the guilt, the fire pit where we threw in our fears and promised to do better. The kid I was back then didn't think he'd make it here. Didn't think he *deserved* to.

"Remember that night?" I ask quietly. "The fire?"

"How could I forget?"

I nod. "I meant every word I burned that night. My past… it used to have me by the throat. But this year, I learned how to breathe again. Learned I could build something out of what was left."

Addie looks up at me, her eyes shining in the porch light. "You did more than that, Jax. You changed your story. You let people in."

"I guess I did," I say, voice thick. "And I'm proud of that."

"You should be." She squeezes my hand.

"I still get scared sometimes," I admit. "Of the future. Of screwing up. Of losing people again. But… this fear feels different now. It doesn't hold me back… it just reminds me I'm still alive."

Addie smiles softly. "It means the fire's still burning."

I grin at that. "Yeah. It does."

She tells me she wrote about her own fears, too. "I promised myself I'd stop letting pain define me," she says. "That I'd start believing I was enough."

"You were always enough," I tell her.

She blushes, resting her hand on my cheek. "I just needed to believe it myself. And I do now."

I kiss her then, slow, unhurried, full of everything words can't say.

When we pull apart, she whispers, "I found myself this year."

I look at her, the girl who changed everything I thought I knew about strength. "Yeah," I say quietly. "Me too."

The laughter and music fade into the background, replaced by the soft rhythm of cicadas and the glow of string lights overhead.

We don't know what comes next. College, distance, the chaos of growing up. But our schools aren't far from each other, and we've already promised. No matter what happens, we'll make it work.

Because this year wasn't just about surviving.

It was about becoming.

I take her hand, my thumb brushing her knuckles. "I guess this was the year we became more."

Addie's smile widens, eyes glinting like stars. "Yeah," she whispers. "It really was."

ACKNOWLEDGEMENTS

This book began as a memoir. I wanted to write honestly about being born with a bilateral cleft lip and palate and the mental and emotional battles that shaped my life. But every outline hurt too much. I would start, remember, and then throw it away because I was afraid of reopening wounds and afraid of hurting the people whose lives touched mine. So I turned to fiction.

Adelina and Jackson emerged first, each carrying a piece of my truth. Then Zahra, Liam, Yoona, and Matthew arrived, giving voice to the parts I still could not speak aloud. Months later, when I finally looked up from my laptop, I realized I had written my story after all, only in a form that allowed me to survive it.

There are so many people who have helped and encouraged me along this journey. I would like to acknowledge everyone at Franklin Publishers for their help with this story. Working with you was a joy. Even when we were deep in work, our meetings felt warm and full of optimism. You supported me as a writer before I ever felt like one.

I grew up in Washington Heights, teaching myself how to write because I did not have the money or the time or the resources to chase this dream properly. I had to grow up fast. I had to work fast. I did not come from a world where people studied the greats or learned craft in quiet rooms. I came from a world where I fell in love with stories on my own and clung to that love because it was all I had. You saw that. You saw my beginnings as a strength and not a limitation. You believed my story mattered, and you gave me everything I needed to bring it to life. I will forever be grateful for that faith.

To my parents, thank you for the kind of love that does not waver. Our beginnings were humble and often judged. We were the ones people whispered about, the family that needed help, the ones who did not quite fit in. But you never let any of that define us. You stood by me through every surgery and every recovery, giving me health even when your own was slipping. You showed me what it means to get back up when life decides to hit harder than expected. You taught me perseverance, heart, and the courage to keep going even when everything felt impossible. *Con Dios adelante, estamos bien.*

To my best friend, who has walked beside me through every season life has thrown our way. Through sickness and through health, from the bottom to the top, from nowhere to somewhere. Thank you for being my constant. You never once treated me as less than, even when I was convinced I was. You insisted that I deserved a life that felt whole and real. You refused to let me shrink myself or believe that my differences made me unworthy. You gave me a version of normal that was actually freedom, and you held onto me in the moments when I questioned whether life was worth staying for. You reminded me that it was. Every single time. You saved pieces of me I did not know how to save.

And lastly, to my partner. Throughout the long nights and the long silences, when I disappeared into this project and could not be fully present, you somehow managed to be present for both of us. You carried the weight I could not hold. You believed in this dream with a devotion that felt sacred, as if you had breathed life into it right alongside me. You see beauty in me on the days when I struggle to find any trace of it. Your love remains unyielding and unconditional, no matter how deep the shadows get. You steady me. You anchor me. You are my safety in a world that has not always been kind.

Thank you.

ABOUT THE AUTHOR

Amber Irene resides in New York City with her partner and their two cats. When she is not writing, she can be found wandering through bookshops, sipping on coffee, or reading books. She gravitates toward stories rooted in perseverance and in finding love in the darkest of places. Her inspiration for writing began with her own journey, which taught her the power of resilience and the beauty of healing.

She has spent close to a decade as a special education teacher in Washington Heights, the neighborhood that raised her. Her work in the classroom fuels her belief that being born different does not limit your ability. It strengthens it. As a writer, she brings that same conviction to every story she tells. She also cries whenever an underdog rises, most recently during Tanjiro and Tengen's fight against Gyutaro in the Entertainment District arc. Naruto and All Might still hold the record for past tears though.

Follow her on Instagram & TikTok: **@amberirene.author**